IN THE TRAP

Hazel & Maeve: The Campus
Mysteries, Book One

Jessica Cranberry

A NineStar Press Publication

www.ninestarpress.com

In the Trap

ISBN: 978-1-64890-478-3

First Edition, April, 2022

Also available in eBook, ISBN: 978-1-64890-477-6

CONTENT WARNING:
Discussion of an on-campus murder of a student (off page); mention of the sexual assault and suicide of a family member (off page); depiction of on-campus drinking, drug use; homophobic slurs; harassment/violence against women; discussion of past trauma of a POV character; de-piction of self-harm (cutting).

"Set at the dawn of the internet age, *In the Trap* is a fast-paced campus mystery complete with one dead body, an anonymous chat room confession, and a burgeoning attraction between two appealing female sleuths, intent on navigating not only campus life but also solving a murder. I enjoyed the subtle indictment of the "boys will be boys" mentality as the university attempts to cover up a series of assault crimes and found myself hoping Jessica Cranberry is already hard at work on the sequel."

—Maggie Smith, author of *Truth and Other Lies.*

"A lonely introvert on an idyllic college campus finds her life upended, first by violence, then by a website where students reveal their darkest secrets, including abuse, assault, and murder. Jessica Cranberry's *In the Trap* grabs readers at the start and doesn't let go until the surprising, tense, and satisfying ending. A definite must read!"

—Merry Jones, award-winning author of *Child's Play* and *What You Don't Know*

In The Trap is a taut, satisfying campus thriller--a throwback to early aughts college days of online diaries, coffee and cigarettes, and "me too" whispers replied to with shouts of "it could be worse" or more commonly "what was she wearing?" Jessica Cranberry isn't afraid to dig deep into the dark aftereffects of trauma, and what happens when we come together to prevent it. Hazel is a compelling heroine whose strength lies in her vulnerability and resolve to do right, and I hope we haven't seen the last of her.

—Lauren Emily Whalen, author of *Take Her Down* and *Two Winters*

"Now why should that man have fainted? But he did, and right across my path by the wall, so that I had to creep over him every time!"

—Charlotte Perkins Gilman, *The Yellow Wallpaper*

Chapter One

Red Flags and Near Accidents

SEPTEMBER 16, 2000

Bell-e-fon-taine. We soared past the exit in Aunt Liddy's old Volvo station wagon, and I couldn't read the sign any other way. Ohio had a couple of cities spelled one way but pronounced another. Bellefontaine was actually *Bell Fountain.* In Versailles, west of here, closer to the Indiana border, people called it *Ver-sales.* I didn't know why; I wasn't really from Ohio.

Aunt Liddy's car was humid, just like outside. We drove a little to the middle and a little to the east. Dark clouds gathered. I could've said on the horizon, but Midwestern storms didn't always work that way unless a tornado was coming. No. The clouds hung close, not a ways off. Their color changed, oppressive ash-gray shifting to ominous lead billows. The sky darkened so hard one might think the whole world was on fire.

With a crack and a flash of silver-white, raindrops fell thick and loud, pounding against the car. The storm's beating percussion drowned out the sound of Aunt Liddy's sappy oldies music, so much so she ended up clicking the station off. I cranked up the air conditioning to keep the windows from fogging up.

The windshield wipers went wild, swiping waves of water away as fast as possible. It reminded me of how Dad used to laugh when he told the story about helping Mom learn to drive. They were high-school sweethearts—of course. In the rain, she'd get lost in the tempo of the wipers and automatically steer the wheel to the rhythm. She'd swerve all over the road until he'd scoot in close and steady her hand, instructing her to look farther ahead, past the wiper blades.

"I better slow down," Aunt Liddy mumbled to herself. Most people talked just to hear their own voices, but especially when they got nervous.

The car's momentum slackened, but the road and our windshield still blurred with splashing water. I couldn't see anything in front of us. Out the side-view window, everything was soaked in the deluge, a blurry, slushy mix of greens and grays.

"Should we pull over?" I asked.

Aunt Liddy chewed her lower lip by way of an answer, and the hairy mole on her chin twitched—in a good witch kind of way. She ran her hand through the cropped mop of curls on top of her head; she was in her early fifties and had already accepted a *Golden Girls* haircut into her life.

I could make out an elongated mound up ahead. "Looks like an underpass. We could pull over underneath."

In seconds, our car slid under the shelter. The beating of the rain silenced for a moment. But Aunt Liddy didn't stop; her knuckles turned white as she gripped the wheel, and we kept going.

"We're not stopping," she said as if I wasn't already aware of her steadfast persistence to get me to college.

"There's no timeline, Aunt Liddy. It's the weekend. We can show up at the dorm whenever."

"We made a plan; we stick to the plan."

This was our screwed-up version of a family motto. I wasn't sure when or how it originated, but Fischers rarely deviated. We did what we thought we were supposed to do. No matter the warning signs, we pressed on.

The rain subsided a little; its pounding beat softened to a patter, and Aunt Liddy relaxed her shoulders. She punched the radio back on, and the soothing tones of "I Can See Clearly Now" filled the car.

As Aunt Liddy hummed along, I worried a hangnail on my thumb, savoring the little sting of pain. It reminded me who I was, where I was going, and that I was doing it alone. The road stayed slick with water and sounded like its own river as we drove over and through puddles.

Suddenly, a sharp bite stole my breath as I lurched forward in my seat, the seat belt digging into my collarbone and chest. Aunt Liddy put her arm in front of me as if that would be enough to stop my head splitting against the windshield. The dashboard was mere inches from crushing the bridge of my nose.

She stomped the brakes and yelled and cursed. Bright red taillights filled our windshield, sparkling and reflecting in the last of the raindrops that hadn't been swiped away. The back of our car started to edge around. Back and forth, fishtailing as Aunt Liddy tried to gain control. Her face flushed pink, expression strained.

Life was supposed to flash in front of my eyes, but I hadn't lived long enough for anything to really show up. I saw my mom smiling and heard my dad laughing, and nothing more. Were they—and everything they'd been through—all my life had amounted to?

Miraculously, Aunt Liddy steadied the car. She laid on the horn. It blared long and loud.

"Did you see him? He cut me off!"

The truck in front of us was massive, with a set of mud flaps showing the curving silhouettes of two naked women. *Classy*. The truck driver stuck his middle finger out the window.

"Stupid dick." Aunt Liddy drew in a deep breath. "He's gonna get someone killed." She turned to me. "I'm sorry. Are you okay, hun?"

I could barely breathe. My heartbeat pounded in my throat and ears. My eyes watered and felt as though they were barely in their sockets. But sure, I was fine and said as much. That stupid song continued. Its singer insisted life was all clear blue skies and obstacles could be seen from far off, which was a damn lie. Trucks came out of nowhere, and so did bad people. Red flags didn't look like red flags until after the fact.

BY THE TIME we arrived on campus, the storm had passed through the college town, and the sky was a robin-egg blue. Green leaves and twigs dotted the wet roads. Traffic was a real bitch. The air, both in and outside the car, suffocated like a heavy wet blanket of humidity held up against my face. Aunt Liddy cranked up the air conditioning, and I rolled up my window, taking in every little detail about this brand-new place I was supposed to call home.

"What do you think, Hazel?" Aunt Liddy tapped her fingers along the steering wheel. "Are ya excited?"

Did I tell her what she wanted to hear? The truth was I'd gone right ahead and stepped into this preapproved, family-planned future, and—fingers crossed—it wouldn't turn to shit.

College. This was the plan, had been the plan since the day I was born, and my parents had started saving. College was supposed to be *the* ticket. To what though? The expectation was a teaching career, like many a Fischer before me, including my aunt. But nobody had ever asked me, and I wasn't so sure what I wanted for my life yet.

"It'll be cool to start something new." I'd moved in with Aunt Liddy in high school, and no one had known a single thing about me. So I already knew starting over brought some freedom. Anonymity equaled a certain kind of power.

"Good, hun. And remember, I'm only a phone call away. Any time—day or night—you call me when you need me. Got it?" Aunt Liddy inched the car into the drop-off zone and shifted into park.

I didn't have time to respond. We were bombarded by volunteers, yanking open doors and hustling me out of the car. They immediately tossed my stuff into a cart on wheels and were busy barking instructions to Aunt Liddy. Once my cart was filled, one of the volunteers took my registration printout and started rolling my stuff away.

"I'll be right back!" Aunt Liddy yelled, and she drove away.

"No, she won't." My escort was a tall, lanky guy with sandy-blond hair pulled into a low ponytail at the nape of his neck. "It'll take at least an hour to find a parking spot. You'll probably be unpacked by the time she gets back up here."

"Busy, huh?" I didn't know what to say.

"Ya think?"

I decided to drop the small talk; I loathed it anyway.

The guy wheeled my stuff near a brick building labeled Robin Hall and left with nothing more than a "Good luck!"

"Thanks," I murmured, pushing my cart inside.

People—families—filled the dorm lobby. Teary moms and proud dads. Younger siblings sat on worn couches with their noses in Game Boys, probably pretending their lives weren't changing too.

"Can I help you?" A cheery voice came from behind a counter set up like a check-in desk at a motel.

"Uh, yeah." My papers were still crumpled in my hand. "I have these." I handed over the forms, mildly embarrassed they were damp with sweat. She rattled off directions— down the hall, take the elevator...

My nerves piled into a lump in my throat, and I moved through the hallway as though in a dream. Fluorescent lights strobed inconsistently as I strolled by a long line of open doors. I tried not to peek, not to spy on these snippets of life as I made my way to my room, but it was impossible not to overhear the kids blowing off their parents' final attempts at nurturing.

At the elevator, I blew out a breath and pressed the button. My dorm room was on the second floor. The names of my suitemates had been mailed to me—printed on the same registration papers sticking out of my back pocket—but that was all I knew about who waited for me in Room 222.

Same as all the others, the door was propped open, and a few people milled about in the hall, simultaneously trying to both help and get out of the way.

"Excuse me," I said to an older woman, leaning against the wall. She seemed around the same age as my mom would have been.

"Is this your room too?" Her hair was styled in an angled bob, and a lot of pink makeup decorated her cheeks.

"Yeah, I'm Hazel." I wiped my sweaty palm on my pant leg and held it out to her like a legit grown-up.

"Nice to meet you. I'm Trish's mom."

"Mom, have you seen my— Oh, hi!" Trish was loud and bouncy and gave off an overly friendly energy. "You must be Hazel. Everyone else is already here."

"Hi. Yeah, I am." We shook hands too.

Trish stepped aside to talk with her mom, and I left my stuff in the hall, entering our new room. One small loveseat and four desks lined the walls. I set my bag on one of the two desks next to the windows and checked out the view. Below us, sidewalks and mature trees punctuated a small court-yard. How pleasant.

Beyond a heavy curtain separating the living space from the bedroom, two sets of bunk beds took up the majority of space in the second room. One of the bottom bunks seemed unclaimed, which was fine by me. I wasn't the type of person who insisted on being on top, so I dropped my backpack on the bare mattress.

Rolling the giant cart into the room proved futile. Even if I'd been able to maneuver it through the too-small door-way, everyone else's stuff cluttered and overtook the whole room. So I left my things parked in the hallway—next to Trish's mom, who kept rolling her lips and picking at her cuticles—and unpacked my stuff, piece by piece.

Trish and another roommate, Kim, had known each other in high school and were busy stringing Christmas lights everywhere. There didn't seem to be a plan or pattern to what they were doing. They tacked twinkling strands along the perimeters of their desks and formed an abstract figure on the wall above the loveseat. The lights cast a soft pink glow around the room.

I went back to the bedroom, unzipped a new pack of sheets, and started making my bed.

"Hey," a smoky voice said.

I stepped out from under the bunk and looked up at a face—a pretty one, heart-shaped with olive-toned skin and big brown eyes—atop the railing. "Hi," I said.

"I'm Maeve Drakos. Greek dad, Irish mom."

"Hazel Fischer. A little bit of everything?"

"People sometimes ask because of my name."

I wasn't sure I would have—asked about her name, I mean. Her name was beautiful, movie-star quality, but its origins probably wouldn't have been the first thing I won-dered about when it came to Maeve Drakos.

OAKLEY UNIVERSITY

"Where tomorrow's leaders don't fall far from the tree."

Go Oaknuts!

Welcome to Oakley University's online diary-hosting website, promoting a shared community experience for all.

Username: dead_papers

Date Posted: September 16, 2000

And so, I'm here. All moved in.

My room is achingly small. It's where I am now, typing away at this little diary at my little desk in my little chair, like a doll in a playhouse. But the furniture is not as cute. It's all industrial-looking. The upholstery, of the chairs and the curtains and the couch in our shared lounge area, is an offensive burnt-orange color. It's a hue screaming to be noticed, desperate not to disappear among its surroundings. But then, a shade has no choice, neither blending in nor standing out of its own accord. And, of course, there's a stain. Right in the middle of my seat cushion is a quarter-sized spot of brown. I can only imagine...

The dorms seethe with stories, are haunted by them actually. Thousands of rooms housing thousands of tales, rotating in and out with the seasons. I know mine. I've known exactly what I come from for some time now. A great and terrible secret that would scare the shit out of you.

Chapter Two

Weak Ankles

SEPTEMBER 20, 2000

The lid to the toilet seat came down with a clatter. I sat down and laced up my new shoes. It was the first day of classes, and wearing the right shoes seemed like an important detail. I'd wanted a pair of Docs, but these chunky-heeled imitations had been marked for clearance. So decisions had been made.

The floor tiles were slick with condensation from the shower. When I stood up, my ankles wobbled, and I steadied myself between the sink and the towel bar. The shoes gave me several extra inches, which meant I was well over six feet tall. I tried not to back away from my size though. Hated that game actually. Some of the girls I'd known in high school were always trying out new ways to make themselves smaller. Whereas I just wanted—needed—to take up space.

Shrinking was for the dead and/or dying.

And I'd had enough of that.

I smoothed wrinkles from the sleeves of my T-shirt and tugged on the hem. It barely reached the waistline of my favorite pair of jeans. With a squeeze of mint-green paste, I brushed my teeth. *This will be fine.*

"I can do this," I whispered to my foggy reflection and wiped foamy spittle off my chin.

"Hazel!" One of my suitemates pounded on the door. "You done in there?"

I gathered my wet towel and pajamas. The bonus to the all-girl dorm was the semiprivate bathroom connected to our living suite—the exact and only reason I'd selected Robin Hall as my first choice. Most dorms had one huge, very public restroom per floor, with shower stalls and everything. *No thank you.*

Steam billowed out of the bathroom as I opened the door. Maeve, who was my height when I wasn't wearing platforms, stood before me in a pair of boxer shorts and a loose tank top. Her eyes were still morning-time squinty, and her pixie cut had gone wild in her sleep. She crossed her arms.

"You can't hog the bathroom," she mumbled, shoving past me.

I ignored her and slipped through the living room and past the curtain at the bedroom's entrance. A fan hummed near the windows, propped up between the beds, producing a slight breeze, the last of summer's muggy death grip. Even so, the room smelled like there were too many bodies inside.

Trish and Kim were still asleep. They'd taped photographs of themselves in sparkling prom dresses to the walls and had pinned up twin posters of the cast from the TV show *Dawson's Creek.*

I stuffed my dirty clothes into the laundry bag tied around the post at the foot of my bunk. A whiff of mildew hit me full in the face. Aunt Liddy had dropped me off nearly a week ago, so it was almost time to figure out the machines in the basement. The rest of my belongings fit into a tall wooden wardrobe with one rail, one shelf, a drawer, and two little cubbyholes near the bottom for shoe storage, or whatever. I grabbed my Caboodle off the shelf.

Back in our common room, sunlight filtered through the window, creating bright rectangular spotlights over the floor tiles. I plopped down at my desk and put on my face—what Aunt Liddy called it. She never left the house without coating herself in an orange foundation that left stains on her shirt collars. I tried *not* to do that, using just beige powder, mascara, and some candy-flavored lip gloss. I ran my hands through my still-wet hair and detangled the knots, then tied it all up with a scrunchie.

The toilet flushed, and Maeve came out of the bathroom. She glared at me. "It's like a sauna in there." She was pretty scowly in the morning.

"I like really hot showers."

"Yeah, well, it's no fun taking a shit in a steam room." Maeve rubbed at her eyes with the heels of her palms.

"Sorry," I said. "There're no windows in there."

"Turn the fan on next time." Maeve ambled back into the bedroom. The drape swished after her.

"Will do!"

"Shut up, bitches!" Kim yelled.

Our bed creaked as Maeve climbed back to the top bunk. I could already distinguish some of the telltale sounds of our dorm. Maybe this place *could* be a kind of home to me.

I pulled the strap of my messenger bag over my shoulder, the leather's earthy smell reminding me of Aunt Liddy. The bag had been my graduation gift. Guilt panged in my heart; I should have called her already. But a big part of me needed to prove I could do this alone, away from everyone and everything from my past. Including Aunt Liddy. I was near the middle of the state now, surrounded by a fresh, screaming city. When I was honest with myself, I was excited, maybe even hopeful, about being here. Sure, my optimism was like an ember in a firepit of ash, but I hadn't felt anything in so long, I wanted to protect this spark. Maybe fan it a little.

I spritzed sunflower-scented body spray into the air and stepped through the mist. Tossing my keys into my bag, I left, clip-clopping through the hall and down the stairwell. The combination of bag and shoes threw off my center of gravity. I wobbled here and there, using the handrail to steady myself as I plodded onward. But then, at the bottom step, I went down hard. My stomach lurched with the shock; my whole body crumpled and collapsed. My butt slammed onto the edge of the last stair.

"Christ!" I sucked in a breath; my ankle throbbed. I sat up and prodded the sore spot, surveying the damage.

Three girls skipped past me, their bookbags shushing against their backs. One of them flung her hip into the door's push bar and held it open for her friends. I glimpsed the shining day beyond her, calling everyone to their start, and here I was, a limp body in a dank stairwell.

"You okay?" the girl holding the door asked.

"Weak ankles." I blamed myself, not the shoes.

"Freshman?"

I nodded.

"Us too. Good luck out there." The door banged shut.

"Thanks!" I called after her. At least I wasn't totally invisible.

But I was still left alone in the hall. Minutes ticked by— minutes I'd specifically calculated were needed to span the distance between my dorm and Maynor Hall.

Stick to the plan.

My cheeks went slack as I blew out a long, deep breath. I tested movement in my ankle, back and forth. A string of popping snaps, like a bowl of Rice Krispies cereal, released within the general area. But without any lingering pain, I put my full weight on my ankle and pressed on.

A buzz of activity swarmed outside the dorm. Drivers swung their cars through the looped driveway, either picking people up or dropping them off. Near the bike rack, a few students fumbled with their locks, eventually mounting their bikes and zooming past my purposeful plodding.

Along the sidewalks and within the patches of green lawn in front of each dorm building, crowds pulsed together and split apart. Excited chatter floated with the wind, along with the exhaust fumes of idling cars at the corner stoplight. At the crosswalk, I opened my bag and searched for my Discman. The headphones' soft foam comforted the rising tide of anxiety in my chest. Sometimes I liked people best when I didn't have to hear them.

Whatever CD I'd popped in last time immediately tuned out the voices and city noise. If I ever let anyone know me again, they'd surely make fun of my music choices. But whatever, "More Than a Feeling" was an awesome song. Classics made me feel good. When I allowed myself to be sentimental, they brought up images of little-me dancing in circles around the living room with my parents.

Mom and Dad *would* materialize if I listened to the right song. With proud smiles and teary eyes, they followed me through the teeming crosswalk, only to be startled off, dissolved, when a police car whizzed by. Anger pulsated through me in the same way the car's sirens blared and the lights flashed. But as time spanned and distance grew long, my feelings and the actual, physical commotion on the street faded. Everything calmed. I could hear the music again, but my parents were gone.

I walked toward the classroom buildings—large structures with hugely varying architectural designs. It was like cruising through a disjointed timeline. Modern constructions of white stone and smooth lines alternated and competed with flat brick saltbox-style edifices. In the distance, looming over the stadium, stood three massive, rather plain and beige towers—the newest student housing.

The oldest lecture halls lined the perimeter of a far-reaching, trapezoid-shaped grassy area, adoringly referred to as the Trap. According to campus lore, each lap around the Trap's perimeter resulted in a year of good luck if done after midnight. I'd have to employ all sorts of tricks to make that happen safely: pepper spray, keys gripped between each knuckle, a self-defense class or two. The map showed my first class in one of the historical buildings with classic stone turrets on the other side of the Trap.

My ankle protested here and there, but I ignored it. Tendons didn't get opinions. A group of girls spread out their belongings in a corner of the university lawn. I dodged a frisbee, accidentally stepping through a triangle of players. In another section, onlookers, dressed like me or like students anyway, encircled a speaker.

I stepped toward the outskirts and pulled the headphones off my ears. Based on the speaker's screeching about Hell, I knew it was a Bible he thumped in his hand. The audience harassed him, and he harassed them back. In turn, each person fed off the frenzy of confrontation. I put my headphones back on and stepped away from the unfolding drama. If not for my class, I could've sat and watched all day. I didn't love being surrounded by people but watching them interact was usually amusing. I'd piece together elaborate backstories for why they might behave a certain way, cataloguing reactions in my mind, trying to understand their motives. Trying to understand mine.

A tall, gnarled oak tree overshadowed the Trap's center. A marker in the paved segment around its base suggested historical importance. I wasn't about to stop and read it though. I had zero interest in looking like a tourist. As I approached the marker, I craned my neck to see if I could snag any words. Over time, maybe I could piece it together as I passed by.

But, without any warning, my ankle buckled again.

There was no railing to grab on to this time, only people. I stumbled forward, out of control, and reached for the guy in front of me. His shirt sleeve slipped through my fingers as he shoved my hands away, disgust registering with the curl of his upper lip. Time slowed and then sped up as I went down like a tree in the forest.

My knee banged into the cement, and my arms whooshed out from my sides to keep me from falling over. And there I stayed, balanced on one knee with my arms out-stretched, looking as if I'd just finished a performance or a magic trick. All I needed was a sparkling jumpsuit and cape.

I'm not much of a crier, but I could have cried then, especially when people picked up their pace as they walked by. Hurrying past my kneeling form, they shot confused, sideways glances at me. I wiped my eyes, then laughed. Surely, somebody else would laugh with me. They would help me up, marking the beginning of a friendship that might span a lifetime. This would all be okay then—worth the embarrassment even—because an alliance would have been gained.

But that wasn't what happened.

As my laughter curled around the nearest branches of the oak tree, the circle of traffic around me widened in total social avoidance. I stood back up on my own, dusted my jeans off, checking for rips or stains. My cheeks burned with humiliation, but I was okay. No blood, no foul.

Stick to the plan.

OAKLEY UNIVERSITY

Username: dead_papers

Date posted: September 20, 2000

At all hours, muffled, thumping club music travels through the cinder block walls. Shrieks and laughter leak, too, alongside the rhythmic basslines. Are these *really* happy sounds? It's such a thin line from one feeling to the next. Ecstasy or fear. Joy to terror. Every one of those emotions could be at the party, teetering on the razor's edge of expression and all sounding so eerily similar.

I should know.

Views: 1

Likes: 0

Comments: 0

Chapter Three

Precious

SEPTEMBER 20, 2000

"Oof, what happened to your knee?" Maeve tossed her keys on the desk next to mine. Her eyes were brighter than they had been earlier. She wore thick black eyeliner, contrasting her brown irises nicely. Maeve had an effortless way about her, from the way the strings of her cut-off shorts fringed her legs, to the bohemian-style blouse falling over one shoulder.

"I fell in the Trap." I sat with my pant leg rolled up, poking at the fresh purple bruise.

A bunch of bananas sat on top of the minifridge, clearly marked with our roommate's name on a strip of masking tape. Maeve grabbed one and peeled it.

"Those are Trish's," I said.

"That looks bad," she said through a mouthful of banana mush, totally irreverent about stealing someone else's groceries.

"It isn't good, that's for sure." I considered telling her the whole story because it was kind of funny. We might've bonded. But before I could, Maeve tapped a pack of cigarettes on the palm of her hand, then leaned out the doorway to ask our neighbor if she wanted to smoke.

From where I sat at my desk, I could see inside our neighbor's open dorm room. She sat across the way, filing her nails. She was short, and her waist-length blond hair made her seem much shorter. Every time I'd seen her, she'd worn a pair of fishnet stockings with a different pair of combat boots—short ones, knee-highs, in different colors and patterns. I placed bets with myself on when there'd be a repeat. It had to be coming; nobody had more than a week's worth of fresh combat boots.

After they left, I let my hair down, rolled down my pant leg, and kicked off my own damn shoes. We were breaking up. Throwing them away would be such a waste, but I had no idea where I could donate them. Even if I did, getting there would involve figuring out the city's bus system, and I hadn't gotten that far yet.

Our trashcan was an overflowing mass of packaging scraps and balled-up shopping bags. Every time someone took out the garbage, it seemed to immediately refill. I slipped on my reliable sneakers—an old pair of brown Chucks—and stamped down the trash until it became manageable. With the flimsy knotted bag in hand, I went searching for the dumpster.

I took everything outside with plans to unload the trash, then hit up the cafeteria and grab some lunch to go. Sitting alone in the dining hall was starting to feel a bit tragic. Aunt Liddy always made us eat together, her usual nonstop chatter providing a soundtrack to my every meal. Now, lunch took all of ten minutes as I stuffed something in my mouth while pretending to read.

Ahead of me, a walled-off area corralled the green metal receptacles. Students had only been here a couple days, but the vicinity already reeked of sweet pickles and, *Jesus*, piss? I set the shoes on the ground and lifted the heavy plastic lid, touching as little as possible. Flies zoomed out. I forced my mouth shut and held my breath. Bag and shoes hit the rest of the collected trash with a swoosh. The lid banged shut, and I got the hell out of there, obsessively wiping my fingers on my pants.

The side entrance to my building wasn't too far from the trash. Sheltered by a bricked stairwell, intermittent puffs of smoke wafted out of the ingress. Girls' laughter sang out—Maeve and our neighbor—and, for whatever dumb reason, drew me nearer.

"I don't know; she seems kinda anal and a little...precious?"

I stopped before turning the corner. Maeve's voice was easily recognizable with its alto register and smoker's scratch.

"Precious?" asked the other voice. Which had to be the neighbor. "What the hell does that mean?"

She must be talking about Trish.

"I can't think of any other way to describe her."

"How 'bout the other two?"

Maeve stopped to inhale; then a cloud of smoke wisped my way. I hated how much I enjoyed the smell. "They might be worse."

Our neighbor snorted. "How so?"

"Besties from the same hometown. I think they'll try for sorority row when they can. Should be interesting."

Wait, what? I was the precious one?

Their banter continued, sizing people up and knocking them down. I wasn't quite sure how I'd already earned a label, but whatever. I'd heard enough. Mean-girl shit had always banged around high school, like locker doors clanging shut. I'd had hopes people would leave those behaviors behind, but apparently not. Apparently, we were all just animals, nipping and snapping at each other until we died. College didn't change anyone.

Backpedaling, I followed a group of guys toward the cafeteria. They moved in the bouncing, energized, easy way some boys do. Dressed identically in low-waisted cargo shorts and trendy tees, they were a pack. When a cute girl walked by, they turned in unison. One of them whistled, signaling the others to start in with the catcalling. Then one noticed me.

"Hey," he said.

But I was still reeling over what I'd heard Maeve say about me. *Precious? What does that even mean?* I looked at the pavement, ignoring him. Maybe he'd take the hint and leave me alone.

"You don't speak?" He let himself fall behind the others and kept pace with me.

Damn it. "I do."

"That's better. Didn't your daddy ever teach you any manners?"

I almost laughed. Dad taught me a lot of things, mostly how to protect myself in ways that might make this guy cry.

"Nope." I held up my hands in an exaggerated shrug. "Born in a barn, I guess."

He laughed. His hypermusky cologne blocked all other smells. I could taste it on the back of my tongue. He patted the top of my head and then tangled his fingers through the waves of my hair.

"See, that's so much better." He gripped my arm.

I blinked away from his gaze and tried to swerve out of his grasp. But his hand made its way past my shoulders, trailed down my spine, and lingered near my lower back. His fingers, right above my ass, pressed firm as he subtly let me know he could reach farther if he wanted. He could grab what wasn't his in broad daylight, and I'd be lucky if he stopped himself. But without another word, he did stop and jogged to catch up with his friends. His leather flip-flops snapped against the callused heels of his feet.

BACK IN THE dorm room, I flipped on the little TV set either Trish or Kim had brought and waited for the screen to fill with the soft-filtered faces of characters I loved to hate. I sat on the loveseat, set my Styrofoam to-go box in my lap, and squirted a bunch of tartar sauce on a fish sandwich.

On-screen, sand sifted through a towering hourglass, and behind it, waves pounded upon a shoreline. String instruments struck a series of repetitive chords, reminding me of heartbeats. As the voice of an elder character declared the show's prophetic tagline, Maeve strolled in. She sat next to me, reeking of cigarettes, and stole a fry.

"Mmm." She angled her knees toward me and took another one. "You watch *Days of Our Lives*?"

"Since I was twelve. You?"

"'Bout as long," she said.

Pretentious. Haughty. Finicky. Synonyms of what she'd called me. My insides burned with...embarrassment? Shame? Indignance? Yes, yes, and yes. But I wasn't in the mood for a confrontation. I had to live with this person. Eavesdropping on private conversations usually went badly for everyone involved. At least, it always did on soap operas.

I set the container between us, and Maeve continued to bogart fries.

"I hate what they've done with Ghoul Girl," she said.

"Chloe Lane?! I love that story line." My annoyance with Maeve dropped away to talk plot points.

"It's tired." She shrugged. "Ugly duckling tropes trigger the hell outta me."

I hadn't thought of that. It had been so satisfying when the other teenagers on the show finally embraced Ghoul Girl. But thinking back on how the narrative played out, Maeve was right. A lot of their acceptance had been based on how sexy the character appeared when she came out from underneath the black cloak.

"Don't get me wrong; I love the show," Maeve said. "I mean, a soap opera isn't the place to expect a whole lot of social commentary. I just wish there'd be a girl who stayed herself for once."

"Trauma shaped Chloe's desire to hide. And really, people change every day."

"I don't know if I believe that."

"What? So you're the same person you were your freshman year of high school? You didn't transform at all?" Maeve didn't answer, so I continued, "You haven't learned new things about yourself?"

"Okay, okay. Point taken."

The music played as the network cut to the first commercial break. I chewed and looked at Maeve. She smiled as though she were my friend and not someone who'd talked trash about me forty minutes ago. She wouldn't fool me. There was no room for a friendship here.

We watched the rest of the show in relative silence. The big baby-swapping reveals were usually reserved for the end of the week, not some random Wednesday. When the end credits rolled across the screen, I tossed the to-go container in the trash.

"I could use a nap." Maeve stretched her long arms above her head. She was tall and sinewy. She yawned and rubbed her eyes, asking, "What's your afternoon look like?"

"Uh..." I fumbled for an answer, though I had memorized my class schedule. I kept up the ruse and checked my planner. "Educational Philosophy."

Maeve's eyebrows raised. "You wanna be a teacher?"

"Not really."

"Then why'd you sign up for the class?"

"It's just what my family does."

Aunt Liddy and I hadn't even discussed what my major might be. Fischers were teachers. Kindergarten to phys ed, all across the Midwest, a Fischer stood at the head of a classroom. They ended careers with thirty years' worth of school portraits—except for my parents. Their case was an anomaly, a glitch glossed over.

"But is that what you want?" Maeve asked.

"No. I don't know. What about you?"

"A gen ed course."

"Well, I better get going." I hated being late almost as much as being lost.

"Wanna walk together?" Maeve slipped the straps of her bag over her shoulders.

Awkward. Why was she being nice to me when she clearly thought I was some precious piece of shit? "That's all right. You go on ahead."

Maeve slid on a pair of mirrored sunglasses and cocked her head to the side a bit. Her eyebrows scrunched, which made me think she wasn't used to rejection.

"If that's the way you want it." She shrugged, letting my casual coldness roll off her.

"I do." I stared at the floor and bit my bottom lip. Protecting myself—my feelings—came first. Period.

OAKLEY UNIVERSITY

"Where tomorrow's leaders don't fall far from the tree."

Go Oaknuts!

Welcome to Oakley University's online diary-hosting website, promoting a shared community experience for all.

Username: dead_papers

Posted: September 22, 2000

I spent a long time at the window today, staring out at the murky river. Its everlasting movement held me there, transfixed for...hours? The ceaseless, rushing movement slashed through the land and rock, dissolving minerals and carrying them downstream.

I lost time imagining what it might be like to exist in such a way, affecting so much without a care, without a worry. Merely being whatever the hell I was meant to be.

The river knocked some pointless memory loose. It's there, wriggling like a worm right before the hook punctures its body and it's remade into bait. What am I to do? The river whispers, *tell.*

My dad owned a hardware store, and I spent most days with him after school, hanging out in the back room, doing homework, and playing pretend. Once I turned thirteen, he brought me up front to work the counter or stock shelves. Sometimes male customers thought I was his wife. It never mattered if my pink cheetah-print backpack was on the counter in plain view or how I looked like a miniature version of my dad—same brown eyes and hair, same round cheeks with dimples.

"She's my daughter, Bob." Or Tom, or Dave, or Steve. His voice sounded like a stripped screw, deformed by force. Or so I thought. These were shoppers. Our livelihood depended on the paying customer always being right. And they wore him down until he stopped correcting them. To those men, a girl didn't have a soul. I was only a face. A body. All they saw were the beginnings of curves, new acres of flesh. Even my dad's pained expression wasn't authentic. He had his own shames—so many of them.

Views: 4

Likes: 2

Comments: 2

Ivee16: I know what you mean.

BlUBrd5: I've never thought about it, but yeah. Something similar happened to me too.

Chapter Four

Acquaintance Past

OCTOBER 4, 2000

I had to run a mile and a half to get to class because I'd missed the campus shuttle. So when I walked in the building, sweat lined my upper lip, and my armpits were swampy. Lecture had started seven minutes ago, and I side-shuffled to a seat in the back of the well-lit classroom. Apologizing as I went down the row, I took the first empty seat.

Educational Philosophy was populated with young and mostly white women, all of them looking over a handout I didn't have. I fanned myself with a spiral notebook and tried to peek at the girl's paper next to me. She scooted the paper closer.

"Thanks," I whispered. She shrugged, popping and snapping bubble gum in her mouth.

After twenty minutes of class discussion, my ears burned with frustration. Annoyance flushed my cheeks every time someone raised their hand for a counterpoint or yet *another* what-if scenario. I hated this—disliked most of my classes to be honest.

Maybe I needed a coffee break. My bag weighed a ton, and when I slung it over my shoulder, it nearly missed the girl's nose. I mouthed *sorry* and *bathroom*. Her lips tightened with obvious disapproval.

I found a coffee vending machine across the hall, fished some coins out of the bottom of my bag, and pressed my selection. A paper cup plopped down into the little cove area, and magma-hot liquid streamed into it. When the last of the not-even-close-to-a-real-cappuccino cappuccino dribbled out, I took the cup and blew over the top. It smelled like mocha, though, and that was comforting, at least.

"Hazel? Hazel Fischer?"

It couldn't be.

I turned as Plainville High's head thespian, Sara Gilchrist, emerged from the elevator and waved. She trotted over in a maroon velour tracksuit and running shoes, flawless as usual.

"Hey, Sara." I sipped my drink too soon and burned the hell out of my tongue. It stung and scorched all the way down my esophagus. I sputtered and coughed, scanning the area for a water fountain.

"Are you okay?" Sara asked. A look of genuine concern wrinkled her forehead.

"Fine. Burnt tongue, is all." My tongue felt thick and numb.

"Oh, yeah. Those things come out crazy hot." Sara flipped her sleek, next-level, black hair over her shoulder. I'd been envious of that hair flip as long as I'd known her.

"How've you been?" Sara asked. "Where are you living? I'm in one of the towers by the stadium. The suites are split into three-bedroom areas which you share with one person. Six people share the living area and a bathroom. It's totally fun. Don't you think?"

Conversations with Sara went like this. She talked fast, verbally jumping from topic to topic until she ended with a pop of a question. After a couple drama classes together, I knew to be ready for the quick pause of inhalation where I could sneak in an answer.

"I'm on north campus," I blurted.

"What's your major? I'm gonna try for theater. Ms. Hein thought I should go for it. Took some convincing on my parents' end, but I think it's the best fit."

I didn't think she cared about my major since she'd started talking about herself right after asking. Instead, she probably wanted a butt-pat regarding her choice.

"I'm sure you'll be a huge success."

Sara got the lead role in every high school play. The rest of us worked our asses off to get the slightest nod from Ms. Hein. But "watch how Sara does this or see how Sara projected here" was all we ever heard.

"Tryouts are coming up." Sara tucked silky strands of hair behind her ears. Her eyes widened.

Pay attention, Fischer. She's getting an idea.

"You should try out with me!" She clapped her hands together under her chin.

I laughed. "No way." A splash of coffee spilled over the side of my cup. The brown liquid almost splattered all over Sara's white sneakers. "Sorry." I looked for something to wipe up the mess, realizing this was my out. "My acting days are over."

"Come on, Hazel. It can't hurt to try."

It can. It will.

"Let me give you my number." Sara materialized a pen and pulled a copy of the school newspaper, *The Campus*

Echo, from her backpack. "There's an article in today's art section with all the details. Call me, and we'll do this, okay?"

"Yeah, maybe." I balled my fists before taking the newspaper. Sara and I had always been competitors. Trying out for a college play alongside her would be a repeat of the same old high school shit I'd gladly left behind. "I better get a paper towel to wipe this up. I don't want anyone to slip." I motioned toward the bathroom. "Catch ya later."

"Good to see you!" She gave a little wave, her delicate, piano-playing fingers fluttering. Sara's eyes glimmered with...sadness? Pleading? Either way, I'd never seen her make that look before. So I made sure not to throw her phone number away.

The Campus Echo

Busy Start for Campus Cops

by Gayle Jackson

According to the data, Oakley crime is on the rise.

"It's part of every new school year," says Oakley University's lead security officer, Dave Mason, in response to an uptick in complaints among Oakley's sprawling campus. "Each fall, as the freshman come in and find themselves doing all kinds of things they've never done on their own before, we get extra phone calls and lots of hits off the emergency blue boxes. But those alerts turn out to be mostly pranks."

The 1990 Clery Act, enforced by the United States Department of Education, has sought to bring an air of transparency and accountability to policy surrounding campus security, requiring universities receiving Title IX funds to keep public complaint logs. Currently, Oakley's crime logs have seen a 50 percent increase in alcohol and theft-related crimes. "Kids are gonna come here, and unfortunately, they're gonna drink," Officer Mason says and assures that of the burglary reports, "Most of those are cases of missing ID or stolen bikes." He advises students to invest in U-locks.

Yet, most striking for current Oakley students might be the number of assault crimes reported in the last week. Data suggests three out of every ten calls fall under the assault category, which include crimes of rape and/or stalking and hazing. Those numbers may seem low, but according to lead advocate at Haven Center, a local nonprofit treatment facility, they can be deceiving, citing many survivors' reluctance to come forward in these cases. The Haven Center representative states even a small spike may point to a much larger problem.

While the Oakley security department advises students to remain aware of their surroundings and travel in groups at night, they assure the population that campus remains a safe place to be.

University president, F. Henry Pepper, was contacted for this story but submitted no comment.

Chapter Five

Singer's Shadow

OCTOBER 7, 2000

Three times a week, I suffered through an econ lecture. I took notes, went to every class, and asked questions in recitation, but the concepts escaped me. Eventually, I realized my grade would boil down to memorizing chunks of text. A couple of my classes had been going this way, and I spent more and more time in the Robin Hall basement study room.

I headed downstairs, armed with a heavy textbook and my travel mug filled with black coffee. Aunt Liddy had always served green tea when I pulled a late night for school. But now, the bitter bite of black coffee fit better.

White-speckled linoleum tiles and dim sconces lined the basement hall. At one end, the laundry room shimmered with a fluorescent-tubed glow. It was always quiet down here, except for the soft tumble of the jumbo-sized dryers or the occasional spraying *whoosh* as washers filled with water.

The space smelled of soothing lavender detergent. A chair leg screeched against the tiles as I scooted it out from under the table. I went about setting everything up: books on the left, angled precisely; notepad slanted to the left, coffee on the right; pen clicked and at the ready; highlighter... *Damn*, I'd left it upstairs. My coffee would be cold by the time I returned from getting one, so I forced myself to ignore its absence and get to work.

I read and copied what I thought might be important. But before long, the letters meant to explain the economy jumbled together. I hated those letters. I squeezed my temples and let out a groan.

"*Hmmhm hmm hmm hm-hmm...*" Someone's humming broke through the silence of the basement.

I recognized a clear, strong voice when I heard one. Aunt Liddy had made me go to church where everybody *sang*, just not well. Elderly voices were tired and tinny; young ones were screamy. The songs all blended into a ghostly Sunday morning wail. But the crispness of someone who could really sing was akin to seeing a rare bird.

Screw it. I needed a highlighter anyway.

In the hallway, the laundry room singer's shadow spun on the walls. This seemed like a semiprivate moment.

I paused at the doorway, listening to the sweet voice rise and break over a stunning melody. The air smelled overly perfumed, like warm dryer sheets. I held my breath and extended my neck enough to see my roommate, Maeve, with a set of headphones over her ears. She folded her laundry and danced. Underneath the spaghetti straps of a tank top, Maeve's tawny-beige shoulders swiveled. Her body accentuated the beat; I could almost see the music. She wore a pair of tired-looking flip-flops, and her long flowy black pants swished over the cement floor.

Maeve turned suddenly. Her laundry basket balanced on one hip.

I wrenched myself back into the hall's dimness, but it was too late.

"What the hell, Hazel?"

"Crap," I muttered. Stepping back into her view, I waved awkwardly.

Maeve yanked the headphones off and tossed them on top of her neat pile of clean clothes. "Were you spying on me?"

"I wouldn't say 'spying.'" My fingers trembled with embarrassment as I tried to emphasize certain words. "I was studying down the hall and needed a highlighter. I heard you singing as I walked by. That's all."

"Well, sorry to interrupt your study sesh." Maeve moved forward. "You wanna let me pass?"

Things had continued to be strained between us. She didn't know I'd heard what she'd said about me, and I was fine with that. If she thought I was a pretentious bitch-loner, it made keeping her at arm's length easier. I stepped out of her way.

The corner of her basket caught on the doorframe and knocked Maeve a bit sideways. She adjusted and kept going.

"Can I ask you a question?"

She stopped but didn't turn around.

"Who were you listening to?" I asked.

She faced me. "Ani."

I shook my head, hunching my shoulders toward my ears.

"Ani DiFranco?"

"Never heard of her."

"That," Maeve scoffed, "doesn't surprise me." She picked up her headphones out of the basket and headed for the stairs.

My cheeks stung as if I'd been slapped. *Precious*. All the easy labels people had assumed about me welled up to the surface. *Bitch. Weirdo. Dyke.* I forced my eyes closed. *They don't know you. It doesn't matter.*

I went back to my hidey-hole. Forget the highlighter; I'd sleep down here if I needed to. I could spend my whole college career in the basement. The way things were playing out, it probably wouldn't last long anyway.

Back at the table, I blew out a few breaths. My mind kept reeling around how much I hated this place. College wasn't what I'd expected. I never thought the experience would be rainbows and party hats, but I certainly hadn't expected to be so lonely either.

I pressed my forefingers to the corners of my eyes, next to the bridge of my nose. I'd made a stupid deal with myself *not* to call Aunt Liddy until one month had passed. One more week. I only had to get through one more week, and then I would have proved myself to...myself. I imagined Aunt Liddy's sugar-cookie-sweet voice urging me to keep going and stay focused on the work.

With a flip of my hand, I closed the textbook. Enough. I sat there, running my hands through my hair, gripping till it hurt. What was I supposed to do here?

Shh, slap, shh, slap, shh slap.

A shuffling sound in the hall drew near.

What now? I straightened my posture and listened.

Shh, slap, shh, slap, shh slap.

Fear bloomed out of a place of realization. I was overwhelmingly alone, with only my heart beating in my ears and a heavy textbook to protect myself. I could run. But the only way out was the way in.

Come on. Nobody's coming after you.

The front desk didn't let nonresidents in after a certain time. But that didn't stop people from sneaking them in. Our neighbor across the hall had her boyfriend roaming the halls at odd hours, seemingly coming and going whenever he wanted. And still, the sound continued, growing louder with each smacking step. Someone *was* coming. Closer and closer.

Shh, slap, shh, slap, shh slap.

I stood; my chair slammed to the floor.

Shh, slap, shh, slap, shh, slap.

I gripped the textbook in both hands and flattened my body against the wall near the room's entrance. I'd smack them in the face—imagined their cartilage crunching and breaking under the book's momentum—and make a run for it.

Shh, slap, shh, slap.

The sound stopped. They were right outside. I could feel their presence in the hollow of the doorway, my sensory perception primed with the flood of adrenaline.

"Hazel? You in here?"

Maeve emerged, and my chest deflated with relief. I mentally smacked myself for being so hysterical. The campus had procedures. Anyone coming in late had to scan or show their ID to the desk attendants. Sneaking dudes in after hours wasn't impossible, but seriously? Literally, no one was creeping around the basement of Robin Hall in search of potential victims.

"Jesus, are you okay?" Maeve eyed the textbook in my white-knuckled grip. She didn't completely pick up her feet in those flip-flops as she *shh-slapped* her way over to my table. She placed a Discman on top of my notebook.

"I'm fine. What's this?" I asked, even though I already knew.

"No one should be denied Ani DiFranco." She took a soft pack of cigarettes from the waistband of her pants. "You mind?"

"Uh, no." I looked around, not sure where she planned to smoke or what would happen if she set off the fire alarm.

But Maeve didn't seem to play by all those rules; she set her own, and that was...intriguing.

Maeve towed a chair toward the study room windows. High and just under the ceiling, they were large for a basement. She stood on the seat and cracked one window open. Her lighter clicked, and after what looked like a satisfying exhale, she said, "Go ahead. Give it a listen."

Placing the still-warm headphones over my ears, I hit Play. An infectious drumbeat filled the tiny speakers, and in the distance, a woman laughed and then wailed. Somehow, the music sounded ancestral and stunned something deep inside me. Like nothing on the radio. Maeve smiled, gave me a thumbs-up, and coughed into her balled fist.

I listened through the first song before attempting to give the CD player back.

"Keep it." Maeve put her cigarette out on the window-sill, shooing smoke through the screen.

"I don't wanna take your stuff. What's the record title? I can find it at one of the music stores on Sharp Street."

"It's *Living in Clip*, and you need it right now." Maeve hopped off the chair. "See ya later, Fischer." She squeezed my shoulder and left.

I pressed Play again and let some of the ice I'd packed around starting a friendship with Maeve melt.

The Campus Echo

Sunflowers Represent Survival at Haven Center

by Gayle Jackson

Outside the Haven Center, a patch of land contains their community garden. It is harvested and bare now, yet just weeks ago, it was filled with tall, bright sunflowers.

"We plant one for every call for help we receive," says center manager, Leslie Barnes. "To us, the seeds represent strength and journey. People will bloom again."

When asked how many sunflowers seeds were expected to be planted next season, Ms. Barnes stated the number fluctuates, but this year, the center has seen a particularly high influx of calls—more than double the reports from the previous year at this time.

"There will be one for me." An anonymous Oakley student has volunteered to join us for this interview. "I was attacked in the Trap my first weekend here."

A chart behind the table in the Center's conference room, where we met for this interview, indicates thirteen new sunflowers will be added to the garden next spring.

"Not all of that number represents campus crime; some students are coming out of abusive home environments and are now seeking help. But yes, many do represent cases of assault crimes that have happened on campus recently. More than half."

Of those thirteen, only a handful have been reported to the police or campus security.

"There are many reasons why someone chooses not to start criminal proceedings—fear, shame, accusations and attacks on their character, a belief that it's pointless. We here at Haven Center provide support no matter how the survivor wants to progress."

The Haven Center offers survivors access to 24-hour crisis intervention through their hotline, victim advocate team, rape exam support, criminal justice accompaniment, and counseling.

"I didn't tell anyone what happened to me right away." The anonymous student picks at a hangnail while she talks and stares at the table. "Dealing with it on my own wasn't working. I stopped going to class. Stopped talking. Eating. I never said anything. My roommate noticed. I don't know how she knew, but she handed me a brochure for the center. The gesture probably saved my life."

When asked what she would tell anyone dealing with this, she said, "Tell someone. You're not alone."

If you or someone you know is a victim of an assault crime, the Haven Center 24-hour hotline has available resources that can help at 1-800-656-HELP.

Chapter Six

The Trap at Night

OCTOBER 15, 2000

Phone calls always caused a low tide of anxiety in me. So calling Sara Gilchrist sat on the bottom of my to-do list for days. We were only slightly more than acquaintances anyway. The conversation would surely be full of halting starts and stops. But I knew it was something I needed to do. Aside from Maeve stealing my fries during *Days of Our Lives* weeks ago, I hadn't shared a meal with anyone since the night before moving day when Aunt Liddy and I split three plates of potato skins at Applebee's.

I needed to call her—Aunt Liddy—too, but the first thing she'd ask would be whether I'd managed to make any friends. If I lied, she would know. So I suffered through an awkward chat with Sara. Our voices butted into each other like bumper cars at the county fair until we finally set up a time and place to meet near her tower on Sunday.

The rest of the week passed in a blur of boring lectures, taking notes, and reading. By the time Sunday rolled around, I was mentally prepared for Sara to talk too much. And as I pulled on a semiclean pair of jeans, I figured her boundless chatter would make the whole evening easier.

"Hot date?" Maeve threw herself onto my bunk and crossed her arms behind her head, exposing her navel. She wore a peasant skirt with an elastic waist that had ridden low, right below the curvature of her hip bone.

"No. Meeting a girl I used to know in high school for dinner."

"Really?" Maeve's voice strung the word with intrigue. "Hazel Fischer, lone wolf? I barely believe it. Can I come?"

"You want to?" I tugged a clingy T-shirt over my head. A waft of the cheapest detergent I could find flared as the fabric stretched.

"Why not?"

"I don't know. She's not a friend-friend."

"I sense some backstory. Do tell."

"It's hard to explain." I searched through a pile of mostly cheap jewelry on the counter above our dresser drawers and settled on my necklace with a vintage silver charm.

"Try me, Fischer."

"Have you ever been around someone and it *feels* like they're competing with you even when you are clearly *not* in a competition?" I focused on pinching the necklace's clasp.

"Explain." Maeve's long fingers traced the font on one of my obscure ska-band bumper stickers adhered to the wall.

"I was only into a couple things in high school, right? Drama was one of them. Well, same with Sara. Only, she was better than me." With the clasp fastened, I rearranged the charm until it rested right in my clavicle divot. "But that never stopped her from making passive-aggressive comments about my work, my size...whatever. Lots of little pokes. Does that make any sense?"

"I get it. So you want me to come? I'm a great buffer."

"Sure." Tensions had softened between us since she'd lent me her music and Discman. I hadn't forgotten what she'd said about me, but she was so nonchalant and irreverent—cool. Being around her made me feel as though I might be all those things too.

It was Sunday evening, so campus was still in the post-coital haze of yesterday's football game. Everything felt sleepy in the Trap—from the students spread out on blankets with paperbacks covering their eyes to the oak trees and their tired, drooping fall leaves. Maeve and I walked beyond the towering main library building and its ornate splashing fountain. Oddly, we were still getting some warm days. With the air overbaked and dirty, we seemed stuck in a season past its prime. Autumn waited, at the ready, poised to kill everything off.

"So if you don't like this girl, why did you agree to dinner?" Maeve asked, her sandals scuffing along the rocky pavement of the commons parking lot.

"It's not that I don't like her." I held open the door for Maeve. The river splashed beyond the building, and while I couldn't see it, I could hear its babbling rush cutting through rock and sediment.

Maeve shot me a disbelieving look as she entered the building. Inside, the air conditioning prickled my forearms with goosebumps.

"Okay, okay," I said. "This is all so that when I call my aunt tomorrow, she won't worry about me being alone all the time. Plus, Sara mentioned tacos."

"Aw, lured by shame and food. Got it." Maeve followed me up a set of stairs, past signs indicating the food court location.

"What about you? Why did you want to come?" I asked.

"Bored." The glibness inflecting Maeve's speech echoed in the stairwell. I didn't know if she was insincere about everything, or if this was some kind of defense she played.

"Is the girl across the hall gone this weekend?" I asked.

"My smoking buddy? Her name is Bridgette. And yes, she went somewhere with her boyfriend."

We approached the landing, which opened into a darkly decorated lounge area with a high ceiling, industrial maroon carpet, and paneled walls. People gathered around heavily upholstered couches and cheap-looking coffee tables, some of them holding hands and sipping warm drinks out of forest-green-and-white cups. They talked and laughed overly loudly, the volume of each interaction a form of approval, a signal of encouragement to the others. All that time wasted trying to fit in. For what? In the end, it never worked out. If you were trying to fit, you already didn't.

"Hey, did Trish and Kim leave this weekend too?" I asked, realizing I hadn't seen them since Friday.

We walked toward a row of floor-to-ceiling windows—the room's only redeeming quality—overlooking the river. Brown water splashed and swirled below us.

"I'm not sure. I haven't seen much of them. Have you?"

"No. Where are they?"

"Aliens must've got 'em."

I snorted. "You think?"

Maeve walked backward, away from the windows, shrugging. "Who knows?" She whistled the unmistakable first notes of *The X-Files* theme song.

"All right, Mulder," I joked.

"If I'm Mulder, that makes you Scully, right?" Maeve asked.

"I'm okay with that."

We laughed in a comfortable way, and one of the knots I lugged around loosened.

"For real, though, should we be worried about them?" I asked.

"Nah. Now that you mention it, I half remember them saying they were going home, but I tune them out a lot."

"Me too."

The smell of grease and chili-seasoned beef wafted through a hall off the lobby. We followed the aroma, which led us to two fast-food chain stalls. Students meandered and clustered in groups around the front of each restaurant. Employees yelled orders while alarms beeped every few seconds. Baskets of fries sizzled in hot oil on one side of the hall. On the other, nacho chips and cinnamon sticks were placed in crinkly little bags.

Sara sat at a table by herself near the neon taco sign. She looked around in an obvious, expectant way.

"There she is."

Sara waved as we approached the table. If she was annoyed there would be a third wheel, she didn't show it at first.

"Hi, I'm Sara." She held out her hand, and Maeve shook it.

"Maeve, the roommate."

"Cool. You should've let me know, Hazel. I would've asked one of my suitemates too."

She was irked; I could tell.

"It was kind of last minute," I said.

"I sprang it on her as she was leaving," Maeve explained.

The three of us grabbed purple trays near the register and slid them along a metal shelf attached to the counter, similar to any other school cafeteria.

"I haven't had tacos in forever," I said.

"Me either," Maeve agreed. "My body is ready."

Sara stood between us while we waited in line. She'd never been so quiet.

"May I take your—" A Black girl, close to our age, stood behind the cash register, but an older man, gut bulging over his belt, interrupted her.

"Let me get this one." The man—his name tag said General Manager—tossed a large set of keys in the air before clipping them to his belt loop.

"I got it," she said.

"You've been screwing up orders all afternoon. I don't want these pretty ladies to have to deal with that." He winked at us. "Be the runner, Tor."

The girl's eyes were barely visible under the brim of her cap, but I could see her lashes rest for a beat. She took a breath, relaxed her shoulders, and then she moved away from the register while her boss took over. The manager's dead front tooth, brush-stroked with shades of gray and purple, showed itself as he blurted every stray thought he should've kept to himself.

"Whoa!" He balked after I listed my order. "That's a big meal for a girl."

"I'm hungry," I said. But it was just three tacos and those cinnamon spiral things—a meal, that was all I wanted.

He chuckled to himself as he scanned my ID. Handing the card back to me, he leaned over the counter, clearly checking out my lower half.

"Best be careful, girl."

"Get fucked," I muttered.

"What's that, hun?"

"Nothing."

He winked, and I could've poked his eye out. Maeve looked as if she might mangle her tray. Sara stared at the counter, requesting only a side of nachos for her entire dinner. The runner set part of my order on my tray and asked if I wanted hot sauce. I nodded, wondering what all she had to endure with this douchebag manager. *Should I say something? Complain?* It would probably make him more obnoxious, and for sure, he'd take it out on his employees. I didn't want to make things worse for anyone. So I said nothing, just like everyone else.

As we settled at a table in the dining area, I asked about Sara's auditions to clear the air.

"Did you try out for that play?"

"Not yet!" Sara tilted in her seat and pulled a slip of paper out of her back pocket. "I brought this for you." She unfolded a flyer and placed it near my tray of food.

"I told you I'm not interested." I popped a fried sugary twist in my mouth and pushed the paper back to her side of the table.

"Why not?" Sara whined.

"Why do you care?" Maeve asked around a huge bite of taco.

Sara's perfect brows creased right in the middle. She snatched the lid off the container of nacho cheese before answering. "You wouldn't know this, but Hazel's very talented on stage."

"That's not what I asked." Maeve wiped her mouth with a napkin. She picked up another hot sauce and tore it open.

"I thought it might be fun," Sara said, defending herself. "That's all."

"You think collegiate-level theater will be fun? You're kidding yourself," Maeve stated.

"How would you know anything about this?" Sara shot back.

"I'm with Maeve on this one, Sara." I unwrapped one of my tacos and picked off some of the lettuce. "I think it's gonna be pretty cutthroat, not like high school at all."

Sara blinked fast, her eyes going all watery. Maeve and I had hit on something she'd either never considered or was obsessively contemplating.

"You're a great actress, Sara." The last thing I wanted out of tonight's dinner was for someone to cry or give up on their dreams. "Acting is not something I want to do anymore, but you should go for it."

Sara nibbled a corner of a tortilla chip. "I'm sorry." She folded up the flyer and returned it to her pocket. "I didn't mean to be pushy." Her cheeks flushed.

"It's okay. I understand wanting someone to go with you." I took a bite and glanced at Maeve, who stayed quiet, but a playful twitch danced along the corners of her mouth as she watched the exchange. Something dawned on me; she was enjoying this. The situation was comparable to a study in soap-opera lite. Was that Maeve's schtick? Pressing people's buttons? Watching their reactions? How weird...

And *why* did I like her even more for it?

"What day are tryouts? I could come and be the person in the seats who roots for you," I offered.

Sara wiped the corners of her mouth with a paper napkin. "You'd do that?"

"Why not? I don't have anything else to do."

"That would be so great! Can you be here next Friday?"

"As long as I don't have class, yeah. Call and remind me though."

Another positive thing to tell Aunt Liddy.

"Awww!" Maeve wadded up her taco wrappers into fist-sized balls. "Look at you two! What a heartwarming moment."

When we got up and threw our trash away, Sara thanked us both for coming, and apparently, she'd become a hugger. Her thin and small frame pressed against mine, her shoulder blades sharp as I held her close. I thought of those parakeets at pet stores with clipped wings.

Outdoors, evening had fallen. Ahead of us, the shuttle bus station gleamed against the night in shining fluorescent light. I hadn't forgotten Maeve's enjoyment when she called out Sara's motives. The ride home seemed like a good time to get some answers out of her.

But Maeve veered off the path leading to the station.

"Where are you going?" I asked.

"Smoke break," she called back to me.

The grass was thick, padding our every step toward the riverbank below. With the sun already set, the streetlights cast billowy red and green orbs over the water's surface. The click of a lighter brought Maeve's face, glowing pale-orange, into view as she lit a joint. The dark returned except for a hot little end of something still burning bright. She inhaled, coughed through the exhale, and then passed it to me. The weed stank like burnt tires and skunk.

I sat with my legs stretched over the grass, nearly reaching the muddy silt, then took a hit. The tickling smoke filled me up and couldn't wait to get back out again. I suppressed it, tightening my core until only a few spasmodic grunts emerged.

Maeve snorted through the breath she'd been trying to hold. My eyes adjusted, and I could make out the cloud of smoke haloing her. She sat next to me and picked something off her tongue.

I lay back, propped up on my elbows, listening as the interstate's constant stream of traffic overtook the river's gentle lapping. We passed the joint back and forth until finally, I broke the silence.

"You think I'm prissy," I said. "And you totally enjoyed watching Sara almost lose it back there."

She stared at me with either suspicion or admiration in her eyes. "Okay, I underestimated you. Maybe you are some kind of detective." Her words seemed heavy with sarcasm.

"Nah. I don't know anything about anybody."

"You figured me out." Maeve offered me the joint again. I pinched what was left in between my thumb and forefinger and sat up.

"No, I didn't. I overheard you talking to Bridgette. I'm *precious*, right?"

Maeve's face remained impassive. I couldn't tell what she was thinking, and I wasn't sure if she'd be mad about the eavesdropping.

"Sorry," she said.

"I shouldn't have been listening."

"I shouldn't have been talking." Maeve faced the river and ran her palms over the freshly cut grass. "The other part, though, about me liking how Sara cracked up back there— You didn't overhear that. How did you know?"

"It was in your eyes. They danced a little when she started getting upset. Were you trying to make her cry?"

"I just asked her a question. I didn't know she would cry."

"That's not really an answer."

"It is. I'm not responsible for other people's reactions." Maeve ripped some of the grass out of the ground, then sprinkled the torn blades over the patch. "And so, what if I did enjoy seeing her get emotional? What's that make me?"

"If *you* don't know"—my voice was barely more than a whisper, probably inaudible over the traffic rushing over the highway encircling campus—"I can't know."

Her face tilted slightly as her lips parted. It seemed a question ran across her furrowed brow, and then she laughed, breaking any tension that might have been building. A high-pitched giggle, sounding nothing like my usual, burst from my throat as the weed did its job. Smoke floated above us, rising and dissipating, like time. Beyond it, the sky was huge and black. The pinpricked patterns of stars glowed and burned, arranged by a god millions of light-years away.

"Here." I handed her the joint, stood, and brushed off my jeans. "I think I have to be done."

"Okay, precious," Maeve said, still laughing.

I offered her a hand up. She took it, throwing me off balance as she pulled herself up. In the next moment, we stood close. Really close. Like kissing close. Did I want that? I didn't know. But before anything could happen, a cyclist buzzed by and broke the spell.

We started back to north campus, unsure of the time or even cognizant of its passing.

"Should we wait for the shuttle?" I asked.

"I wanna walk."

I agreed. The campus seemed different at night. Draped in darkness, it filled me with a creeping thrill.

"For the record..." Maeve stopped near a panic station. The electric blue lit up her eyes, reminding me of a squid's inky defense mechanism. "I'm sorry you heard me talking shit. Now that I've gotten to know you better, I actually don't think those things about you."

Behind her, the Trap glowed gold-orange under the black sky and twisted tree limbs. Pathways split off in a million directions, lined with lampposts. Shadows saturated the ground, a patchwork of darkness. If I thought about it too long, it might seem as if pieces of earth had been removed, cut away.

"Hazel?" Maeve snapped her fingers. "You there?"

"No worries." I was only half aware of her apology. Somehow the air was damper now, and I held my breath until I felt the tiniest of aches, then let it go. "First impressions are weird."

"I was just trying to connect with someone or fit in, ya know?"

"I do."

"But you don't, Hazel. I can't tell if you don't care what other people think or if you're clueless."

"Both."

"How? How do you do that?"

"I focus on what I'm supposed to be doing, what's directly in front of me. Like, I'm here to learn how to be a teacher, and that's all. If I make friends, cool. If not, okay."

"I think there's more to it."

I shrugged and started walking again because I needed to move. Maeve pierced through people's bubbles. She'd done it with Sara, and I could feel her poking at the one I'd blown around myself.

Her peasant skirt whooshed over the quiet walkway until we were side by side.

"People don't last." There. I'd said *some* of it. I'd told her my certain truth. Everyone came and went; no one stayed forever. And the less people I let know me, the less pain I experienced when I lost them.

Something about my answer was enough to stop her questions, or she was high enough and easily distracted. Either way, my bubble survived another day.

Only the two of us meandered over the Trap's pathways. Something I hadn't thought possible with a university this size.

Low to the ground, something, a creeping, spectral form, skittered along the path. I jumped, and Maeve fit her hand into mine. Touch almost always felt overwhelming, like a little kid screaming over too-loud fireworks. But in this moment, the cool, soft touch of Maeve's hand was reassuring.

"Probably a rat," she said.

"Oh. And ew."

We kept walking like that, though, hand in hand. The journey stretched out before us, taking hours or minutes. I didn't care.

"I'm hungry." I wasn't sure if I'd spoken until Maeve answered.

"Me too." But she let go of my hand and ran toward the old tree near the center of the Trap, laughing. She collapsed under the canopy of branches.

"Aw, come on, Maeve. I wanna order a pizza or something." I jogged over to her, registering how my voice sounded too loud in this time and place.

"Go on without me." She sprawled awkwardly over the grass.

"I'm not gonna leave you out here in the middle of the night." I might have been stoned, but not enough to abandon her. "It's getting late. Plus, you're hungry too. Remember?"

"The grass feels so good, and you have to see the color of the sky right now."

"I can see it. Midnight-blue. It's the best color."

"It is?"

"Yeah. From the crayon box." I craned my head toward the sky. The color came through between a cross section of black branches and gold leaves. "Midnight-blue is my favorite. What's yours?"

"Periwinkle." Maeve stood and dusted off her skirt.

"I might've guessed that."

"How?" she asked.

"I don't know. It's a vibrant color."

She paused. "You think I'm vibrant?" She butted me with the side of her hip.

"Maybe." I caught my balance. "You're vibrant, and I'm precious."

"What a pair." She smiled, then stretched: her arms reached high, head tossed back, navel exposed, her aura all glittering stars.

My cheeks flushed as I stared. "Come on," I croaked. "We shouldn't be out here."

"Why?"

I gave her an incredulous look. "You know why. You read the newspaper. It's getting late. There've been attacks."

"We're together."

"We're high." I stuffed my hands in my pocket. The night air had grown thick with humidity, morphing into a version of itself that choked off deep breaths.

Maeve twined her arm around mine, and we turned back toward the path. But a spattering echo of hoots and hollers stopped us in our tracks. Ahead of us, a group of dark figures swayed and pulsated. Even from a distance, I could tell they were dudes, a whole school of them. They cut through the Trap, surging toward us, trampling the grass.

"They're drunk," Maeve said. We stayed beneath the tree's canopy.

That fact, combined with the reports coming from the *Echo* recently, sobered me right up. This could be bad—very, very bad.

"Do you think they've seen us?" I asked. "We might be able to get around to the other side of the tree until they've passed." The trunk was massive. It would provide enough cover.

"What's this?" A deep voice sounded thick with booze and something else. Spittle? Chew? Bubble gum?

It was too late.

"I said, what's this?" he slurred. "We know you're there. Come party with us!"

"Yeah!" a couple of the others yelled.

No fucking way. Maeve and I exchanged a glance; she felt the same. I wished we were already home, that I'd convinced Maeve to get up and leave the Trap five minutes earlier. That was all we would have needed. Just five minutes.

Two of them broke away from the main group and headed our way.

Fear crept under the collar of my shirt. My ears burned. I had nothing. The Mace, which Aunt Liddy had made sure I had, sat on the dresser next to a bunch of scrunchies and my deodorant.

Maeve let go of my arm and slipped her hand into her purse. She brought out a cylindrical shape. She looked me in the eye. Her thumb shifted in a familiar way. She'd moved the cap to the unlocked position.

"We'll be okay," she whispered.

I gave a terse nod, and we both faced the guys who now stood right outside the oak's shelter. They reeked of alcohol and smoke. One of them kept both his hands deep in his pockets. The other swayed with the slightest breeze; the drink in his red plastic cup sloshed over the side with each stumbling overstep.

"Show us your tits," the barely standing guy demanded. His eyes were slits, and he snuff-snorted before taking another sip.

My breath, my voice, my pride: all failed me.

The guy with his hands in his pockets shrugged. I caught his gaze for a second, but his shoes must have been more captivating. We were nothing to either of them.

"Show us your tits." The demand came louder this time.

"It's not Mardi Gras." Maeve spoke with a joke in her tone, trying to deescalate this hellish situation. "You don't have any beads." Her shoulders were straight and high. Her chin jutted forward in obvious defiance.

The wobbly guy stepped closer to Maeve. His movement was enough to finally trigger his buddy, who grabbed his arm. The action stopped his movement but not his ugliness.

"You're a dyke, ain't ya?" He spat, and a glob of mucousy saliva landed near Maeve's feet.

"Come on, dude." The friend tugged his arm. "Let's go, Ryan."

"Back off." Ryan shrugged off his friend. "Am I right?" He stalked toward Maeve, leading with his crotch.

"Because she won't flash you?" My voice didn't shake, but my cheeks were aflame with fury and rage and...fear. *Damn it.* "You come at us with disrespect and expect a free show? Get outta here." My tone dismissed him while my heart beat straight dread into my veins.

The guy's friend shook his head at me. A warning? Screw him. He wasn't here to help anyone or act the hero. He seemed fine with letting his buddy spout off and intimidate us.

Ryan came closer to me. His breath reeked of cheap booze, and his teeth were weirdly small—rodentlike. "Maybe it's you that's into pussy." He meowed, licking his hand and rubbing it over his brow, impersonating a cat. His drink dropped to the ground; the rest of its contents splashed onto my jeans.

Squaring up, I stared through him. "Go fuck yourself."

"I don't have to." His upper lip curled, exposing eye teeth protruding like fangs. "There's a hole right in front of me."

I clenched my fists and bit my tongue to keep myself from screaming.

"Ryan, stop." The friend grabbed him more forcefully this time. "Let's get out of here."

This time when his friend urged, the rest of Ryan followed. The two of them took a couple steps backward.

I stood straighter then, pulling my shoulders all the way back too. We were taller than both of them. Ryan's gaze never left mine. His beady, possessive, ferret eyes flared with anger because I wouldn't give him what was mine. I had no doubt he would've taken it had his friend not been there to gently, politely persuade him to stop.

After his friend tugged Ryan away, and we were sure they were leaving, Maeve and I blew out a long breath. It all could have gone so wrong. Adrenaline pulsated through me; my neck and shoulders released the tension propping them up. Feelings came out in heaving gasps of breath. We smiled anxiously and forced ourselves to laugh the whole thing off. Maeve's laughter became a melody erasing all the could-haves in that haunted little scenario.

But only for a second.

"Hey! Come back!" someone yelled.

Even in the shadows, I could see Maeve's expression transform—relief, then fear.

I turned my head as a loud *smack* clapped its way through my whole body. My ass rang out with the tingling sting of Ryan's thick palm. The hit came so hard I stumbled forward, and he jogged away, laughing.

"Sorry!" his friend shouted.

"Yeah, sorry!" Ryan called out, mirth still singing around the edge of his words.

Maeve stared at me, her eyes searching mine.

"Are you okay?" she finally asked.

"Yep." I bit my lip and looked past her to the white marble staircase of a nearby building. I focused on the structure, something solid, secure. Steps that had been there for many years—decades, maybe a century.

"I should've sprayed him." Maeve slipped the canister back into her shoulder bag.

"It's fine. He's gone now."

I ran my hand through my hair. I was okay, still intact. But as we continued home, my ass burned as if that guy's hand were still there.

OAKLEY UNIVERSITY

"Where tomorrow's leaders don't fall far from the tree."

Go Oaknuts!

Welcome to Oakley University's online diary-hosting website, promoting a shared community experience for all.

Username: dead_papers

Date posted: October 16, 2000

Shadows swim in the river, still whispering. Moments I have lived float along the water's surface, churning over the bedrock. I don't know this power the river has—to wrench flashes of history from minds—but I'd like to harness it.

A black form, a wraith, overtakes the rippling waves, twisting any clarity I might have had. I *am* split into halves—standing at the banks and just below the water's surface. I see myself, restocking an endcap at the hardware store as an old man approaches. The river roils at this point, frothing and foaming, making it hard for me to see what I already know comes next: the featherlight touch between my legs. I jump, confront him, and smack his gnarled, arthritic fingers away. He acts confused and stutters through an excuse. My skin crawls.

The river stills. My other half floats downstream. We are separate now.

I wake with terrible headaches. The moonlight illuminates the room in grays and blacks. I'm alone, my roommate gone again.

On the phone, Dad says, "It's nothing. Go back to sleep. You need your rest."

It's the advice he's always given. Dismissing me within the gaslight. I shouldn't focus on these things, which is all I would love to do—forget. But the river's constant babbling and bubbling keeps me remembering. It murmurs to anyone all the things I wish had never happened, all the things I wish I never knew.

What am I to do? It's a goddamned river. It will not stop.

With my head still pounding, I go to the banks for a closer look, and with the saturated, soft ground beneath my feet, the form of another woman takes shape. Instinctually, I know she is a witch, a sea hag, living and swimming and seething under the water. She rises out of the stream. Her black gown clings to her body, and the water flows around her feet. The rapids drag her back, then push her forward until she stands in the damp silt before me.

Tell. Her mouth so close I can feel the breath of her words on my lips. She stinks of marshland, the air around her heavy with mold and decomposition. Rivulets, shining silver in the moonlight, course and drip over her face and black hair.

"I can't," I whisper.

She moves so fast then, thrusting her wet gray fingers into my ears and mouth, poking and prodding until what she searches for breaks loose. I gag and cough and sputter. Once I settle, I see what she has taken. She pinches the secret between her thumb and forefinger, a writhing worm of recollection.

You must.

She bends and releases the creature into the river. I expect it to swim away, to use its wriggling flagellum to propel through the water. But instead, it grows large, matures into something like a 100-year-old catfish with a long and gaping mouth. A slippery body of scale and myth, it hides in under-water caves, outwitting us all. The hideous thing multiplies in the water. Suddenly, the river teems with green and gray fish bodies, writhing and squirming.

"What do you want me to do?"

Catch them. The witch's eyes glow gold. Her lips never part, but I hear her say, *Fry them. Eat them.*

Views: 8

Likes: 2

Comments: 3

bizzybee3: This is kinda weird.

Bonnielass32: hang in there. it gets better

skullznhardons: Psycho.

Chapter Seven

There's Always One

OCTOBER 16, 2000

Our curtains bellowed and stilled with the breeze. A ray of sunlight streamed through the open window, drawing a line between our two sets of bunk beds. The dorm had the feel of emptiness—a rare peace holding the promise of absent suitemates. In the church pews with Aunt Liddy, she and her friends would talk about the Holy Spirit and how they felt it move through them during services. I never knew or understood what they meant. Then I shared a room with three other girls, and when they were all gone at the same time, there was a certain holiness in the silence.

I stretched, long and hard, before placing my bare feet on the fluffy, pink rug between the beds. Then I tossed the comforter over my pillow and went to the living space.

There was only enough coffee left in the carafe for half a cup. White and umber swirled and bloomed together as I poured the milk into my mug. It wouldn't be nearly enough caffeine, and it was lukewarm, so I went through the motions of starting another pot.

A built-in shelving unit next to the minifridge was our pantry. We each had a designated shelf and one common shelf for shared things: coffee and extra-large jars of peanut butter. Kim worked out the system the first week after Trish had a hissy fit about disappearing bananas.

The wall-mounted phone hung next to the door—beige upon beige, with a long, curled, plastic-coated cord. I balanced the receiver between my ear and shoulder. My mother had drilled Aunt Liddy's phone number into my memory at a young age, and in the end, it had turned out to be a necessary precaution.

"If there's ever an emergency and you can't get ahold of me or Dad, call your aunt." The memory flooded my vision—blue and red lights flashing through our old living room, painting the sofa in a spinning pinwheel of color.

It had been years now. So long ago that in my head, Mom's voice had been replaced with my own. *When had that happened?* A new wave of panicky grief rolled over me. Mom's voice was gone, another piece of her stolen away by time, my stupid memory, and that man. Those three pecked away at her presence like proverbial vultures.

Thunk! Something bright red smacked the window and exploded with a watery swish. The scarlet pieces of a water balloon fell away from the screen bit by bit.

I dialed Aunt Liddy, and her phone rang for a long time before the answering machine came on with a recording of my own voice and a long, solid beep.

"Hey, it's me. I got a minute alone here and wanted to call and see how you were doing. Give me a call back when you get—"

"Hello!" Aunt Liddy shouted. I pictured her standing in the kitchen, disheveled as ever, with locks of her brown-and-gray frizzed hair poking out from under the wide brim of her sunhat. "Hazel, is that you?" There would be a smudge of potting soil running the length of her forehead.

"Hi! Yeah, it's me."

"Oooh, it's so good to hear your voice!" she sang.

"Yours too." Her familiar tone actually brought tears to my eyes. I wiped them away and smiled at the thought of her dirty gardening hands and the "Lettuce Eat!" apron she always wore.

"I was out in the greenhouse taking care of some watering. What on earth have you been up to? And why haven't you called?"

Her frankness always cracked me up. She never beat around any bush, even with a small independent garden center to run. After teaching geometry for twenty years and with district budget cuts looming, Aunt Liddy took an early retirement and made her second passion into a living.

"I'm sorry," I said.

"That's not an answer."

"I needed to see if I could do this all by myself."

"And?"

"I did it."

"Alrighty then. Tell me about your classes."

"There's not much to tell. Everything's harder than I expected."

"Well, that's true of most things in life. Have you made any friends?"

"I have prospects."

"Hazel Frances Leevi Fischer, did you spend this entire month not speaking to a soul? Now, I know you think it's fine to do that, but you must put yourself out there and—"

"I went out to dinner with some girls the other night. So you can chill."

"Good." She sniffed. "I will chill."

"You know I'm slow about these kinds of things."

"I know that, dear. I also know you are perfectly fine to hermit yourself up."

"Don't worry."

"It's what grown-ups are supposed to do."

"How have you been?" It was time to change the subject. "How's the nursery?"

"Stop that. You know good and well I'm doing the same old things I always do. You're the one having adventures. Give me the dirt on your roommates."

"You met them. Trish and Kim can be...particular."

"They sound fun." Aunt Liddy half cackled. When she laughed, the loose skin under her chin shook. She called it her turkey neck, and I could imagine the slight jiggle.

"Maeve is the other one. Good taste in music. Interesting outlook. Kinda funny. I like her. She's one of the people I went out with."

I left out all the details regarding our encounter with those guys in the Trap. But Ryan and his hand had left an imprint I wouldn't soon forget. His slurred demands hung around like a bad dream I needed to shake off. But those kinds of details would send Aunt Liddy over the edge. She'd drop everything to drive up here, track those guys down, and beat them senseless.

"It's so good to hear from you, Hazel. Do you think you'll plan a trip home soon?"

"Maybe. I gotta figure out the buses, but I'm sure some of the other girls can help me out."

"You know I can come get ya anytime."

"I know."

Trish and Kim waltzed into the room. They were busy shouting at someone down the hall until they noticed me on the phone. Trish mimed an apology and slipped into the bedroom with Kim following behind her.

"I gotta go. People are getting back now."

"Okay." Aunt Liddy's voice wilted a little. "Don't wait another month to call me, ya hear? You've gone and proved yourself. There's no need to keep it up."

"I promise," I said and hung up after we both said good-bye. We never said, "I love you."

Those were the last words my parents had said to me before everything in my family broke bad. And now, I would never get another chance to tell them both at the same time, to feel our little triangle of a family intact and whole. So I resolved never to tell anyone. Again.

Aunt Liddy hadn't pushed me on this. Instead, we made promises and just knew love was there.

"We're headed outside to lay out. Wanna come?" Kim asked. She had already changed into cutoff jean shorts and a floral bikini top with a lot of boob padding.

"It's October." I hadn't brought a swimsuit. The thought had never crossed my mind. "And I have class. Don't you guys?"

"It's a warm day though. So we're skipping." Kim had brown hair like mine, but instead of my uneven waves, hers was wedged sleek and straight around her face. Her lips formed a slight natural pout.

"Might be the last day of the year for it. You should come." Trish paired a fluorescent pink one-piece with a pair of matching nylon athletic shorts.

"I don't have a suit. You guys go. Enjoy it."

"Okay, we will."

They left on the breeze they came in on. They were nice girls doing nice things. They spent their time munching popcorn through the latest *Dawson's Creek* episode, gathering information on which sorority to join, or spent weirdly warm October days splashing around in a baby pool on the dorm lawn. Sometimes I wished I could do all those things too.

I poured fresh coffee into my mug, went into the bathroom, and turned on the shower. I might not spend the day lounging in the sun, but the idea of skipping class was alluring. Nothing could stop me from heading down Sharp Street to wander through stores and art galleries. *Hmm...*

"Hazel!" Maeve's voice rang out in the living room.

"I'm in here!" I opened the bathroom door.

Maeve stood by the window, her hair standing on end. She turned to me; her dark eyes seemed frantic, and mascara was smudged all around them.

"What happened?"

"C-can I use the shower first?" she asked.

"Yeah, sure." I stepped aside and let her in, still wondering what had happened but not wanting to pry.

She closed the door without saying another word.

At my desk, I flipped through my planner and checked today's syllabus. Nothing was due. What would missing one econ lecture and a women's lit discussion hurt? With Maeve in the shower now, at best, I'd already be a few minutes late. It *was* time for a personal day.

Maeve emerged a few minutes later, wrapped in Kim's robe, her cheeks flushed pink from heat or scrubbing; I wasn't sure. Her eyes were still as big and round as they'd been before the shower. She ignored me, heading straight for the bedroom.

As I went to use the shower, I caught a glimpse of her staring at herself in the full-length mirror. She touched her reflection, and the act worried me.

"Are you okay?" I called out.

Maeve startled as if she were unaware of my presence. She caught my eye in the mirror's reflection. "I fell," she said.

"I know what that's like. Did you hit your head?"

At my question, she touched the back of her head gingerly. "Uh, yeah."

"Hold on." I turned off the water and slipped into the clean clothes I'd set near the sink.

When I remerged, Maeve wasn't where I'd left her. I found her sitting on my bunk, staring at her scraped-up hands. The cuts were minor; nothing bled, but the first layer of skin had torn in a few spots. Road rash.

I sat next to her. "Can I feel the bump?"

She nodded slowly. Her lips parted, and I could see her snaggletooth, one cute canine that didn't fall in line with the rest. Most of the time she hid it, not always showing her teeth when she smiled.

Maeve's hair was cropped close in the back, so the lump was easy to find. She winced when my fingers grazed over the spot.

"I'm sorry. Do you feel like you might throw up?" I went through the list of questions my mom had used every time I hit my head when I was little.

"No."

"Did you throw up or pass out when it happened?"

"No."

"Okay, good. Want some ice?"

Her eyes searched mine. For what, I couldn't have guessed. Recognition? Maybe this fall was worse than I thought, and I needed to get her to the hospital. Sadness? I had 100 percent hit my head and then cried over it later. Like a delayed reaction, my brain had tried to keep everything together and get me to a safer area to lose my shit.

"I'll get you some clothes first." I hopped up and pulled out her dresser drawer.

"Don't." Maeve noticed the robe and tightened it around her chest. "You have horrible taste."

That was when I knew she was fine. "Okay, bitch."

She gave a weak smile. Her hand gripped the bunk bed post, and she wavered when she stood. Her eyes closed, as if the small action pained her. I went to the bathroom and rifled through the shelves. There, behind the package of toilet paper, was a little plastic bottle of ibuprofen. The pills rattled around inside when I popped off the lid. I shook two into my hand, rinsed out my coffee mug, and refilled it with plain water.

By the time I got back to the bedroom, Maeve had managed to pull on some leggings and a T-shirt. Her hair was still a wet and spiky mess, and she gingerly tested the sore spot every few seconds.

"Here you go." I offered her the medicine.

"Thanks."

A sudden scream rang out. The sound flew through our open windows, past the heavy curtains, and bounded around the room. Maeve and I exchanged what-the-fuck looks. We hurried to the living space windows to see what was going on outside.

There, the scene revealed several girls I recognized from our dorm. Their legs were slick and shiny, and they were scattered around an inflatable pool filled with three fully clothed guys. The guys splashed and kicked; water sprayed everywhere, and the girls screeched as if they were being murdered. The boys laughed harder and kept going.

"Looks like they're having fun," I said.

"Just wait." Maeve stood next to me, her eyes still looking a little glossed over. "Someone will take it too far."

And sure enough, as if on cue, a fourth guy crept into play, standing behind Trish and Kim. Most of his features were blurry from this distance. I could see he was white and wore sagging shorts. His face was mostly hidden under the brim of a ball cap. He held a fountain drink and took off the lid. Then, without warning, he dumped it over Trish's head. She shrieked as brown liquid and clumps of ice dripped down her neck and shoulders.

"Oh shit," I said.

"There's always one." Maeve shook her head and winced with the too-quick movement. Her hand fluttered to her head injury.

Kim reacted swiftly. She leapt up and smacked the guy's arm. "Asshole!"

The boy looked down at her, his smirk unmistakable, even from our second-floor window. She continued to admonish him while he laughed and put his hands on her bare waist. He shifted his hips toward hers until they were touching, then brought his mouth to her ear, probably whispering something offensive. Kim shoved him. Hard. He stumbled backward, and another guy stepped up, hopefully to aid her, but that was never a given.

"Should we get the RA?" I asked. I remembered how I'd felt in the Trap, how fear had held us immobile. We could've used the help.

Maeve didn't answer. Her facial features went hard, and red splotches formed on her neck.

The jerk stumbled backward and straightened up, leering at Kim as he backed away. Kim ignored him, rushing to Trish's side. Trish wrapped her hair up in the towel and stomped toward the dorm.

The party continued outside. Somebody cranked the music up, and a wave of nervous chatter overtook the small crowd. But I braced myself for whatever drama might unfold in our living room. Maeve sat on the loveseat with a book in her lap, and I opened a notebook at my desk and started doodling. Sure enough, within seconds, the door flew open, and Trish hurried in with Kim right behind her.

"I don't understand why you're mad at *me*!" Kim grabbed for her friend's arm, but Trish yanked away.

"You turned that whole thing into a big scene!" Trish yelled.

"*I* did? Not the guy who threw a fucking soda on you? You're not even making sense!"

"We all could have had a laugh and it would have been over, but no. You had to step in and turn it into a whole big thing. Like you always do!"

Her words dripped with a history I knew nothing about but was immediately interested in. I snuck a peek at Maeve, whose eyes never left the page she was surely pretending to read.

Trish slammed the bathroom door, and we all listened to the familiar sound of the shower squeaking on.

"Fine. Fine! Next time, I'll sit there and do nothing while some dude makes you look like an idiot!" Kim flew into the bedroom. She came out with a T-shirt over her bikini top and jingling keys clipped to a beltloop on her shorts. She marched out.

Maeve and I were left with the room's lingering sense of spectacle and the rush of water spilling through the bathroom pipes.

Maeve mouthed, *Wow*! Her eyes round and wide.

"I better get you some ice," I said. "For your head."

"I'm coming with you." Maeve grabbed her purse.

Outside, in the smoker's stairwell, she paused, a cigarette set between her lips. The lighter's igniter ground and clicked a spark alive. She sat on the steps. Her shoulders fell with the first deep intake of breath and smoke, and she rolled her head, shoulder to shoulder.

"Want one?" she asked.

"No. Yes. I quit a while back." I desperately wanted one. The pull remained strong. In my dreams, I still smoked and woke up feeling guilty. My dad used to get so mad when he smelled cigarettes on me.

Maeve nodded as though she understood.

I stepped out from under the awning and peeked around the side of the building. The swim party was still going strong. R. Kelly's voice played over the front lawn. The guy that instigated Trish's incident had come back. He spread himself out on a blanket next to a couple girls who seemed annoyed by his presence. He talked while they stared in different directions. He was either oblivious to their feelings and cues, or he didn't care. Another girl emerged, carrying a stack of CDs. Without her combat boots, I hardly recognized our neighbor as she plopped down on a beach towel.

"Neighbor girl's with 'em," I announced.

"Is she?" Maeve came up beside me and stubbed her cigarette out on the bricks, leaving behind a charred smear of ash. "She's branching out."

We turned and started for the cafeteria. The warm weather juxtaposed some already-turning leaves, bringing nature's chaos to the forefront. *Stick to the plan.* The motto floated through my consciousness with the balmy breeze. *There is no plan.*

"How'd you know that guy would pour his soda on Trish?" I asked.

"I didn't know the specifics. But in any group of people having fun, there's always one dude with something to prove, willing to do something more dickish than the rest. And *voilà*! Hypothesis tested and proved. Again."

"That common, huh? I don't know..." I said. As we approached the cafeteria, a lanky guy held the door for us. "See. A nice guy. Maybe they're not all bad." I didn't know why I was arguing. For the most part, I agreed with her.

"Who said anything about them all being bad?" Maeve grabbed a tray from the stack at the beginning of the line. "But did it feel that way in the Trap?"

Anything could've happened to us that night in the Trap. We'd had little to no control over how the scenario would play out. Those guys had known it too. Even three-sheets drunk, the power was theirs. They'd had it all along, forever.

The Campus Echo

Assault Reports Ignored by Campus Police

by Gayle Jackson

Several students have come forward this week claiming to have filed assault complaints with the campus security department that were either denied or ignored.

"They didn't take down any of my information," says an anonymous source. "I was attacked in the Trap, and they didn't even write down my name."

"I was told to schedule an appointment," says another, "because I waited several days to report. Then they kept asking me if I'd been drinking, what I was wearing...that kind of thing."

University hospital social worker, Tonya Jones, says, "This is unfortunately a frequent occurrence. When people come forward, the instinct of those who should be in this listening, support role too often turns into a shaming accusation toward the victim."

Overall, the campus security department has reported steady decreases in campus assaults with intermittent spikes since it started collecting and analyzing data in the early nineties. When asked how the department would be handling the accusations brought forth by students, lead officer, Dave Mason, declined to comment.

"We always know reported numbers only represent part of the whole picture," says Jones. "It's difficult to grasp the scope, but anyone denying a problem exists is simply lying to themselves." Some national statistics state three out of every four sexual assaults go unreported.

In the meantime, these students are seeking legal recourse. This is an unprecedented move for Oakley University. Never before has the university institution been taken to task regarding sexual assault.

University president, F. Henry Pepper, in a typed response, stated that his office cannot comment on any legal proceedings, but he encourages all students to take common-sense measures, especially at night. *Continued on Page 9.*

Chapter Eight

Recognition

OCTOBER 20, 2000

Before leaving for Sara's tryouts, I dragged a brush through the windblown knots of my hair, then headed back into the chilly winds of a fall that had finally started to arrive. The air carried a crispness, making my eyes water as I trudged across campus to the Cardinal Union Theater.

Sara paced the length of the auditorium's lobby. As I approached, she massaged her fingers and palms. Her mouth moved as if she were speaking to someone, yet she was alone. Before auditions, I used to practice that way, too, whispering a breathy rush of lines as if they were some kind of prayer. Midpace, Sara stomped her foot and shook out her hands, surely cursing a forgotten or misplaced word.

"Hey," I tapped her on the shoulder. She jumped, then threw her arms around my neck. Her tight grasp indicated tentacles of need.

"I'm so glad you made it!" Her voice was muffled by the collar of my fleece.

I straightened my spine and awkwardly patted her back.

"I told you I'd be here," I said, strands of her hair stuck to my lip gloss.

Sara flipped her hair over her shoulders. "I know, I know. Still, I wasn't sure you'd show. We were never super close in high school, so I would've understood if you needed to be somewhere else."

Yeah, right. She'd badgered me for a full week.

"Sara, shut up." I recognized an anxiety spiral when I saw one. She needed the verbal equivalent of a slap across the face. "I'm here. We're friends. And you're going to be great up there. 'K?"

Her shoulders rose with a deep intake of breath. "If you say so."

"I do."

Just then, a short, beefy guy sauntered over. He wrapped his arm around Sara's waist and pulled her in close. Sara giggled as he nuzzled her neck.

"Knock it off." She playfully smacked his chest.

He stopped kissing her but kept their bodies touching. He nodded at me, flashing a beady glance my way. I immediately knew not to trust him.

"Hey," he said, his mouth barely opening as he forced a greeting.

"Ryan, this is Hazel, a high school friend."

Hearing his name, an alarm bell went off in my head. The guy who'd slapped my ass as if it belonged to him—his name had been Ryan. But it couldn't be the same dickwad from the Trap last week. Could it? There were probably hundreds of Ryans on campus.

"Nice to meet you." I held out my hand, firmly putting myself in the no-hugging category. Ryan reached for it and smiled. His teeth were small, complementing the rest of his narrow facial features. All except for a pair of inward-pointing canines that seemed like fangs.

Fangs. I'd noticed them right before he'd looked me in the eye and said, *"There's a hole right in front of me."* It was him. The realization knocked the breath out of me all over again.

"Sara, can I talk to you for a minute?"

"Oh,"—she checked her watch—"I can't now. They want everyone auditioning seated in the front rows by four o'clock. I gotta go. Wish me luck!" She smiled at Ryan in the dreamy way some girls do when they're busy imagining a future wedding. They home in on the dress, the flowers, the attention, instead of seeing the monster in front of them.

Ryan grabbed Sara's ass as she hurried away. The scene transpired as if it happened in slow motion. Two of his fingers tucked right up under her skirt while he palmed and squeezed the rest. Nothing like how he'd smacked me but still aggressive enough to leave a lasting impression.

"Break a leg!" I called after Sara. My voice sounded low and sluggish in my ears. All the while, I struggled against the shrinking feeling taking over my whole body.

Time sped back up, and Ryan turned toward me.

"Wanna sit together?" he asked, without even a hint of recollection.

"Nope." I headed for the theater entrance, trying to slow my pulse and praying he wouldn't follow me.

The theater was already dark, except for the stage. And the spotlights allowed for easy navigation through the rows of seating. I sped-walked down the aisle, spotting an empty seat next to someone slouching low with their feet propped on the chair in front of them. I checked for any trace of Ryan. At the door, he surveyed the room as though he owned everything inside.

"Taken?" I asked, pointing to the empty seat.

The guy wiped his nose with the back of his hand. "All yours." He moved his backpack to give me more leg room.

"Thanks."

He sneezed in response and pulled a small pack of tissues out of his pocket. After he finished blowing, he whispered, "Don't worry. It's allergies."

"Okay." I smiled politely. My hands were trembling, so I folded them together, clasping and unclasping my grip on the reality of this situation. I had to tell Sara about her boyfriend.

"You okay?" He nodded toward my fidgeting hands. "Cold or something?"

"Oh, no." I stopped with the clenching and wiped my palms along the legs of my jeans, then gripped the seat handles. "I'm fine. I'll be fine." I sat up taller and looked for Ryan again; he seemed to have disappeared.

At the front of the room, the director, a middle-aged guy with round glasses and a fair amount of chest hair showing, introduced himself and hopped on stage. He started a speech about the history of drama and its important role in society. I sighed. At this rate, my whole night would be spent sitting here next to allergy boy.

"I like your necklace."

"Oh, thanks." I touched the charm dangling at my clavicle. Some days, I forgot I was wearing it. Other days, it strangled me.

"I'm Doug, by the way." Doug wore a fraying hemp choker with a polished white shell nestled within the rope. His hair was brown, and he parted it down the middle like a lot of indie/emo guys. I recognized The Promise Ring band patch on his backpack.

"Hazel." I introduced myself and motioned toward the patch. "They're great."

"You know them?"

"I saw them when they played in Indy last fall."

"No shit? I was at that show!"

The girl in front of me turned and gave us an annoyed look.

"Cool," I whispered.

"So you're not trying out?"

"No. I'm so over drama."

He smiled, and honestly, it was a great smile, the lower half of his face parenthesized as the corners of his eyes wrinkled. He had a genuineness about him, and I trusted him. Slightly.

"Same," he said. "My roommate is auditioning, and I didn't feel like doing laundry tonight."

"You spend your Friday nights doing laundry?"

"I know. It's so lame."

"So do I."

There was that smile again.

"Well, maybe one Friday, we can skip doing laundry together?" He bit his lower lip—a move that probably garnered a decent amount of attention.

"Sure."

He pulled out his planner, clicked a pen, and offered it to me. I wrote my phone number and name down. When I gave it back to him, I wondered if he'd really call. He placed his forefinger to his lips and pointed to the stage, where the first actor started their monologue.

Doug and I didn't have much time to talk after that. The director kept the auditions moving at a good pace—one person after another with no room for applause. When Doug's roommate stood on stage, Doug gently elbowed me and told me so. I did the same when Sara went on.

When the lights came up, I squinted until my eyes adjusted. The director announced when the casting list would be posted, and everyone dispersed with a lot of yawns and stretches.

As Doug and I stood to leave, I could see we were around the same height. He slipped his backpack over his shoulders, and his forearms had a natural veiny thing happening. If I touched them, the wild blue twines would bounce back with a rubbery give.

"Nice meeting you, Hazel."

"You too."

Doug walked away and greeted his roommate with a series of high fives. I scratched my head, looking for Sara. She was still near the stage. Ryan stood right next to her with his arm around her waist. She didn't seem aware of how his eyes flashed with possessiveness while she talked to some of the other people trying out, but I noticed. One thing was certain— I wasn't leaving Sara's side until I had a chance to warn her.

I followed the steps down to the area in front of the stage where actors milled about, congratulating themselves and patting one another on the back. Bodies shoved against mine as I wound my way through the crowd. I spotted Sara talking to someone with shoulder-length strawberry-blond hair and wireframe glasses. Ryan was now nowhere in sight. Maybe he'd gone back to wherever he came from; I imagined a dingy cave.

"What did you think, Hazel?" Sara glowed. I couldn't see into anyone's future, but no matter what, theater suited Sara. She belonged here, and a sudden pang of jealousy clanged in my chest. I'd yet to experience the flush that came with having a passion or fitting in somewhere.

"You were great up there. That monologue was a good choice."

"It got me the lead back then. I hope it does now too."

The person with the glasses nodded along. It seemed Sara had another fan, one who flinched when she noticed

Ryan sneaking up behind Sara. He shushed the two of us with his finger held close to his lips. Without warning, he wrapped his muscular arms around Sara's waist and picked her up.

"Eeeeek!" Sara yelped, her feet kicking in the air.

I stepped back so as not to take a wedged heel to the face. Ryan laughed as though the whole scene was hysterical, but he didn't see how red Sara's cheeks were when he put her back down.

"Idiot!" She smacked his arm and ridiculed him through clenched teeth.

"What, babe? It was a joke!" He held out his arms and nodded at the encircled group of strangers, egging some observer to take his side.

"You embarrassed me in front of everyone," Sara whisper-screamed. She checked herself in front of the surrounding crowd, smoothing back her hair and taking a few gulps of air.

"Come on. Nobody cares," he said.

Even if they weren't being totally blatant, drama kids soaked this shit up. There was many a side-eye, judgement beaming like laser lights.

"Go home," Sara said with a forceful edge to her voice.

Sara's other friend twisted the hem of her sweater around her fingers. I bit my bottom lip, the bulging pressure reassuring as hell. Ryan could blow this whole thing to the next level. He'd made me feel tiny in the Trap; he'd certainly do the same to Sara. At the collar of his shirt, a triangle of exposed skin flushed bright pink. A few tense seconds ticked away as he balled up his fists, sniffed aggressively, and then, finally, stalked off. A pressure release fanned over me, and the crowd's nervous chatter picked up again.

Maybe Ryan actually cared about Sara. Maybe Maeve and I were the only ones he didn't view as real people.

"Great," Sara said. Her demeanor deflated as she turned back toward us.

"He just needs time to cool off," Sara's friend offered.

"Sure, but now that's the start of my reputation."

"You can't predict or control how people will see you, so why worry?" I was grasping. Theater folks gave every ounce of spectacle its due weight; it was their nature. Sara would merely have to figure out how to spin it.

"She's right, Sara. People have short memories. I'm Shirlee, by the way." She extended her hand my way.

"Hazel."

Her palm was sweaty, the handshake like holding a doughy biscuit.

"I know who you are," Shirlee said. "Sara's mentioned you."

"People don't forget, you guys." Sara's pitch was at a near whine. "My acting should be what's on everyone's mind tonight, not how Ryan made me squeal like a pig in front of everyone."

"Stop," I said. "None of this will mean anything come opening night."

"You were great, Sara. Try and leave it at that, okay? I gotta go study. I'll see you back at the dorm." Shirlee swung a miniature leather backpack over her shoulders, which were slightly rounded. "Nice meeting you."

"Same." When Shirlee was out of earshot, I asked, "Roommate?"

"Kind of." Sara gathered her hoodie and purse from the first row of seats. "She's not who I share a bedroom with, but we share the living area and bathroom. She's a little weird, but she's also the only one around, usually."

We started toward the double doors as the crowd dwindled. The only kids left were the suck-ups shaking hands with the director.

"So, how'd you meet Ryan?" I asked.

"We met at lunch one day. I spilled my tray, and he stopped to help me clean up."

"What a guy," I said flatly.

"He's a little handsy, but I like him."

Sara led us outside toward the housing towers. "You don't have to walk me home."

"I don't mind. I wanna see the tower suites." *And tell you that your boyfriend might be a psychopath.*

Outside, evening shadows lengthened. More daylight had been lopped off with the changing seasons. Alongside the paved path, the river gurgled. A humid, wet sediment smell filled the air. Beyond the towers, the sky burned orange and gold.

For the remainder of the trek, we ran out of words. Sara probably replayed the minutiae of her audition, while I tried to figure out the best way to tell her what I knew about Ryan. Which was what really? That he'd gotten overly drunk, same as anyone else on campus. That he'd thought he had the right to smack me—she already knew he was handsy. That he'd made both Maeve and me feel as if we were things rather than people.

Sara turned, leading me up a ramp toward her building's entrance. The lobby was more modern than the one I was used to on north campus. In the middle of the room, a big circular desk corralled multiple volunteers. Behind them, shiny silver elevator doors dinged open and close. Off to the right, in a bright room sectioned off by glass doors, students played Ping-Pong. The knock-knocking sound of the bouncing plastic ball barely resonated. Sara breezed by the amenities.

"Wow!" My amazement slipped out in a whisper.

"Is it much different from yours?"

"Yeah, kinda. Everything's older there. No rec room, that's for sure."

Sara pressed the button at the elevator, and within seconds, a cluster of young adults staggered out. We stepped inside and were met with an unmistakable fart smell.

"God." Sara pressed number eighteen, and away we went. "It always reeks in here."

When the doors opened again, we were greeted by loud music and a squirt gun fight. Playing as if they were at war, a few guys chased one another through the halls, ducking and weaving around university-issue couches and chairs.

"Sara!" They all stopped to greet her with a salute.

"Hi, guys."

"Who's your friend?" A guy stood up from behind a chair and was promptly hosed.

"Cool it, Chauncey!" yelled the guy doing the spraying.

Sara rolled her eyes as she fit her key into the room marked 1802. The lock clicked behind us, and we entered a long, rectangular living area. An uncomfortable-looking couch sat in front of a small TV, and beyond that was a dinette set—a blond circular table with four chairs.

"Here's the bathroom." Sara indicated a room that looked exactly like a truck-stop public restroom, down to the tiled floor and tan metal stalls. Two showerheads poked out of the far side wall. Flimsy opaque curtains hung limp on the rods.

"How many people to a suite?" I asked.

"Six."

Sara unlocked another door labeled *A*. The entire building was a maze of cavities, a Russian doll of partitions. Sara flipped on the lights. This smaller apartment consisted of two desks and a bunk bed.

"Must be nice, sharing this with only one other person."

"Honestly, I wouldn't know. She's barely ever here." Sara propped the door open, nudging the stopper with her foot.

And that seemed true. On Sara's side of the room, a corkboard tacked with pictures from high school hung next to a puppy calendar displaying an adorable pug dressed in a candy corn costume. Her matching red-and-white polka-dot bed set decorated the bottom portion of the bunk bed, and textbooks, pens, and a rainbow assortment of Post-it notes littered her desk. Her roommate's side was barren in contrast. A messy upper bunk, with a set of plaid flannel sheets tangled in a drab crocheted blanket, provided the only clue someone else lived there.

"Loopholes," I said.

"What?" Sara asked.

"Your windows are like loopholes. You know, from medieval castles."

"Uh, no. I don't know."

"The design let archers fire arrows at invaders." Although they were useless against the bad guys already inside.

I snooped around some more, scanning her roommate's desk, then nosing around Sara's pictures from senior skip day. I pretended an awkwardness hadn't settled between us. But truthfully, we had almost nothing in common. The bed squeaked when Sara sat on the mattress edge. She picked up a threadbare stuffed puppy dog and played with its droopy ears.

"College isn't quite what I expected," she said quietly.

"I know what you mean." As I leaned against the painted cinder block wall, the cold crept through my layers of clothing. "Look, I need to talk to you about Ryan."

Sara's eyes snapped away from her toy and narrowed on me. She was already defensive; nothing I'd tell her would make a difference. Still, I couldn't stay quiet. He'd treated Maeve and me like shit, and his girlfriend should want to know.

"Last week..." I continued after Sara's nod, "...we left here and ran into some guys in the Trap. One of them was pretty drunk—Ryan."

I stopped and rolled my lips together. Did I tell her the specifics or get glossy concerning the whole thing? I settled on a mix of both and said it as fast as I could, as if ripping off a bandage. "He wanted us to flash him. When we told him no, he hit me."

A vertical wrinkle divided Sara's forehead. "He hit you?"

"Yes. Well, he smacked my ass. I thought you should know."

"So, he...didn't hit you?"

"I mean, not in the face. No. But he's a pretty angry guy. Or at least he was in the Trap. But even tonight, you were mad! You were pissed at how he just, like, *manhandled* you."

"Get out." Sara sighed, dumping the stuffed puppy in a heap on her pillow.

"I'm only trying to help."

"Right. Like you tried helping Penelope in high school."

Shit. I should've known she'd bring that up. "That was totally different! Luke and I—"

"You stole him from her, and now you're trying to do the same thing with Ryan. He was joking around after my audition. I made it into a bigger deal than it needed to be."

"Sara, I am so *not* into Ryan. And, Jesus, Luke kissed *me*, okay? Not that it matters now." This was going all wrong, and I hated how defensive I sounded. "Look, I can call my roommate. She was there. She'll tell you." I grabbed the receiver and started dialing our dorm number. "We smoked a joint down by the river, and then she went running off in the Trap—"

Sara's manicured fingernail appeared as she pressed the dial tone button. "You were high?"

"Yeah, so?" I countered. But the receiver slipped in my grip, and I hung it up myself.

"I think you should go, Hazel. Thanks for coming today."

I paused at the door and said, "Let me know if you get a part in the play, okay?"

Sara already sat at her desk, writing in a notebook. I'd probably never hear from her again, but at least I'd warned her. Maybe now she wouldn't be blind to some of those red flags Ryan waved.

I used the bathroom before the long walk back. When I came out, Shirlee sat curled up on the sofa with a paperback. She pushed her glasses up her nose but kept her gaze focused on her book.

"I believe you." Her words were a gust, powerful and quiet. Would they have made a sound had I not been there to hear them?

OAKLEY UNIVERSITY

"Where tomorrow's leaders don't fall far from the tree."

Go Oaknuts!

Welcome to Oakley University's online diary-hosting website, promoting a shared community experience for all.

Username: dead_papers
Date Posted: October 20, 2000

This truth wasn't something slowly divulged over time. No flashes of red flags anywhere. For all seconds prior, he was only a dad. A good man. So it stood out—this instance where my world hollowed out. Similar to watching a tragedy on the news, like seeing the blackened shell of the federal building in Oklahoma City or watching kids run and cry and hold one another at Columbine, I'll never forget where I was or what I was doing the moment I discovered the truth about him.

He'd sent me to clean the bathrooms during a shift at the hardware store. The men's restroom always smelled of an odd chemical tang and old piss—that night was no different. A smattering of graffiti covered the walls. I remember thinking "Jesus was here" written in red marker in the last stall was funny. As I sloshed the mop over the tiles, I noticed a set of smudged footprints on the toilet seat. *Why would anyone be standing on the toilet*? I thought.

Instinctively, I looked up, and a ceiling tile was a tad off-center. I climbed up and pushed it back, predicting something good must have been stashed up there. I hoped for weed—how sweet and so naïve. I wasn't tall enough to see but was able to feel around. I almost gave up, and then my fingers graced over something hard and plastic. I brought it down; it was a bottle of lotion. I dropped it, disgusted.

At that point, I probably knew this was going to be terrible. I'd found a big stack of magazines in the basement once. It had been gross and awful—realizing your parent has...desires. *Gag.* But how could I stop?

Some morbid sense this was going to be so much worse than expected kept me looking. Rubbernecking, as if there might be some terrible accident up ahead. I couldn't *not* look; I had to know if brains had been bashed, to see if body parts lay at odd angles. Because...it was hidden away. In a ceiling. At Dad's store. He'd surely expected no one to ever look up here, that he'd get away with whatever this turned out to be. So instead of giving up, I stretched farther. I stood on my tiptoes, balancing with one hand against the stall and the other up in the ceiling, and pulled a stack of glossy photos out of their hiding place.

This wasn't simply porn: posed, shaved, overly made up and fake. This was gritty and realistic, but in an uncanny, off-putting way. Each picture contained a woman, usually in varying stages of undress but sometimes not, taken from an odd, faraway vantage point. The subjects seemed unaware they were being watched. Curtains were mostly drawn, and faces were a little blurry, but there stood a woman in a black bra. Her arms were behind her back, tugging at the clasp. The next shot showed bare breasts as a T-shirt slipped over her head. A different photo showed a woman reading on a bed, lounging in a silky nightgown. One of the straps had slipped off her shoulder. Clearly, the photographer had been standing outside their homes, peeping and studying these women.

As I flipped through the stack, the imagery escalated. Tears wet the flushed cheeks of a woman blindfolded and gagged. The distance from the previous photos dissolved;

he'd been in the room with them then. Then came the extreme close-ups: bound wrists, bare and scraped knees, a man's fist wrapped in someone's hair—the homemade tattoo of an *X* on his forefinger showing. My hands shook as I held them and slowly realized what it all meant. I knew that *X*.

I could barely breathe—still can't—let alone form the thought regarding my own father. He loved me, defended me. I never told him about the old man in the store groping me, but he would've done something. Killed the guy, maybe. But then, what was this? How could he do this to other women? I couldn't separate myself from the woman I was turning into, yet he could? He was able to be a man who stalked and abused and destroyed souls, then turned around to protect mine at the same time?

He could be a father and this...this devil.

Catch them. Fry them. Eat them.

I hear it like a mantra now. An anthem.

But my only power is telling. And that never seems to be enough.

Chapter Nine

It's a Date

OCTOBER 21, 2000

It was Saturday. Our dorm room had been quiet. Trish and Kim had left early to meet their moms for a shopping day. Maeve was out, too, but I didn't know where.

I picked an apple off our shared-food shelf, then went to the lobby and checked my mailbox. Tucked inside the cubbyhole was a pink package slip, a first; the only mail I'd gotten so far were credit card applications. I showed the notification to a cheery redheaded volunteer at the front desk.

"Got a package, huh?" she asked before disappearing behind a shelving unit.

"That's what the note says." I crunched into the apple I'd grabbed, hoping to avoid more conversation. It was mealy on the inside, dry and mushy at the same time. I spat it out in a large trashcan, filled with unopened junk mail.

The volunteer reappeared, still examining the slip. She went up to a line of boxes behind the desk. "It's a big one. You might need to grab a cart to help get it upstairs. Or I can help?" She stuffed the notice in her back pocket and pushed the box out from behind the counter. "I'll need to wait till Carla comes back to cover the front desk. Should only be a sec."

"I'll be fine." The image of a ruby-plastic iMac computer covered the box. "Who is this from?" A dumb question: only one person would send me a gift of this magnitude.

"Not sure." But the girl tapped an address sticker on the top. "You're so lucky. No more schlepping to the library all hours of the night. Not that any of *us* should be doing that!"

I nodded but was only half listening. I wasn't even sure she'd stopped talking before I hefted the box—my very own computer—into my arms and headed toward the elevator near the stairwell.

People milled about the hall, and I tried not to get annoyed at how they wouldn't get out of the way. I kept having to stop and wait for them to pass while a corner of the box dug into my hip.

At my dorm, I banged on our door with my foot. Strands of hair stuck to an outbreak of sweat on my face. Trish opened the door, but her gaze stayed focused toward our bedroom.

"You look fine!" she yelled, then noticed me. "Whoa! What you got there?"

"What's it look like?" I'm not sure how she missed the giant picture of a computer on the box.

She stepped back, holding the door open. I needed every inch of room, and even then, my knuckles scraped against the frame as I waddled inside. Fighting the urge to drop the box, I squatted, carefully lowering it to the floor beside my desk.

"Oh man! How great to have one in our room!" Trish exclaimed.

Kim came out of the bedroom in a baby doll–style sundress and a cropped pleather jacket. Her eyes lit up when she noticed the computer. "Nice! How soon can we get it working?"

"I don't know." I ran my keys under the tape and opened the top. A pamphlet of directions and warrantees were the first thing I noticed. "My aunt set up the one we have at home." I flipped through the instructions, and the words went blurry at the mention of ports, cables, and drives. I knew how to use a computer, basically. I could type things, play solitaire, and sometimes I would log onto AOL and talk to randoms. But anything behind the scenes of the screen was a total mystery to me. "I guess I should call her."

The phone's ring filled the room.

"Oooo-oo-ooo!" Trish waggled her fingers as if something spooky had happened. "Maybe that's her."

"Hello?" Kim smacked Trish's shoulder playfully as she listened. They'd made up quickly after the pop-spilling incident. "Yeah, she's here." Kim placed her palm over the talking end and said, "Someone named Doug for you, Hazel." She batted her eyelashes and made a cutesy, teasing face.

"Duh-ggg!" Trish drew his name out into extra syllables. "Who is Doug?" she sang.

"Nobody." I snatched the phone from Kim and headed into the hall. They cackled behind me, crooning Doug's name and being stupid about the whole thing.

"Hey."

"Hey, this is Doug."

"I heard." There was an awkward too-long pause I scrambled to fill. "I wasn't expecting to hear from you so soon."

"Did I screw that up?"

"No, no. I'm glad you called."

"What are you doing tonight?"

"My aunt just sent me an iMac, so I'll be trying to figure out how to set it up."

"You wouldn't know this yet, but I'm kind of a big deal when it comes to computers."

"Oh, yeah?" A little muscle spasm shot through my cheek, and I realized I'd been smiling through the conversation so far. "Would you wanna come over and help? I can promise pop and...peanut butter. I think all we have is a giant jar of peanut butter."

"I've got pizza money. It's a date."

I gave Doug directions to the dorm and hung up, nearly exploding with nervous energy.

Trish and Kim fluttered around me. They asked about Doug, a flurry of questions I didn't know any of the answers to yet. I understood why they were excited, but all their energy did for me was highlight the fact that I'd invited a stranger into my home. They were heading out again, dinner with their moms and then some frat party once their moms were tucked back into their hotel rooms. Doug and I would be alone unless Maeve came home.

"Do you want us to stay?" Kim asked. She must've picked up on my pacing and nervous hand-wringing.

"It's okay." They were both already made up and dressed for a night out. "I met him at my friend's audition."

"We can totally give you our first impression."

"It's fine, really." I'd picked up zero bad vibes regarding Doug. He'd seemed perfectly nice, but I had been a tad focused on warning Sara about Ryan. I could've missed something. "I'll leave the door open. There's always a few stragglers in the dorms on Saturday nights."

"'K, bye!" they sang together, waving as they left. Their excited chatter drifted down the hall.

I unpacked the rest of the box from Aunt Liddy, and when the phone rang again, I knew it was Doug. The all-girl dorm policy insisted male guests call up to the room, and a resident had to escort them through the building. "Hello?"

"I'm here."

"I'll be right down." I hung up and took a few deep breaths. Anxiety coiled around my chest, taking a centimeter more of my breath with each inhale. But this was normal for me, and there was nothing to do but keep moving. I checked my reflection in the bathroom mirror. My teeth seemed white enough, nothing stuck between them. My hair was all over the place, but whatever. I blew out a few deep breaths, swiped on some lip gloss, then left to meet Doug downstairs.

The auditorium lights had been low, so I'd thought his eyes were brown. But in the brightness of the lobby, I could see they were hazel. He wore a slouchy pair of brown corduroy pants and a short-sleeve dress shirt. His hair scarcely brushed the tops of his shoulders, framing his angular jaw. He was cute in an indie rocker way.

"Hey, you!" he greeted. Instantly, I started calculating a proper greeting. Hug? Handshake? What was the protocol when you'd met someone just yesterday?

"Hi!" I waved. Apparently, I was going with not touching.

He bit his lip and looked around the lobby. "You wanna take me to your computer?"

"Oh, yeah! Sure, this way."

We walked side by side through the hall and up the stairs. Every once in a while, I dared peek at him. He caught me and smiled, but as for conversation, it stalled. What had seemed natural at the theater wasn't now. My keys jangled as I unlocked the dorm and let us in. He checked out the small room, then crouched next to the computer stuff.

"These are so easy," he said. He lay on his back and scooted underneath my desk.

I stood there with nothing to do but watch him plug things in.

"Want a drink?" I blurted.

"Sure."

The fridge made a familiar slurping suction sound when I opened it and grabbed two frosty cans. He thanked me and popped the top, and so did I. The carbonation tickled my upper lip as I sipped and searched for a conversation.

"How do you know so much about computers?" I asked.

"They've always been my thing."

I prayed he'd add on to his answer because, Jesus, what the hell could I ask next? Thankfully, he continued.

"We had a tech club at my high school. Everybody kept saying computers were the wave of the future, so I figured it might be smart to know my way around them."

"All I know how to do is instant messenger."

He smirked and gave half a laugh.

"And solitaire," I added. "We used to have a Carmen Sandiego game too." *Idiot.*

"That's cool." He slipped his head and shoulders back under my desk. "Lucky the dorms have ethernet now."

His shirt lifted as he worked, and the top line of his box-ers stuck out over the top of his pants. His stomach was flat with a vertical trace of hair. "Have you seen the online dia-ries?" he asked from down under.

I had no idea what he was talking about. "No." I sat on the loveseat so I could see part of his face. "What's that?"

"People putting, like, journal entries on the web."

"For anyone to read? Why?"

"I don't know." He placed the pop can on the desktop and booted up my computer. "Almost done." He sat at my desk and attached the keyboard to the monitor. Typing and clicking on a few things, he showed me how to get online and installed AIM. "Okay, you're all set up."

"Wait, show me the diaries."

"There're a couple different sites that host them. I'll show you the campus one."

"It's specific to this campus?"

"Mm-hmm." His fingers moved over the keyboard, quick and fluid as though he'd been practicing all his life. "Here. Take a look."

I bent over his shoulder to read the screen. He smelled refreshing, a simple mix of minty toothpaste and Ivory soap. My suitemates smelled of either cigarettes or Clinique's Happy perfume.

The homepage illuminated with a header image of the Trap, all paths leading toward the historic oak tree in the center. He typed a username and password into the log-in screen, and his online diary popped up. The most recent post appeared a couple hours ago, and I couldn't help but wonder if my name was written somewhere in it. Underneath, Doug scrolled through a seemingly endless array of posts.

"All these people tell their secrets online?"

"Sure." Doug scratched the back of his neck. "If you wanna read other people's stuff, you have to create an account."

"Would I have to write too?"

"There's a mandatory introductory post you make. Let me show you what I did." He scrolled through a backlog of old writing; it was apparent he frequented the site often. At the bottom, he clicked on his introduction. A series of x's he'd used to create an image of a smiley face filled up the screen. "It's up to you what you share."

"Oh, good! You're home. Now I don't have to—"

Both Doug and I turned. Maeve breezed in wearing a T-shirt and running shorts. She puffed heavy breaths, and her cheeks were bright red. Her hair was slicked back with perspiration.

"Oh! I didn't know we had company." She stopped short, her sneakers squeaking on the tile. "I'm Maeve." She approached the two of us with her hand outstretched, and I had to step out of the way for them to shake.

"This is Doug," I gestured to him.

"Nice to meet you," Doug said.

"Same, same." Maeve glanced at me, one of her eyebrows cocked inquisitively. "What's all this?" She waved her hand around the perimeter of the new computer, but I had a feeling she wasn't just talking about it.

"My aunt sent it," I answered, as if the computer was all she'd been referring to. "Doug's helping me set it up. Did you need me?"

"Cool." Maeve's eyes danced with questions. "And no. I can catch you later." She stuck her head out the door. "Bridgette, tell me you're desperate for a smoke break," she sang at the neighbor.

After she left, Doug asked, "Still up for pizza?" He seemed oblivious to Maeve's impish ways, her curiosity, her brand of fun that attracted all sorts. Instead, he smiled at me, his eyes projecting an earnest calm.

"Always."

THE CAMPUS STREETLIGHTS emitted an orange glow that beat back the darkening sky. It felt as if we walked inside a jack-o'-lantern, minus the slimy pumpkin guts.

Doug pressed the crosswalk button, and we waited for the light to change, along with a line of cars stretching as far as I could see. Some vehicles had cracked windows, with puffs of smoke emerging, while others vibrated with the bass blaring out of expensive stereo systems. A group of girls gathered behind us. One of them bumped into me, and I grabbed Doug's arm, steadying myself on the edge of the curb.

"So where are you from?" I asked after regaining my balance.

"Not far actually. Both my parents work at the campus hospital, so we live close."

"Oh, a city boy."

"More like a suburb boy. And you?"

Explaining this was always fun. I'd spent most of my life in a small town near the Illinois/Indiana border, a weird place where people ended most conversations figuring out whether something was on Central or Eastern time. None of that mattered after Mom died though. I'd moved to my aunt's home in Lima, Ohio, and got stuck squarely in one time zone.

"Lima."

"That's up north, right?"

The traffic light changed. We were halfway through the intersection, when the Don't Walk countdown started. Headlights beamed over our shuffling legs as we broke into a quickstep.

"North and a little west," I answered as we stepped onto the sidewalk and continued. Should I go all in with my personal tragedy on a first date? Or save it for later and explain why I hadn't been upfront? Neither way ever felt comfortable. "I moved there for my sophomore year of high school. I used to live in Illinois, near Champaign." Because when I said I was from Illinois, most people assumed Chicago.

"There's a Big Ten school there, right?" Doug talked over the group of girls who'd merged into our path, separating us.

"Right!" I shouted over a pair of glitter-sprayed pigtails.

The group passed, and Doug and I reconvened. He slipped his hand over mine, and it kept us from being split up again. My insides didn't explode at his touch or anything. Bursts of star trails didn't shoot out of his eyeballs. But his touch was warm, firm, and connecting.

We walked by the record store and passed Poetry Joe, a campus legend. Nearly every student on north campus had their own experience with him, receiving an individualized poem for a couple of quarters on a blurry night walk home.

"Hey, pretty mama!" Poetry Joe called out to me.

"Hey," I answered back.

"Wanna buy a song for the pretty lady?" Poetry Joe asked Doug.

"No thanks," Doug said.

"Suit yourself." Poetry Joe turned and started slant-rhyming anyway. "You ain't never gonna get none, if you don't know how to give some..." His scratchy slurring faded behind us.

"He's probably loaded," Doug muttered.

"What?" I asked, a little taken aback. What was he implying? I wasn't quite sure, but I didn't like it. I unclasped my hand from his.

"My RA told us those homeless guys make tons of money off the freshman every year."

"I...don't know if I believe that." *Ugh.* "Poetry Joe is a street performer. And even if he wasn't, everyone deserves help. Giving a dollar, or whatever, doesn't hurt me right now."

"It's what I was told." Doug shrugged and shoved his hands deep into his pockets. "Thought you might wanna know."

"Well, whatever."

"Yeah."

The walk was pretty quiet after that.

Max's Pizza, always voted best slice, was the best part about living on this side of campus. The pies were cut into thick squares with a bite of spicy heat in their sauce. The food was pricier, and they didn't accept our ID debits, so you had to have cash or an actual credit card to eat here. The smell of fresh dough and melted mozzarella hung around the building. Doug held the door open for me.

Near the entrance, a chalkboard sign asked us to wait to be seated. So we did. The tables were standard pizzeria fare. Vinyl checkered tablecloths and red candle votives counted for much of the restaurant's ambiance. A group of guys sat at a four-top, loudly splitting a pitcher of beer. A couple in the back, near a hallway marked with a restroom sign, made eyes at each other. The kitchen was visible through a partitioned wall cut-out. Every now and then, a bald head appeared at the window and shouted, "Order up!" He slid hot trays filled with gooey, cheesy goodness onto the counter. At the line, waitstaff lingered.

"This place is supposed to be great," Doug said.

"It is." Maeve and I had splurged here a few times.

A tall guy in a black polo shirt and matching apron greeted us. "Two?"

Doug nodded.

"Right this way." The server grabbed two plastic-covered menus and motioned for us to follow him. He led us to a table near the other couple who were now sitting on the same side of their table, totally making out, groping in full view.

After the server left with our drink orders, Doug peeked over his shoulder. "They could use a room, huh?"

"Uh, yeah."

"You wanna sit on my side?"

"No, that's okay..."

Sirens blared outside; blue and red flashed through the dim restaurant. A line of emergency vehicles honked their way through traffic. The view out the restaurant's big picture windows showed cars inching toward the curb. An ambulance swerved into the other lanes, and two police cars did the same.

Everyone seemed to stop and notice, but I went back in time and saw my mother, wobbling toward an ambulance. An officer tried to help her, but she shrank away from him, crying out until the paramedics and my dad rushed over to help her.

"Wonder what's up?" Doug asked.

"Maybe a wreck," I said and pushed the memory away.

A waitress delivered our glasses of pop and pulled out a miniature notepad. We decided on a medium pepperoni. I tied the paper wrapping of my straw in knots and prayed for the food to arrive quickly. Small talk wasn't my strength.

"What kind of music do you like?" Doug asked.

"All kinds. My roommate got me into this folk singer, Ani DiFranco. Heard of her?"

"No. I like indie rock. Some pop-punk."

"Do you have a major?" I asked. We'd now covered all three of my go-to conversation topics.

"Computer science. You?"

"Education, teaching. I don't know if I'll keep at it though."

"Why's that?"

"It's what my parents did." I danced around my parents and what had happened, giving him basic facts.

"Did? Like, past tense? Are they retired?"

Shit. "Uh, yeah, not really first-date material."

"Okay. Next time, then."

"Maybe." I smiled but didn't show my teeth. An old Galaga arcade game sat in the corner, its electronic theme song sounding off. A distraction might save us.

"Got any quarters?" I asked.

"I can get some. You're into video games?" Doug sipped his pop and nodded toward the machine.

"I'm down if you are."

"I'm so down." He smiled, excitement twinkling in his eyes.

He must be a gamer. And he thinks he's gonna whoop me.

Doug hopped up from the table and went to the register to ask for change. Another line of emergency vehicles sped past the front windows. The blaring honk of a fire engine led another string of police cars down the street.

I clenched my fists; a wave of nausea threatened. I did not want to see my mother again. I didn't want to think about this anymore. I only wanted to do normal adult-ish things tonight.

When the traffic quieted and the feeling subsided, I met Doug at the arcade game. He held a stack of quarters and slid a few into the machine's slot. The joystick took some getting used to, but I made quick work of shooting down...the spaceships? Alien insects? Not sure. When I died, Doug took his turn. I watched for the pizza while he zeroed in on destroying whatever those little buggers were. He beat my score, but barely.

"Pizza's ready," I said.

"Yes!" He cheered for himself. "I beat the pants off ya!"

I winced at the phrasing. "You did not beat my pants off, and honestly, you probably never will."

"Okay, okay. Sorry. Video games are kinda my thing." We walked back to the table. "They go hand in hand with all the tech stuff."

"If you say so." But I smiled so he'd know I wasn't offended or anything.

He smiled back while using the spatula to dish out slices.

This pizza needed a knife and fork. The flavor made me say a little gratitude prayer.

"Holy shit, this is amazing," said Doug.

"Told ya."

"Oh my god." Doug talked through a mouthful, and I laughed at his facial expression, which was a mix of unbelieving ecstasy.

"Ew. I think I just saw your o-face."

Doug nearly spit out his food, laughing. He dabbed the corners of his mouth. "You're kinda funny."

I shrugged and popped a pepperoni in my mouth. "I saw what I saw." If I had embarrassed him, he didn't show it. And honestly, that put points in his favor.

We finished eating, and Doug paid. Everything concerning the walk home was quieter, which, in retrospect, should have been a red flag. For a Saturday night, the sidewalks should have been pulsing with partiers. But I was too focused on the lack of witty banter between Doug and me. The vibe between us had settled somewhere near friendship, and I hoped he was picking up on it too.

As we crossed into campus territory, it became clear something big was happening. From where we stood on the street corner, I could see the treetops of the Trap. They flashed red, white, and blue—more emergency colors. Whatever had happened, happened there.

A group of girls rushed along the sidewalk; Maeve was among them.

"Hey!" I yelled, waving her over.

She trotted toward us. "Did you guys hear?"

"No," we said, simultaneously.

"Campus is on lockdown. There's a dead body in the Trap."

OAKLEY UNIVERSITY

"Where tomorrow's leaders don't fall far from the tree."

Go Oaknuts!

Welcome to Oakley University's online diary-hosting website, promoting a shared community experience for all.

Username: dead_papers

Date Posted: October 21, 2000

I put the pictures back, wiped off the seat, and pretended I never found them. I went about my business, like a good Midwesterner. I made myself believe the photos weren't his. The building was old; anyone could have left them there.

But I watched him more closely, scrutinized everything he did. I turned his words over and over in my mind until I found his polished, shiny lies. I wanted to scream, "I know what you are!"

It never happened.

I keep his secrets still, even as they smother me. Slowly and deliberately, his transgressions press me out of existence.

The other day, I saw sets of scarring slashes on a roommate's upper thigh. She noticed my staring and quickly pulled her skirt over them. I guess I wasn't supposed to ask; there must be some unspoken code around talking about what she was doing to herself. She told me to shut up, then explained it was just something she did when she felt like she might explode. She said it felt like a release.

So I tried it. The next time—which is nearly all the time—I felt like my lungs wouldn't allow another wave of breath into my body. I found the box cutter I'd used on move-in day and a clean towel. Then I went to the bathroom and closed the stall door. The lid to the toilet seat came down with a clatter. I lowered my jeans and sat. My thigh was so pale, and I imagined the red river flowing beyond the surface of my skin, a whole universe I carry around inside me. Could I ruin it?

Like a god.

I slashed quickly, just once without it registering; my brain took a beat to catch up with what had happened. Then came the singeing, searing pain. I pressed the towel to the cut and swiped tears off my cheeks. I was truly my father's daughter then, doing dirty work in a bathroom stall.

As the pain dulled and the blood clotted, there was no release for me.

Catch them. Fry them. Eat them.

No sweet relief. The river witch won't let me forget. She is water, so she is everywhere, in every state: solid, liquid, gas. I can hear them all now. Under the swirling rapids, right next to my stories, are her stories. And her stories. And her stories. Not just my dad's victims, but they're there, too, screaming below the surface...to be set free.

This is my inheritance.

Views: 21

Likes: 1

Comments: 6

SpinMeRound3: This is so fucked up.

Purplehippo5: I think you need to see a doctor.

BlueJay6: I've been there. Seek help! Much love.

GodisEvrywhre1: You'll be in my prayers.

BeccaSaysHi: I've been where you are. And it does feel hopeless, you can't see any other way. Cutting is not the answer. Please, find someone to talk to.

SpaceCowgirl7: This shouldn't even be allowed online.

Chapter Ten

Junk That Binds Us

OCTOBER 21, 2000
Continued

That giddy glint, her love for drama: Maeve carried it with her always. But in extreme measures—like announcing there was a dead body in the Trap—she couldn't even come close to hiding it. Her mouth twitched at the corners, seemingly desperate to laugh. She ran a hand through her cropped hair and watched for the Don't Walk sign to change. There'd be no holding her back soon.

"Wait, what?" I asked.

"You heard me. Somebody found a body in the Trap. I'm gonna go see."

"Is that wise?" Doug asked, taking a step back from our little circle of three.

"Probably not." Maeve lit a cigarette. "You guys coming?" Her eyebrows arched high as she blew smoke over her shoulder, away from our faces. The traffic light glowed red, and she crossed the street.

Doug hesitated.

"Are you in or out?" I asked.

His head drooped with his shoulders. He shoved his hands into his pockets and fell in line behind me. But before we could cross, the signal changed again. A car engine roared, wheels screaming against the pavement.

"You don't have to come!" Maeve shouted, standing on the opposite street corner.

"I can't leave you guys alone out here," Doug mumbled, as though he had no choice in the matter.

"We won't be alone. We have each other. And I've got Mace." I pulled the canister out of my pocket and showed him. "Don't worry."

A crease formed between Doug's eyebrows. "You brought pepper spray on our date?" He took another step backward.

"Don't be offended. You and I barely know each other." I tucked it away. "And you don't have to look out for me. We're not...anything. Right?"

"Okaaay." Doug blew out a long breath. "I'm not trying to disrupt an investigation or be on the news." He folded his lips inward. They were nice enough lips. "So you guys go ahead. I'll call you later, Hazel." He held eye contact with me and took a few steps backward before turning and jogging away.

"Bye," I called after him.

His hand shot up, but he didn't say anything or turn back around.

"Finally." Maeve's chin rested on my shoulder. She must've recrossed the street in the time it took for Doug to bail. "Shall we, love?"

I shrugged her off my shoulder. "Why do you wanna see this anyway?"

"Have you ever seen a dead body, Hazel?"

Yes. I thought of Mom but didn't answer.

"The whole thing is very *Stand by Me*-ish, right?" Maeve practically skipped through the intersection, and I trailed a few steps behind her.

"There's nothing romantic about death, Maeve." I kept my pace steady and my senses on high alert. We had no idea if this was a suicide or a homicide or what. The sidewalks were well lit, but beyond the circles of light from the street-lamps, nothing existed but shadow and darkness. Room enough for either one of us to step into and disappear for-ever. It happened all the time.

"I didn't say there was." She breezed past the last few classroom buildings before we needed to turn toward the Trap. "Wait." She stopped short. "You've seen one, haven't you?"

I ignored her question, bypassing her and rounding the corner. The Trap exploded before us in a sea of crime-re-lated activity. Spotlights, cameras, and news vans gathered footage of attractive reporters while snippets of the emer-gent tragedy rolled behind them.

"Whoa," Maeve whispered.

Some students lined up around the caution tape, ready and waiting to volunteer for interviews. We stayed in the shadows, the periphery of gloom cast by the buildings and mature trees. The main array of activity unfolded under the historic oak in the center of the Trap, where merely a week ago it hosted the incident between us and Sara's boyfriend.

Alongside the center of the Trap, parallel to the big tree, and not swarming with reporters, we found a vacant set of stairs leading to one of the newer buildings. A bulb was ei-ther burned out or the fixture itself was broken. Either way, it kept the stairs dark, and we camped there. Between all the vehicles, people, and distance, I doubted we'd get a glimpse of anything. But Maeve stared on, her eyes glued to the scene.

Walkie-talkies crackled in the distance, and engines rumbled in neutral. Diesel fuel was the night's perfume.

"What do you think happened?" I asked.

"I don't know. Probably some dead girl out there."

"What makes you say that?"

"Isn't it always?"

I didn't answer. Statistically, Maeve was probably right.

After a time, my ass tingled with numbness. I stood and stretched. As I tilted back and forth, a flicker of shine glinted on the sidewalk below. I descended the steps, leaving Maeve to her grisly fascination.

I crouched to get a better look. The charm attached to a ropey strand of leather lay shining in the moonlight, and a shock of recognition coursed through me. There on the sidewalk, in front of my own eyes, was the same choker I wore every now and then. I touched the braided cording, and my finger came away smeared with a smudge of something obscure and wet. My heart raced as I imagined blood. The snap of a twig sounded off behind me. I looked toward Maeve.

"What did you find?" She sounded smug, but she always sounded that way.

"I-I don't know," I stammered, not sure what to do next. I should've yelled, should've called the investigation over our way, should've not touched something a mere twenty yards from the crime scene tape. And now I was connected. The web of fate, or star stuff—the junk that binds us—wound a sparkling little path around my wrist, the charm, and a body lying still under the oak canopy.

Maeve came down the steps. She squatted over the necklace but didn't touch it.

"Do you think that's mine?" I managed to squeak out. "H-how could that be mine?"

"Nonsense." Maeve took a slip of paper out of her back pocket and looked around until she found a stick. "Lots of people have necklaces like this one." With the tip of the stick, she nudged the charm onto the paper and folded it.

"Should we tell them?"

"Nah." Maeve tucked the object back into her pants pocket. "We're good."

"I think there's blood on that thing. That means we're standing in part of the crime scene. We could be fucking up everything."

"Yeah, we could," Maeve snapped, looking past me. "But you just touched it, which means your fingerprints are on it. That places you at the top of the suspect list."

"Wait. We don't know for sure this was a murder, right? It could have been an accident, or a suicide." My voice broke over the word. There was a rustling in the bushes nearby, maybe an animal displaced by the tragedy unfolding in the Trap, but then a flash of two gold circles made me think of a pair of glasses. Was someone hiding in there?

Before I could say anything, Maeve grabbed me by the elbow and dragged me into an alley between two neighboring buildings. It soon became clear she wasn't going to stop. She was leading us home.

"Maeve, we can't steal evidence!"

That got her attention. She came in close, her face nearly touching mine. In the alley's darkness I could only make out a vague outline of her shape. "We can do anything."

OAKLEY UNIVERSITY

"Where tomorrow's leaders don't fall far from the tree."

Go Oaknuts!

Welcome to Oakley University's online diary-hosting website, promoting a shared community experience for all.

Username: dead_papers

Posted: October 21, 2000

We went on vacation once. I was little but still remember the beach mist, cloaking us in a white bubble. We couldn't see ahead of us, and we couldn't see behind. There was only the moment we were in. Nothing else existed, not even a timeline. I wore red-and-white polka-dotted galoshes, and I loved them so much. I held Dad's hand, and he carried my plastic bucket along the shore. There was no one else—no mother or siblings to speak of. We climbed over rocks, and hidden between the spaces were new, ever-changing worlds—tide pools. The cold water held surprising, weird creatures—some prickly with spines, others as delicate as Jell-O. They were treasures, wild mixes of color and texture. Dad explained how the waves washed the creatures ashore. I imagined them as they went about their business in the sea, only to have their whole lives upended by some wild, esoteric force.

I guess this was all to say life always contains a bit of horror. It's only natural.

Likes: 2

Comments: 1

sarajalltheway: I love the ocean too.

Chapter Eleven

Death and Charm

OCTOBER 21, 2000
Still

This was crazy. Stupid. Unwise. Ill-advised. But Maeve's quick pace had me jogging to stay near her.

"Maeve!" I kept my voice low, which was probably unnecessary as the commotion from the death scene grew farther and farther away. "Maeve, stop!"

We stood in the shadowy middle between buildings, an alleyway with lights shining at both ends but not in the center. I could only make out her figure as she doubled back.

"What? What do you suggest we do?" Her words were clipped and tight.

"I don't know. Not this though. Someone's been hurt."

"Someone's dead, Hazel. Do you actually want to march a necklace with someone else's blood and your fingerprints over to those officers?"

I did not want to do that.

"Do you?" She punctuated her question by stomping her foot.

"No," I answered.

"Then it's settled." She headed in the direction of our dorm.

"But what are we going to do with it?" I asked, rushing to keep up again.

"We'll decide later. Once we have more information."

That...sounded reasonable.

Beyond the windows of Robin Hall, occupants paced; their silhouettes created quick little eclipses within the frames of their rooms. With the campus lockdown in full effect, I wasn't quite sure what that meant for those of us trying to get into the building. But the desk attendants scanned our IDs, and we walked right up to our room like any other night.

Trish and Kim had the television news on. They sat on the loveseat as a journalist reported the latest, which wasn't much more than what we already knew. A body was found in the Trap, and authorities weren't releasing details at this time. Nobody knew the victim's identity. But we could guess she was one of us.

The lack of sound—the usual ringing phones and constant hum of chatter—took me by surprise. Everyone's doors were open, and all the TVs were tuned to the same local stations. Beyond that, a pin could drop. After we'd stood there for a while, Trish noticed us.

"You're back," she whispered. Her smudged mascara made raccoon circles around her eyes. She sat with her legs crisscross-applesauce and seemed dazed. "We were worried about you guys."

"Come on. Let's get you to bed." Kim tried to get Trish off the couch.

"I wanna keep watching," Trish whined. "You've seen those articles. That's probably some poor dead girl out there."

"They won't have any new details tonight." My voice sounded like someone else's, as though it came from up above, as if I narrated this particular campus tragedy.

As Kim pulled her up, Trish stumbled. Her bare toes caught under the shaggy rug. Maeve stepped forward to help steady Trish, and the three of them hobbled beyond the bedroom curtain.

I sat at my desk and stared out the window. A breeze picked up, and leaves tumbled along the sidewalk. I opened the window to hear the crackling dead-leaf sound and smell the burnt-sugar smell of autumn. If death brought something that sweet, maybe it wasn't meant to be so scary. I hoped whoever was left in the Trap tonight had felt that way before passing, but...doubtful.

Maeve came back into the living room and sighed as she slumped onto the couch. An undeniable heaviness came with stealing evidence from a crime scene. At least, that was how it felt to me. She signaled for me to stay quiet, then reached for her back pocket. A dusting of maroon flecks covered the slip of paper with what looked like my necklace still inside. The charm shimmered in silver and what was likely crusted blood.

"I have to make sure mine's missing."

In the dark bedroom, Trish and Kim both lay quietly in their bunks, but there was no way they were asleep yet, especially after the shock and flood of adrenaline over what was unfolding in the Trap. I was sure their minds were busy wondering who'd been left out there, quickly followed by the certainty of how easily it could've been one of us. Any one of us. How fortunate we all were not to have been *that* kind of victim, at least not tonight.

I grabbed the little porcelain dish off my dresser. Another gift from my mom, the dish had miniature pink roses encircling a bible verse from Proverbs. I knew the phrase without looking at it: *A merry heart doeth good like a medicine; but a broken spirit drieth the bones.* Mom and I had laughed at the cutesy painting juxtaposed by such grim words. It seemed a bit off, but those were the things she'd loved best. And I did too.

Back in the living room, I lined all the rings and coins and tangled chains on my desk one by one. My necklace with the silver-plated charm was absent from the bunch, which meant it probably sat folded in the dirty piece of paper in Maeve's hands. I couldn't imagine someone taking it. At first glance, the charm—a wise-looking little owl perched on the lower part of a crescent moon—seemed to be a cheap trinket, found at any mall. But it wasn't. It was vintage with a hallmark on the backside. Mom had worn it every day. After she was gone, I wore it, but only when it didn't feel as though it might choke me. And now, the facts were clear; my necklace had somehow gotten itself to the edge of a crime scene. Either by some freak accident or by someone else's hand, I was squarely involved in another death.

The Campus Echo

Homecoming Tradition Ends in Tragedy

by Gayle Jackson

Homecoming is a tradition that celebrates alum from across the nation. At Oakley University the weekend culminates with the rival football game and the win or lose "Big Dipper" celebration, where current students plunge themselves into the Skullkey River.

Unfortunately, this year's party will be forever framed by tragedy. Little information is known regarding a death occurring in the Trap last night. A campus-wide lockdown went into effect shortly after a 911 call was placed around 9:00 p.m. Authorities have indicated this is a suspected homicide, and the victim's identity will not be released at this time.

The tragedy comes after several people have come forward with accusations of assaults being ignored by campus security, all occurring in the Trap. The university and head of campus security have declined to comment at this time regarding any criminal proceedings. University President Pepper asks all students to comply with emergency procedures, to stay together, and look out for one another. When asked if classes would resume Monday morning, Pepper states that the university will follow guidelines put forth by local police authorities, and students will be notified via all available means as to whether classes will occur.

OAKLEY UNIVERSITY

Username: dead_papers

Date posted: October 22, 2000

I find myself still clinging to the rocks, like a brittle sea star in a tide pool. Sure, I've lost an arm here and there; it regrew. I survived. Regeneration is a powerful, powerful thing.

Were I to lose all five arms at once? Well, then I'd be fucked for good. There'd be no regrowth. I'd be nothing but a dead core, unable to move on. And so I couldn't—wouldn't—let that happen. It was reasonable, I think. Logical, even.

Instinctual.

Especially for me. Someone with my genetics.

So many of you were present in the mist that formed around the Trap last night. Each of you bore witness to my unveiling; you transferred your strength to me. And I became big and powerful and not quite of this world. Raw energy, electric and intoxicating, coursed through my veins.

After the deed was done, I stayed out of the light. I teetered on the edge of shadows. I chose the dark because—as my dad must know—that's where all the power is. The depths of the ocean are as pitch-black as the deepest caves.

It is here, in the cavernous darkness, where I learned the most about myself. It is here where I have evolved past the monster's daughter and into a beast of my own making.

My wandering took me toward the river—*of course*—where shouts and screeches howled over the water. There's rarely another soul down here, but last night, the riverbanks teemed with wet, slippery bodies. I needed the water. The frolicking, splashing people provided a cover. For around this time, my powers waned, and reality settled. And so, I snuck into the water with the others. I dunked myself under the freezing current. The witch clutched at my neck, nearly stealing my breath, until she recognized, then welcomed me—thanked me for what I had done.

And now, as I type this, I can't help but find some small amusement in the fact that you all, in your silly homecoming ritual, have bathed in the filth. As the river washed me, the vile sludge wound its way through her waters and floated among the rest of you. Some of it probably got in your hair or your mouth. Can you taste it? You will. It devours from the inside, and we are all complicit.

JasmynBell34: I don't know exactly what this is supposed to mean, but have some respect. Somebody died last night.

Chapter Twelve

Well, Shit

OCTOBER 22, 2000

At some point, Maeve and I went to bed. Only exhaustion allowed me to close my eyes. Because now, as I blinked awake, last night's realization sent my heart racing.

If I didn't lose my necklace in the Trap, who did? Either Trish or Kim could've borrowed it, but my stuff wasn't really their style. Plus, they were usually sticklers about asking before taking. Maeve though? She took whatever she wanted, whenever she wanted it. But that meant... No. I wouldn't let the idea fully form, aborting before it took on a recognizable shape. I trusted her. Period.

After a quick shower, I threw on some semiclean jeans and a T-shirt. In the living area, I flipped on the morning news and started coffee. Maybe if I initiated my normal routine, everything would magically go back to the time before someone died on campus, and my necklace hadn't been there to witness it.

The coffee percolated, filling the room with a toasty nut aroma. A girl's chatter next door bled through the walls. The cinder blocks were cold against my ear and cheek, but I couldn't make out anything more than a mumbled conversation. I poured myself a cup of coffee before it finished brewing, the stream sizzling on the burner, and turned up the sound on the TV as the local meteorologist reported today's weather. On the other side of our door, someone's keys jangled, then clicked into the deadbolt.

"Good morning!" Maeve walked in, whistling. Her hair was still damp, and her face was shiny clean. She had a fancy coffee from the corner store and a newspaper tucked under her armpit. "How are we feeling this morning?"

"Not great," I mumbled.

"Well, shit. Are you coming down with something?"

Had she lost her ever-loving mind? "I don't think that's it, Maeve." I raked my hands through my hair and pulled it up into a topknot, giving Maeve my most incredulous look.

She shrugged and started taking apart the newspaper at her desk. I sat on the loveseat and propped my elbows on my knees, willing the news for an update on what had happened last night in the Trap.

"Look at this!"

Why hadn't I considered the newspaper? I didn't have to listen to Traffic Jam Joe scream over the whoop-whooping lash of helicopter blades. I clicked off the TV and read over Maeve's shoulder.

"Ani's coming to town." She folded the paper around the upcoming events section. "We should go!"

"A concert? That's what you wanna talk about this morning?" I sighed, feeling disgusted with her nonchalance, her easy way of compartmentalizing.

I crossed my arms and moved toward the windows. A normal Sunday unfolded below. Most people were dressed in hoodies and pajama pants as they moseyed along, completing whatever errands they'd saved for the week's end. Some carried a slew of plastic grocery bags, while others held Styrofoam containers of takeout. It appeared the lockdown was over, and we were supposed to return to daily life as if someone's dead body hadn't been caught in the Trap last night.

Maeve's fingers dug into the flesh above my elbow like a set of clamping pincers. She smelled of the cucumber bodywash her mother sent in care packages.

"Hey," she said through clenched teeth. "I'm just trying to act normal, okay. I'm as freaked out as you are, but if you start acting like a little bitch, people are gonna notice. So get your shit together." She let go, and I rubbed the spot she'd pinched. "I'm going for a smoke."

She gathered her smoker's pouch, an elongated coin purse with an old-fashioned clasp. Her hand rested on the doorknob as she paused before leaving. "You may wanna take a look at the front page." Then she disappeared into the hall, leaving the door open behind her.

Our neighbor across the hall stood in her living room, still dressed in a bathrobe. She raised her mug as if to say, *Cheers*, but instead said, "Weird night, huh?"

"Totally," I agreed.

My coffee somehow tasted both bitter and watered down. I searched through the rustling papers spread across Maeve's desk for today's biggest headlines. Snapshots of last night's death scene filled most of the front page, but not a whole lot of details were being disclosed to the public yet.

At approximately 9:00 p.m. last night, emergency responders were called to the scene of Oakley University's campus courtyard, commonly referred to as the Trap. Upon arrival, it became clear the victim, recently deceased, was a student enrolled at the university. Police aren't releasing the victim's name at this time and ask if anyone has information regarding what's being described as a "gruesome and meticulous" attack to contact...

Words like *gruesome* and *meticulous* suggested this wasn't something completely random. Of the shootings I'd seen play out on the news, I'd heard them described with *shock*, *terror*, and *horror*. Meticulous implied something else.

The folded piece of paper containing my charm necklace sat on Maeve's desk—totally out in the open for anyone to find. Since it was mine, I took it back.

I went to the bathroom and unfolded the paper. The necklace was a ruin. The band was stained a deep maroon, and flecks collected on the paper like spilled confetti. I grabbed the shower cleaner, but it was empty. So I squirted pearly globs of hand soap all over the charm and scrubbed. The foamy suds became slick and white, but gradually, they turned a reddish-brown. I pretended not to know why. As I rinsed the charm, I examined the crevices, knowing for certain the only way to get it spotless would be to soak it in bleach, maybe take a Q-tip to the crannies.

I couldn't stop thinking about all the bodies in all the compartments in all the buildings on campus. All except one. That one was sectioned off differently now. That one would be in a refrigerated drawer in some cold mortuary.

Stop.

Where we all end up eventually.

Don't go there.

Just like Mom.

Fuck. Get out. Get yourself the fuck out of this room right now.

I finished patting the necklace dry and left, not knowing where I was headed. As I passed the other dorm rooms, snippets of pop music and images of girls painting their toenails melded together. Some rooms still had the news on, but only a few people actually stood in front of the screens, shushing their less-concerned roommates. Life had gone back to normal too quickly.

I checked for the bulge in my back pocket. Still there. It was hard to believe a piece of jewelry could hold the information needed to crack the case wide open.

"Crack the case?" I whispered, the phrasing clunky and—somehow—comfortable in my mind.

My sneakers thudded against the stairs as I descended. I found myself in the basement, the study room door already propped open and the lights on. Voices emerged. When I got to the doorframe, I noticed bookbags scattered on some of the tables. This was no longer a private place.

A group of people huddled near the back wall around a line of newly installed computers. Candy wrappers and pop cans littered the space. A girl sat on a table, swinging her legs. She finished off a fountain drink, filling the room with a slurping *smack* as she sucked the last of the liquid through the straw. An electric-blue color tinted her smile.

As I turned to leave, someone in the back of the room called to me. It was Trish. Her hair looked clean, and her face was fresher without the bright-pink lipstick she usually chose. She waved me over to the group nearest the computers.

The staggering scent of French vanilla body spray overwhelmed my senses as I stepped closer to the group. I cleared my throat and fought the urge to cough and shoo the smell away. A girl, whose face was covered in beautiful orange freckles, gave me an unimpressed look.

"Have you seen this?" Trish asked.

I peeked around the mass of people, rising onto my tiptoes. "What is it?" Some of the girls shot me suspicious looks as if I were cutting in line.

"The online diaries," Trish said over her shoulder.

"Doug was talking about them last night. Is that what everyone's doing down here?" Factions clustered around each of the five computer monitors.

Trish nodded. "Then you've heard of dead_papers?"

"Uh, no." I snorted.

"Come look." She grasped my forearm, and we maneuvered through the grumpy crowd.

"There're other computers," I suggested, thinking of mine, all alone in a quiet, empty room without all the smells and the closeness.

Tricia brought me right up behind Kim, whose manicured acrylics clacked over the mouse as she scrolled through a post.

"What is this?" I asked again.

Kim glanced over her shoulder at me. She brushed a stray strand of hair back into place and chomped a pink wad of gum. "Someone's confession."

OAKLEY UNIVERSITY

"Where tomorrow's leaders don't fall far from the tree."

Go Oaknuts!

Welcome to Oakley University's online diary-hosting website, promoting a shared community experience for all.

Username: dead_papers
Date posted: October 22, 2000
I killed him.

Views: 123

Likes: 3

Comments: 52

djhuffinstuff: hahaha, good one.
Builttolift: What the hell?
Ponyboy5: Is this a joke?
Jilly10: Not even funny.
Emsaysso: You're sick.
CarlaVale: What is wrong with you?
SarahSea: This isn't even a little bit okay.
KatieOK: This account should be flagged and reported.
John1281: I can't believe someone would post this.
Kendall1679: Y'all nuts.

AndreDidnt: Un-fucking-believable.

MiraJB: Shady

SoccerTJ77: Whooooa, man.

Load More

Chapter Thirteen

Something Sour

OCTOBER 22, 2000

Bodies crowded around me. Someone's boobs pressed against my back. An elbow caught me in the rib. The skin beneath my back pocket, where my necklace was tucked and hidden, burned. My throat dried up, puckering with the knowledge of something sour. I tried to push against the horde. But they pulsed forward, each wanting to catch a glimpse of someone's idea of a joke. A bad joke, an internet prank, that was all this could possibly be. A film of sweat broke out on my upper lip. My breath caught in my throat, then came shallow and fast. I needed to get out of the basement study room immediately.

"Spider," I whispered.

No one moved. I cleared my throat.

"Spider!" I shouted, and enough people backed away for me to get out of the room without causing a total scene.

"Hazel, where are you going?" Trish called after me.

I pointed up, hoping that would be enough information. But when I got to the first-floor landing, I burst out of the fire door and gulped in the fresh autumn air—or the air that should have been fresh. Instead, it stank of Maeve's burning cigarettes. Whatever. At least, no one was pressed up against me.

"What's up? You look like you've seen a ghost," Maeve said.

I shook my head and stepped out from under the awning. I gripped my lower back, needing the extra support. The sky was an impossible blue, and the sun shone on Maeve's quizzical face. Her brows scrunched over the top of her sunglasses.

"Not a ghost." I licked my lips, trying to formulate the words to describe whatever the diary entry meant. "A murderer?"

"What are you talking about?" Maeve snubbed her cigarette on the brick wall, leaving behind a coal-black smudge.

"Come with me." I grabbed her by the wrist. "You've gotta see this." For a split second, I wondered, *Is it her*? Then I snuffed out my suspicion, alongside the burning end of Maeve's last cigarette. She might be capable of a lot of things, but killing someone? No. Although, if that post was a fake, meant to grab attention and manipulate emotions... Well, I *had* seen her do that before.

Waiting for the elevator was out of the question; I needed to move. We raced up the stairs, taking two at a time. Back in our room, I held down my computer's power button. We waited through the machine's internal humming and clicking as it booted up.

"What's going on, Hazel? You're acting weird."

"I can't explain it." The monitor screen blinked bright, its main screen, an image of gently rippling waves. I clicked on the internet browser. "You have to see it." I typed in the web address and waited again. A quiet whirring could be heard, but with the cable connection, the old screeches of dial-up were absent, leaving only a pregnant silence as we waited. "Ugh, I have to set up an account."

"For what?" Maeve asked.

"The campus diaries."

"I have one." Maeve pulled her chair next to mine. Her arms stretched over the desk to reach the keyboard, and her fingers graced over the clacking buttons. I tried to watch where her fingers went. Would they spell dead_papers? *Jesus, stop*. Of course they wouldn't. Maeve was not a psychopath.

We were in. I filled the search box with the dead_papers username, and a tiny hourglass appeared.

"What's up?" Maeve asked. "This could take a minute."

I slumped my shoulders, needing her to read it herself. I wasn't a great storyteller, but I didn't see what choice I had as the hourglass kept tipping over itself while we waited. "Someone made a diary entry confessing to murdering whoever was in the Trap last night."

"What?" Maeve's brow furrowed with either disbelief or confusion—maybe both.

The hourglass disappeared, and dead_papers's feed filled the screen. I scrolled through a dozen posts until I found the one posted in the early morning hours. Three simple words—*I killed him*—showed up in the monitor's negative space, like an Etch A Sketch carving.

Maeve's jaw dropped. She brought her thumbnail to her mouth and chewed.

Feeling my wits returning, I asked, "How long before you think the university takes this down?"

"I don't know. What are the other posts like?"

I clicked on the back arrow and selected one of dead_papers's earliest posts. Maeve and I leaned in to read.

OAKLEY UNIVERSITY

"Where tomorrow's leaders don't fall far from the tree."

Go Oaknuts!

Welcome to Oakley University's online diary-hosting website, promoting a shared community experience for all.

Username: dead_papers

Date Posted: September 19, 2000

In middle school, I noticed my friends acting differently—their eyelids were shiny with sparkling purples and blues. They were so cool, so fashionable. I always complimented them and never dared to disagree with anything they said. And then, finally, praising them got me somewhere. An invite.

"You should come with us to the spot," Ashley—I think her name was Ashley—invited me.

"What's the spot?"

Glances were exchanged. The whole of them sucked in their cheeks so that their lips formed *knowing* pouts, and then they burst into fits of giggles. I laughed with them—excitedly, nervously, naïvely. They were bringing me into the folds of their magical group with mystery spots.

After school, the girls took me by the elbows and led me to an empty bathroom that smelled of cheap perfume, hair spray, and used pads. They took their time, swiping all those colors on my face—shimmering pinks and purples—a wand sweeping black mascara over my lashes. And I loved it. So. Much. When I blinked, I wished my eyes wouldn't close all the way, so I could see every speck of the glittery pastel shadow painted on my lids. I was one of them.

And their attention, it was intoxicating. They *oohed* and *aahed* over the change in my appearance, then offered me watermelon Jolly Ranchers and the latest gossip regarding a maybe-pregnant girl who'd been absent a lot lately.

When the time came, we marched across the play-ground toward a chain-link fence surrounding the perime-ter. As we got closer, I heard the mix of boys' laughter—low baritones unpredictably breaking into high-pitched squawks. The girls around me tittered like little birds.

A section of the fence had been blocked off by a slab of plywood that was easily pulled aside. We entered a little cove surrounded by weed trees, growing and reproducing too fast for upkeep. The grass had been worn away, so every time someone moved, brown clouds of dirt plumed into the air.

A popular boy shouted, "Newbie!" His orange hair was cut short on one side and hung longer on the other. A row of spiked hair separated the two styles—a side-spike. On his arm was Shelley, an eighth grader with the right clothes and the ability to form her bangs into the perfect tidal wave every day.

Everyone in the circle turned to look at me, and I waved awkwardly. My friends prodded me toward the center as every set of eyes beamed their appraisal of my worth.

"What size are your jeans?" asked some random girl.

"N-nine," I stammered and hated myself for it.

"Her hips are bigger than her shoulders." The random girl rolled her eyes toward the tree line, disgusted by the way I was made.

"He likes 'em that way. Don't ya, Adam?"

This boy, Adam—I'd never seen him before—stepped forward. He was nodding and rolling his hands together as if they itched to get ahold of me. He seemed bigger and older than the rest of us. As he came closer, I could make out stubby patches of facial hair.

I looked back to my friends, all standing in a row behind me. Their smiles were probably meant to reassure me. They'd already been initiated and knew what came next. I hadn't a clue and started sweating. Fear crept up out of my guts; it turned to heat, flushing my chest with what I knew would be pink, blotchy hives. What was supposed to happen next? This guy, Adam, seemed more and more like a man than a kid. I hadn't wanted to *do* anything. I'd only wanted to be a part of their crowd, to seem cool by association. But as I stood among them, I realized they were animals, a pack of wolves, snapping and snarling at one another. I needed an immediate escape.

A wetness spread between my legs. I hadn't pissed myself, but the gush of hot-warm liquid indicated otherwise.

"What is that?" someone asked.

"Aw, fucking gross!" Derrick shaded his eyes and looked away. "She's bleedin'." More disgust.

I looked down to find a maroon stain blooming on my khaki shorts. My face burned as I stepped back, trying to get out of the circle of kids who were all sniggering and appalled. Someone, a kinder soul, tossed me a sweatshirt to tie around my waist. I fumbled with it, not caring how this would play out later. I knew enough in the moment to be thankful—that if there was a god, she had just saved me.

I sat back in my chair and waited for Maeve to finish reading. Her upper lip curled as she tried not to laugh at the last line.

"Is this a joke?"

"If it is, it's not funny," I said.

Maeve scrolled down the page and clicked on another one. "Are they all like this? Little snippets concerning... I mean, what do you call this?"

"I don't know." I scooted away from the desk. "A close call? Harassment? Hazing?"

Maeve clicked on another post. After a while, she said, "Oof, have you seen this one about her dad?"

"I haven't read any of the others. I just found out they exist."

I went to grab a drink, and the minifridge came open with a *shwuck*. The can was cold and wet in my hand. I popped the top and slurped what bubbled over. "What's it say?"

"That her dad is, like, a sexual predator or something. Maybe an actual serial rapist. *Jesus*. This is so fucked up."

My mind stuttered over "rapist." *Mom. Dad.* Their lives, our family, had been ended by someone with similar inclinations. Someone who came out of nowhere and ruined lives in the course of an afternoon.

"Hazel? Are you okay?"

"What?"

"I asked you a question, but you're all pale again."

"It's fine. What did you say?"

"I said, 'Can you even imagine being raised by her dad?' He's like a bona fide monster. You've gotta read these."

"We should print them out."

"You think?" Maeve rotated in her chair, turning back to the screen.

"I do." I took another sip and noticed my reflection in the bedroom's full-length mirror. I was all hips, had been a size 9 in middle school, too, just like this dead_papers person. Although no one had ridiculed me over it, and I was well into 14/16 territory now. Was I not supposed to be? Fuck that. "It's blowing up; check out the comments. If the university doesn't shut down this account, the police will. I want a hard copy before it's gone."

"This person actually thinks there's a witch in the river, Hazel." Maeve had gone back to scrolling. "No one is gonna take this seriously. Why would we need a copy?"

I reached into my pocket and grabbed my necklace. "Because of this."

"Oh." Maeve held out her hand. "Give me a drink." I passed her the half empty can of pop. She took a long gulp and hiccupped. "The library lab is open until midnight."

I shooed her suggestion away. "It's too close to the crime scene." No matter what, I wanted to steer clear of the Trap for as long as possible. "They put computers in the basement. I didn't see if there's a printer down there, but probably, right? It was packed with people though…"

"You want anyone we know seeing us print this stuff out?"

"No. You're right. But where else?"

"Oh!" Maeve snapped her fingers. "The grad dorm! They have a full computer lab. And it's right behind north campus commons. Nobody will know us there."

"Okay." I nodded, liking the idea. "Okay, yeah. Let's go." My hoodie smelled of Max's Pizza, and I thought of Doug tucked away in his dorm room—almost always safe. I fingered the cannister of Mace I'd kept on my keychain since our encounter with Sara's boyfriend in the Trap. "I'm ready. You?"

"Yep."

We stared at each other for a second. I might never know what exactly went on in Maeve's head, but I was grateful for her. The circumstances were odd and fairly shitty, but at least I wasn't facing them alone.

OAKLEY UNIVERSITY

"Where tomorrow's leaders don't fall far from the tree."

Go Oaknuts!

Welcome to Oakley University's online diary-hosting website, promoting a shared community experience for all.

Username: dead_papers

Date posted: October 22, 2000

People will feel sorry for him. "*A life taken too soon*," they'll say. A boy—but really a man already—who showed so much promise and drive and confidence. His whole life was ahead of him!

Once I'd dipped under the water and washed his blood off my hands, the river witch—the goddess—showed me all of what his future might have been: a successful career in business, the too-big house on a private lane, a pretty wife pretending not to know of his sins as she doted on their two and a half children. He could've had it all. If only, if only...

If only he hadn't crept across my path.

They'll call me a ruthless bitch and say no one deserves what happened to him.

Yet, his children would have been grim souls, twisted from the inside out. And that pretty wife, well, her spirit would have shriveled and dried up over the years, leaving no more than a corn husk of a person.

He was the real monster. And I? Well, I am a monster's spawn. And that is a tale as old as the gods.

I just wish I hadn't left behind that necklace.

Views: 3012

Likes: 22

Comments: 256

sislove: You need to stop.

Badguy1222: You think you're some kind of vigilante? Not cool.

Complicatedjane2: This isn't funny.

ByteM3: Look back at all these posts. Bitch be crazy.

BgDckJ: No one person has the right to be judge and jury. If this is even real...

Butt3rflyw!ngs: You need a therapist.

Savvyf#ckR: Get yourself offline and into treatment. This ain't a joke!

CutiePie666: Badass.

AnnieAnn: I don't know what to believe.

TomStranger: cough, cough, bullshit.

Beesnsuch: Someone needs to tell you this. The river's not talking to you, psycho! Get help!

MallyMo: You can't know someone else's future.

Babyblu: A real person died last night. They had parents and people who loved them. I don't know why you think this is a good time to get attention, but it's real gross.

AndySameAsU: Yikes.

PrettySkinnyGirl: Honestly, I see a lot of myself in some of your early stories. But this prank goes too far.

Sk8r3127: This is wild.

DaizyChainz32: It can't be real.

JessieC: Got enough attention yet?

GreenEyedGuy: I can't believe the university hasn't wiped this account.

TiredCat: Why would they do that? Freedom of speech, dude.

Lily4square: Has anyone contacted the police?

Maroon52: I'm sure they're on it.

Markman: Lol, OK.

Load More

Chapter Fourteen

Ctrl + P

OCTOBER 22, 2000

In the short time it took to walk to the grad dorm, I'd gathered expectations of finding a sparkling new facility—a twin to our dorm, only with more bricks and mortar stacked higher into the air, Adams Graduate Hall was a letdown.

"How'd you know about this place?" I asked, zipping my jacket. October was finally starting to act like itself—crisp and cool, with crackling leaves under every step.

"Bridgette's boyfriend."

"Who?"

"Our neighbor across the hall? Jeez, you're bad at names. Anyway, her boyfriend lives here. He let me print a paper last week."

"Will he need to let us in now?"

"They broke up yesterday, so I wasn't planning on calling him."

"How are we gonna get in then?"

"Girl"—Maeve popped the collar of her peacoat and mussed her hair—"I've got wiles for days."

I laughed, knowing she was right. No doubt, Maeve could manipulate herself in and out of a multitude of situations. We reached the door, and I held it open for her. As she sauntered past, her shoulders were raised high as if she were royalty. She already belonged, and I didn't expect anyone to question her.

The grad dorm lobby was bigger than ours. The ceiling consisted of drop tiles, some water stained and damaged. The floor was a giant sheet of icy marble. A mustard-yellow couch and a quartet of beaten-down chairs created a perimeter around a coffee table piled high with magazines. Bronzed metal doors—mailboxes—filled an entire wall, each with a number inscribed on the front and a lock. There weren't a ton of people around. Two guys huddled over a foosball table in the corner. The whooshing clack of pushes and pulls echoed throughout the lobby.

Maeve pressed the bangs of her pixie cut over to one side of her forehead and smoothed on a quick layer of shiny lip gloss. I let my hair down and fluffed it, then borrowed her tube of gloss. When I rolled my lips together, they tasted of artificial sweetener. Together, we made our way to the front desk.

"We need to use the lab?" Maeve asked.

"Top floor." The volunteer behind the counter sifted through mail and barely looked up.

We made our way to the set of stainless-steel elevator doors located behind the desk at the end of the lobby. I pressed the button, and we waited. Overall, I was surprised by the lack of security since someone had been *gruesomely* and *meticulously* murdered just last night. What made me think there would be cops combing every building for clues, or plainclothes officers peeking over newspapers? None of that was happening. This was the real world. The institution wasn't looking out for me. In fact, the college itself wouldn't recognize me beyond the eight digits on my social security card. They—like the great and powerful Oz working furiously behind the curtain—weren't actually going to do anything, and that included ensuring anyone's safety.

Ding! The elevator doors swooshed open to an empty compartment. Maeve selected the twentieth floor, and we ascended. The elevator stopped several times, picking up other students along the way. I absorbed their details—people-watched. That girl's eyes were puffy, watery and red. I imagined a family emergency for her. The guy chewing gum was a little aggressive about it, so he was probably a bit of an asshole who always had something to prove. Someone mumbled, "'Scuse me," and we shuffled around to make room. The girl next to me had her wet hair wrapped in a bun, and it smelled of coconuts, a whiff of the beach. By the time we reached our destination, all kinds of bodies filled the compartment.

The elevator sounded one last time, and everyone swarmed out. I followed Maeve through a bright hall lined with knotted-pile carpet. The path was so worn I could have found my way to the lab without Maeve or the signs. It seemed the computer lab was the twentieth floor's only destination.

We stood in line and watched the students in front of us sign in. When our turn came, Maeve scrawled her name and handed me the pencil. I did the same. The person who was supposed to be monitoring all of this clicked away at Minesweeper. The sign above his head said No Food or Drinks, but his knee bobbed up and down as he sipped a Mountain Dew, and there were a couple Twinkie wrappers in the trash can next to his desk.

Maeve wound her way through the rows of computers. The lighting, bright and fluorescent, was typical for a computer lab. Hints of auburn streaks glinted in Maeve's hair.

She arranged two chairs together at the end of the last row, then untied the belt of her peacoat as I sat down. In a few short seconds, we were back online. I typed in the username I'd seen her use back at our dorm, Maeveorama3, and looked away as she entered her password. Although it was urgent to get the dead_papers diary printed, there was definitely a part of me that wouldn't have minded sifting through what Maeveorama3 had to say.

I looked around the rest of the room, quiet except for the tap-tap-pause-tap of typing. Someone backspaced furiously. Maeve popped her neck while we waited for the dead_papers feed to load, and a sudden wave of panic washed over me. I grabbed for the edge of the desk.

Since last night, everything had taken on this surreal quality. Extreme moments, one after another, had snowballed, and it hadn't occurred to me that we'd started investigating a murder until then. How was this actually happening? I felt moments away from slapping myself when Maeve clicked Print. She went and stood in front of a row of whirring printers. As each sheet emerged, she grabbed it before letting it hit the tray. A guy behind her kept sneaking peeks at her ass and fumbling his hands around in his pockets.

I wiggled the mouse. The screensaver's slow-bouncing geometric shapes disappeared, and up popped the diary entries, with the newest one entered mere minutes ago. I read through this girl's private thoughts. Although they weren't confidential; she was broadcasting them. It was possible each post had been carefully picked and crafted. Each one had a cadence, a rising tempo, all leading to an inevitable crescendo of death. I got the sense this dead_papers person had kept an audience in mind. When somebody sat down at the keyboard and knew people might read their shit, how truthful could they really be? Weren't they just carefully curating an agenda?

Maeve plopped down next to me. "Did you see the new one?"

"I'm reading it now."

"What do you make of them?"

"I'm not sure. I mean, this could be someone playing a prank. A crappy one, but still, it's a possibility."

Maeve shook her head. "I think they are all true."

"Even if they are based in reality, they only represent one person's perspective. That's not *exactly* the truth."

"This is her truth. Ours, too, when you think about it." Maeve tapped the stack of papers on the desk, straightening them.

"What? No. My dad isn't..." I wasn't sure how to complete my sentence. Luckily, Maeve took over for me

"No, no. That's not what I mean. How many times have you been harassed by a guy? Or an older man."

I shrugged.

"Belittled? Objectified?"

"No more than anyone else."

"That's what we all say, *if* we even talk about it in the first place. Whoever this dead_papers person is, I respect how she's putting it out there."

"How can you say that? She's claimed to have murdered someone." I checked the room for listeners, but most of the people near enough to eavesdrop had headphones on.

"Well, yeah. That's not gonna do her any favors. But I'm just talking about how she started telling her stories in the first place. That's brave."

"Okay." I sighed. There was a lot to figure out in this conversation. Most days, I pretended I'd never *felt* threatened in my life. But that was a total farce. I'd been backed into corners, groped without consent. Yelled at on the street. Told to smile constantly. Smacked in the Trap. Not to mention what I saw my mom go through. Examples could be rattled off in seconds, right off the top of my head, but I wasn't going to haul off and kill someone.

I changed the subject. "What we need to figure out is how this person and my necklace are connected."

"You don't think..." Maeve scratched her head. Her short hair stuck up all over the place. "It couldn't have been Trish or Kim, right?"

OAKLEY UNIVERSITY

"Where tomorrow's leaders don't fall far from the tree."

Go Oaknuts!

Welcome to Oakley University's online diary-hosting website, promoting a shared community experience for all.

Username: dead_papers

Date Posted: October 22, 2000

Now you all have something to say? Funny. I've been writing about violence and betrayal all along, and very few of you paid attention. Were you not entertained when I told on my dad? Were the tiny indiscretions not grisly enough for the average reader? Minor assault—as if there is such a thing—not enough to make your heart pound? They were for me. I've been sliced at too. Whole chunks of who I was meant to be have been stolen over the years. Yes, the cuts scabbed over and healed. And I shouldn't expect to wander through this life unscathed. That's too naïve, even for me.

But see, all those tiny cuts are connected, so they reopen and bleed together. The smallest comment cost me pints. Dripping red blotches of myself have been left everywhere I've walked. A man who told me to smile more—slash. Witnessing a so-called friend slip something into another girl's drink—gash. Finding out my father has committed unspeakable crimes against women—stab. And finally, that guy in the Trap who thought women were his for the taking—strike.

Only this last time, I wasn't the one doing all the bleeding.

Views: 541

Likes: 21

Comments: 312

LadyJournalist: I can't get ahold of you any other way. But if you're interested in going on the record, email me at gejackson@oakleyecho.edu.

Load More

Chapter Fifteen

In an Instant

OCTOBER 23, 2000

Maeve and I had made a deal to take turns keeping an eye on the dead_papers feed from our dorm. We planned on running to print new ones as they were added. I took the night shift and stared out at the earth slowly turning toward yet another day.

I'd set up my own diary account the way Doug had shown me. And now, the cursor line blinked like a pendulum: say something, show yourself. The lure was real. I could put it all out there: what had happened to Mom—the assault, the suicide—and then Dad's ruined attempt at an afterlife. But I didn't *want* to share any of that with anyone. It changed the way people thought of me. Their eyes filled with either pity or grisly fascination; at the funeral, they'd acted as if they wanted to console me when all they really wanted was their fix of gratitude and gossip. So I typed a smiley emoticon and clicked Post.

The number of open diaries seemed immense. The site's landing page included links to all kinds of random entries. I typed in the username, dead_papers, and it appeared at the top of the feed. There was nothing new, though, so I searched Doug's username: GuidedByNachos. Pretty cute.

He had two new posts. At any moment, I expected Doug to call or message me, explaining some eerie sixth sense dedicated to this account. But he didn't. Little electric shock-waves jumped through my nerves. What if he'd typed up something regarding our ho-hum date? *Click.* And sure enough, there was the narration of last night told from his perspective. The words *sweet* and *quirky* popped off the page. It was a nice Midwestern way of describing me, especially compared to Maeve calling me *anal* and *precious* all those weeks ago.

Had she written anything about me lately? I was scared to look. Scared to even explore the fact that I wanted her to be writing about me. There'd been a moment between us I hadn't forgotten—a second, a beat in which I thought we might kiss. But it had passed. And then got steamrolled by all *this*.

The clock on the computer said two hours had passed; I felt as though I'd lost time. Another two, and my shift would be over. My vision blurred as I scrolled through posts and updated the feed. When I closed my eyes, a hazy blue square floated on the back of my eyelids. I stretched, rolling my head from shoulder to shoulder, savoring the quiet pull of muscles too tight with anxiety. Clicking on Maeve's desk lamp spotlighted the chaos she preferred. Pens and stacks of paper cluttered her workstation, some unused loose-leaf, some bearing notes. I cleared part of it away and opened my econ text. Every few minutes, the screensaver kicked on, and I leaned over to wiggle the mouse and click Refresh.

Hours passed that way. My eyes were heavy, and I only wanted to lay my head down on the cool page for a second.

The *do-do-ding* of AIM startled me. I blinked away sleep, smoothed my hair back, and checked the computer.

It was an instant message from Sara. *I'm sorry.*

No worries. I typed, unable to think of anything else to say. I hoped, for her own sake, she'd broken up with Ryan. The program emitted the sound of a door closing as Sara logged off. But then, she logged back on.

The police might come talk to you.

Wait, what?

I was with them all day and have been going back and forth about whether to warn you.

What? Why?

Ryan was the guy killed in the Trap.

SaraOnStage is typing...

When they asked me if I knew anyone who might have had it out for him, I told them what you told me. About what happened between the two of you in the Trap.

Wait, so...you think I killed your boyfriend?

No, no. No, I don't. I was just telling them everything I knew.

SaraOnStage is typing...

SaraOnStage is typing...

But I didn't wait around to see what she had to say. I logged off, needing the door-closing chime to sound as though I'd slammed it shut. It didn't. The chat closed the way it always did, with the chime staying cool and calm as if I'd casually left. Yet my body responded. My breaths came quickly, keeping pace with my racing heart.

"Any word from our girl?" Maeve yawned, then reached for the oversized coffee can. As she peeled back the lid, she came closer to where I sat. The spoon made a swishing sound as Maeve scooped out the grounds. "You want some— Whoa! You look awful. Did dead_papers post again? Were there any new details?"

"It's not that," I managed to whisper.

"Then what is it?"

The conversation with Sara had disappeared as soon as I closed the chat box. The only thing for Maeve to see on the screen was the diary homepage.

"Sit down."

"You're freaking me out." She set the coffee can down and pulled her desk chair close. She sat with her knees turned toward me. "What's up?"

"Remember the guy in the Trap the other night? The one that hit me?"

"How could I forget?"

"He's the murder victim."

"No way." Maeve's eyes grew wide. She shook her head.

"And the police know we knew him. They know about the other night."

"How?"

"Sara told them."

Maeve stood and paced around our tiny living room. "You're gonna have to fill in some blanks for me, Hazel. How does Sara know about what happened?"

"When I went to her audition, he was there. They were dating." My words sounded clipped—cut off, cut short. "So I *had* to tell her what had happened. I tried to warn her about him. But she got super pissed and told me to leave."

"And now she's gone and told the police." Maeve rubbed her temples. "Christ. What are we gonna do? Your necklace was there."

"You don't need to remind me. I'm well-fucking-aware." I grabbed her purse and dug out a cigarette. "I don't know what *I'm* going to do, but keep your goddamned voice down."

I stuck the familiar cigarette between my lips, and my blood pressure dropped. With Maeve's lighter tucked into my pocket, I made for the door, then doubled back. I grabbed her entire pack of smokes and left Maeve to watch over the dead_papers account.

OAKLEY UNIVERSITY

"Where tomorrow's leaders don't fall far from the tree."

Go Oaknuts!

Welcome to Oakley University's online diary-hosting website, promoting a shared community experience for all.

Username: dead_papers

Date posted: October 23, 2000

Would it matter if I told you I hadn't planned on killing anyone? Would you believe I was minding my own business? Running an errand? It probably wouldn't change anyone's opinion, but it's the truth. It wasn't even that late when I decided to leave the safety of my dorm and venture across campus.

I saw what he was doing—how he gripped her arm, how she tried to break away, realizing I knew him. I'd had doubts about his character; something about him reminded me of Dad, but still, I thought maybe she was going to be okay. I crouched behind the bushes to make sure.

The sickly-sweet smell of liquor decorated the area as he stepped toward her. His eyes were far gone with drink. He was out of his gourd—blacked out, as they say. But that didn't stop him from acting.

He pushed her to the ground. Her bare knees scraped against the concrete sidewalk. Each notch of his zipper pounded like a sledgehammer. Panic surged when he touched the top of her head.

"'Old on," he said.

Hold on.

He turned away, and urine poured over the cement. That was when I made my move. I was done letting this happen. Done going quietly into the night. He grunted and whistled while he pissed. I touched her shoulder, careful to keep my face in the shadows, and indicated for her to get the hell out of there. He finished and found me standing before him. He didn't seem to notice I was a completely different person. He fancied himself some kind of god, never suspecting he could fail or be hurt. I'd already spilled my own blood, and it did nothing. But what about his? His blood might bring relief or a certain brand of consolation. I gripped the box cutter I'd stashed in my jacket pocket. It made me feel safe. It made me feel strong. A hero's weapon.

Rage and fate turned out to be a killer combination.

beaniebabe43: Why are you doing this?

dame567: Yes. YES.

Bone69247: Crazy bitches.

Jgreene75: This is wild.

DangerWillRob: Is this real?

Sarahsaidso: I don't think it is.

Partyboyjames: Nobody should be out at night alone, especially a woman.

Gothamy: What's that supposed to mean?

Partyboyjames: Nothing. It's a fact. The newspaper has been saying it for weeks.

Gothamy: So she deserved it? Because she didn't follow

some arbitrary guidelines.

Partyboyjames: That's not what I said.

Load More

Chapter Sixteen

From *The Campus Echo*

OCTOBER 23, 2000

"Police have released the name of the university stabbing victim this morning. Ryan Newsome is said to be..." The early morning journalist glossed over the shortlist of Ryan's accomplishments, which mostly consisted of coming from a prominent white family.

I stood near the doorway, reeking of the half pack of cigarettes I'd smoked through. Maeve sat on the loveseat, sipping from a mug and catching up with the news. She looked up, lips pursed in a way that couldn't mean anything good. I slouched next to her without a word, and she handed me her cup.

"Drink up, buttercup."

"How can you be so chipper?" I sniffed the coffee, craving the comfort.

Maeve held her forefinger to her lips, then pointed to the bathroom door. The spray of the faucet sounded. "She posted again," she whispered.

"Dead_papers?"

"Who else?" Maeve nodded. "Check it out."

I went to my desk, cradling Maeve's warm mug in both hands. On my computer, another short post from dead_papers gave enough horrifying detail to make me want to look away but simultaneously kept me glued to the screen. I bit my lip, rereading certain parts.

"This is shocking." I pulled back the curtains and let in the morning light. A dull throb pounded right under my eyes. Being up all night had left me running on empty. "So now she's some kind of avenger?" The words *gruesome* and *meticulous* echoed from yesterday morning's reports. "At least, that's how she's set this all up to look."

"Detailed enough not to be a prank. Don't ya think? She already mentioned your necklace."

"I don't know. It could be a coincidence? The police haven't released any crime scene details, so dead_papers could be making the rest up. Nobody would know." I sat at my desk.

"Unlikely. My gut tells me she was either there and saw enough to write about it, or what she's describing is true."

"And none of this helps us—me." Because I was the one in trouble here. That was my necklace in the Trap. My lucky charm had witnessed the grisly scene between Ryan and whoever killed him, and thanks to Sara, the police would probably be questioning me at some point today.

"I've been thinking—" Maeve started, but the sound of camera flashes brought our attention back to the TV screen. The words PREVIOUSLY RECORDED in all caps hovered near the upper right corner. A bald man in a navy police uniform shuffled behind a podium. The crowd of reporters hushed, but the shutter clicks from cameras did not. He cleared his throat and sipped from a Styrofoam cup before checking the mic and launching into his script.

"The victim, found the evening of October 21st, was that of twenty-year-old university student, Ryan Newsome." The officer wiped above his upper lip with a white handkerchief. He lifted his gaze, scoping distinct points within the audience. "The department is following several leads, and that's all we can say at this time. Our condolences go to the Newsome family."

"Hazel, I was wondering—"

"Shh, I want to hear this."

Journalists erupted with questions, and the officer chose one with their hand raised in the front row. "Thank you, Chief Standish. There have been some reports regarding the violent nature of the crime. Based on your expertise, is this the type of crime scene found in serial murders?"

Chief Standish blinked rapidly before providing a generic, neutral answer. "That's yet to be seen." He pointed to someone else.

"Thank you, sir. Gayle Jackson from *The Campus Echo*." The camera panned to the profile of a Black woman in a powder-blue oxford shirt. She wore her credentials on a strand around her neck. "Is the department looking into the university's online diary system?"

The question obviously threw Chief Standish. His professionalism cracked with a chuckle. Then he said, "Not that I'm aware of." He moved to point to another reporter, but Gayle spoke again.

"Then you're also not aware of someone claiming to be the murderer on the forum?"

This sent the room into a tizzy of movement and sound. Chief Standish floundered through an answer and quickly called the press conference to an end. He walked away from the podium with files tucked under his arm and his Styrofoam cup crushed in one fist.

"If she knows about the diaries and works for the university…" My thoughts rolled like a pinball, slamming and ringing around in my head. "…then she might have access to the system accounts and who they belong to."

"My thoughts exactly," Maeve agreed. "I watched the press conference live while you were out and have been trying to figure out how to get a meeting with her ever since. But also—"

"We only need the newspaper's contact information, which should be on their website, right?"

"Yes, I found that and her." Maeve wiggled the mouse, and the computer screen came back to life. She hovered over my shoulder and, with a few clicks, navigated to *The Campus Echo*'s homepage. "She's the one who's been reporting on the campus assaults."

The bathroom door opened, bringing both a cloud of steam and Kim dressed in her bathrobe. Maeve and I exchanged a shut-up look.

"Jeez, make a girl feel self-conscious," Kim joked as she shook out the towel twisted around her hair. "You guys stopped talking as soon as I walked into the room."

Maeve and I both stuttered through an awkward laugh.

"God, you guys are weird." Kim huffed and went into the bedroom. Tricia's snores could be heard, and then there was a smack. Kim shouted, "Wake up, bitch!"

I scooted my desk chair closer to the computer screen. "Where are the newspaper offices located?"

"Not far from here." Maeve tapped the screen where the address was listed. I double-clicked on the map section and studied the buildings between us.

"That's where I need to be." I chewed on my lower lip, thinking of the implications.

"What about classes?"

I waved away the question. "Mondays are always a late start for me. But if I need to, I'll skip later."

"Who will watch the dead_papers feed? We still need to print the last one out."

"What's your schedule? Can you do that?"

"Don't worry about it. Of course I can."

"Okay, cool." I tossed back the rest of the coffee and slipped my jacket on. "I'm going to stake out that journalism building. One of us needs to be there to meet Gayle Jackson. If she's been following all this, maybe she knows the identity of the poster. Or at least has access to it."

"Fair enough, but Hazel, wait."

"What?" I was in a hurry. My gut told me Gayle Jackson was the lead I needed, especially with Sara's little police report looming over my head.

"Were you wearing your necklace at Sara's auditions?" Maeve seemed worried. "What if you lost it while you were with her?"

This question slowed me down. The day after I warned Sara, Ryan ended up dead. Then, she turned right around and told the police about me. She could have had my necklace if I'd been wearing it and it broke or something. Dead_papers had already mentioned leaving it behind in her posts. Could dead_papers be Sara?

"I don't know. Maybe?"

Maeve shrugged. "It's something to consider. Someone might really be trying to set you up. I don't think you should be alone."

"Well, join me then." My mouth was dry with the possibility of Sara being behind all this. I had firsthand experience of her being a bitch in high school, especially after the whole Penelope/Luke fiasco she'd dredged up the other day. But she wasn't violent. Then I thought of my dad, a mild-mannered algebra teacher—until he snapped one night at a bar. Everyone was capable of anything.

"Got it. I'll be there as soon as I get the next post." Maeve gathered her stuff into her little purse. She checked her ID as I zipped up my fleece and blew out a breath.

"Should I hug you?" Maeve asked. "I feel like I should."

"I hate hugs."

As I went to leave, Kim emerged from the bedroom dressed in a short skirt and long-sleeved collared sweater.

"Do you guys think this makes me look fat?" she asked.

"Nope," Maeve and I said in unison.

IT WAS STILL too early for a lot of Monday morning foot traffic. But I kept my head down, not wanting to make eye contact with anyone. The crisp morning air nipped at my cheeks and nose; the year's first sparkling frost tipped the grass blades. I held out hope the chill would keep me alert enough to spot Gayle Jackson and have a coherent conversation with her, but I was tired.

One of the oldest buildings in the communications sector of campus housed the *Campus Echo*. Next to it, the slanted lines of the university's center for the arts offset the *Echo*'s plain, brown brick structure. According to the website, the *Echo* was located on the building's top floor. I looked up at the windows in the upper rooms, most of them aglow. Some staffers were probably already up and at 'em, tracking leads and reporting the latest. Gayle certainly had been.

Inside, a warm draft of air poured over me. The hall splintered in two directions. Beyond the hall, a large study/lobby area loomed, which was typical of the classroom buildings. What was not typical was the display; an encased antique printing press centered the great room. A velvet rope surrounded the massive, industrial-looking structure. The press itself appeared to have stopped mid-action, with a pile of browning paper stacked at one end: blank and clean. Past the giant wheels and weathered belts, within the twists and turns of the machine, slips of paper could be seen in various stages of print. Some of the newspaper's earliest issues hung framed on the walls, next to portraits of standout editors and journalists who'd gone on to successful careers after college life.

A snack cart vendor was stationed opposite the exhibit. I paid for a muffin and sat on one of the cushy benches near the elevator. If I were going to have any luck spotting Gayle Jackson, it would be when she was going up or bustling out of that thing. The seating area reminded me of being at the mall, with steps leading down into a conversation pit. Leafy plastic vines flowed over large terra-cotta planters. Across the way, a few students studied at a line of carrels.

After a while, I caught sight of Gayle breezing through the museum portion of the building's main floor as if she'd seen it a million times. A pair of sunglasses covered most of her face, but a braided bun bulged over her right shoulder. Her heeled boots clacked over the tiles as she passed by. She jabbed her finger impatiently at the elevator button. In seconds, the doors opened, and she was whisked toward her job on the upper floors.

I had no plan beyond finding her. What exactly was I supposed to say to someone in this scenario? *"Hi! You're covering a murder I might be implicated in. But don't worry; it wasn't me!"* A horrifying introduction. Maybe she'd be upstairs long enough for Maeve to get here and help with the conversation flow. Or maybe I'd just continue to follow Gayle around campus until I figured something out, but that seemed creepier still.

The elevator doors sprang open once more, and Gayle emerged, wheeling a handcart of filing boxes, as if she'd been fired. For whatever reason, seeing the boxes gave me more courage than it probably should have.

"Ms. Jackson!" I called.

Gayle's sunglasses stayed on. She turned in my direction, and a wrinkle formed above her black plastic frames.

"Do I know you?" Gayle's honey-thick voice sounded the same as mine when I was upset. Her head tilted, and she tucked a tissue farther up her sleeve. Those sunglasses were hiding something, probably feelings.

"Not yet. They fired you?" I asked, eyeing the cart.

"I don't have time for this. I need to get out of this building." Her voice cracked over the last word.

"I saw you on TV this morning. Asking about the online diary."

"You don't look like press." As she said this, she inched her sunglasses down her nose, taking in my jeans and fleece combo.

"I'm not looking for... I—I have information for you."

"Are you dead_papers?"

"No."

"Do you know who is?"

"No."

"Then it doesn't matter to me." She started walking away.

"Wait!" I grabbed the sleeve of her trench coat.

"Don't do that." Gayle snatched her arm away from my grasp. "I can't help—"

"My necklace was found near the crime scene," I whispered.

Gayle took her sunglasses off; coppery eyeshadow perfectly smudged the lids of her brown eyes. Without a word, she indicated a bench on the other side of the room away from both the elevator and the display. I caught a whiff of her floral-heavy perfume as I followed her and the cart to the bench.

After she sat, Gayle asked, "Say that again?"

"Off the record?"

Her shoulders slumped a little, but she nodded assent.

"The night of the murder, my friend and I were sneaking around trying to figure out what was happening when we found a necklace covered in blood near the perimeter of the crime scene. It was mine."

"And I'm guessing you didn't put it there," Gayle offered.

"Right. I don't know how it got there."

"Is this *the* necklace mentioned by dead_papers?"

"It has to be, yes. And then today, I found out a friend who was dating the victim told the police I had it out for him."

"Did you?"

"Kind of," I admitted. "But not in a murdery way."

"Shh. Keep your voice down." Gayle scoped the room, and I followed her lead.

The food cart guy zipped money into a leather pouch. A couple holding hands strolled near the printing press. Whispers traveled around the room.

"There's a reason the newspaper's called *The Campus Echo*." Gayle rifled through her purse. "Why are you telling me all this?"

"I saw you on the news. You seemed to know more than anyone else there." I worried my hands, pinching the skin around each knuckle. "You mentioned the online diaries."

"Have the police contacted you yet?" Gayle clicked a pen and jotted down some numbers in a miniature spiral-bound notebook.

"No."

"They will. My advice is to call your parents and get a lawyer." She tore out the paper and handed it to me.

"My parents are unreachable—dead."

"Sorry to hear that. My cousin, David, is a lawyer." She tapped the flimsy offering in my hand. David's name was written under a phone number in hasty, slanted handwriting. "He might be able to help you, but not me. I'm officially off the job." She stood and left, wheeling her boxes of office belongings with her.

This wasn't how I'd expected things to go. I'd presumed an investigative reporter would have a natural curiosity for the truth. With each of Gayle's footsteps, my world sank into the echo of her clicking heels.

Nobody was going to save me. I'd learned the lesson a long time ago, back when the person who loved me the most was dredged out of the river. This was merely a chapter review of the same truth.

"Hold on!" I yelled this time, and the title of the newspaper rang true as my voice bounced around the journalism building's main hall. "Sorry," I mumbled. I kept my head down and quickstepped to catch up with Gayle.

"Look, I've got nothing for you," Gayle said, her patience clearly running thin.

"I need help."

Gayle rolled her eyes and sighed. "And I need a job." She licked her glossed lips in what I hoped was a moment of reconsideration.

"Just... Can we go have coffee or something? And talk about this?" I asked.

"You buying?"

"Sure." For a second, she looked as if she might leave again.

"Make it breakfast and you've got a deal."

"Let's do it."

I HELPED GAYLE unload her boxes at her car. She rolled the cart to the sidewalk, muttering about her ex-coworkers and how they could come down and get it themselves. Then we entered the blaring sounds of everyone else's Monday morning commute. At the crosswalk, cars rumbled to a stop. Some, with their windows cracked open, emitted snippets of early morning DJ banter. People packed the bus stop, and nearby, a man in a tattered T-shirt and jeans spit rhymes for spare change. It was Poetry Joe. But his beard was filled with more salt than pepper, and he was achingly thin. Most days, I didn't think about his omnipresence; he was always there, always would be. But this morning, I worried, especially with a killer on campus and the nights getting colder.

"What are you standing there for? Walk." Gayle motioned toward the sign and was already a quarter of the way through the crosswalk. I jogged a few steps to catch up. When we stepped onto the curb, Gayle continued south, and I followed. We passed the comic book store and a vintage toy shop. The city held on to nostalgia, making its vibe cool and artsy without being too pretentious.

At the corner, a small storefront displayed a sign that read The Donut Trap in red letters above a pink awning. A neon Open sign glowed in the front window. Bells jingled when we stepped inside. The place smelled sweet and greasy at the same time. Donuts of every shape and color filled the display cases—a rainbow of carbs and sprinkles.

"The usual, Bobby," Gayle ordered.

A guy behind the counter with brown skin and a peppering of facial hair above his upper lip prepped Gayle's order, which consisted of a chocolate éclair and a plain yeast donut. He placed a cup of steaming water on a red tray, and Gayle took it over to a side table with tea bags, coffee stirrers, cream cups, and napkins.

"A small coffee, please. And a chocolate donut with sprinkles." I reached for my wallet. "Actually, can I make that a milk instead?" I needed caffeine like I needed an enema. Bobby and I exchanged cash and change, and I carried my tray to Gayle's chosen table.

She sat in front of the store window, people-watching while she dunked a tea bag into a steaming cup over and over, seemingly lost in thought. Thinking of the boxes, it was obvious her job at the school paper had been pulled out from under her. I could've shrugged off my pre-teaching courses any day, but for Gayle, losing journalism was maybe a dream-crushing event.

"Hey," I started softly, not wanting to startle her. "You okay? Why'd they fire you?"

Her gaze stayed on the folks filing past the shop. Her shoulders slumped, and she rested her chin on her fist. "My editor's been stealing my work; a coworker noticed, and I got reassigned to *Lifestyles*. I wasn't even supposed to be at that press conference, but—" She sighed. "I don't know why I'm telling you this. It's fine. Nothing new, that's for sure." She turned her eyes on me and said, "Let's cut to it. How do you think I can help you? And why should I?"

"You asked about the dead_papers diaries at the press conference. Does the journalism department have access to the school's database?"

"Maybe? I'm no computer expert... What'd you say your name was?"

I told her, then shoved my hair away my face and unfolded the top of the milk carton.

"So what do you think I can do? And again, why would I?" Gayle dipped her tea bag one last time and removed it with a plastic spoon. The water had taken on a deep reddish-brown color.

"I don't know, exactly. I'm not a computer person either." An overwhelming feeling spread through my chest. I needed dead_papers's true identity before the police came to question me. But how to go about getting it? I pressed a scratchy napkin over my closed eyes, trying to think this through in seconds. Crusted flecks of black mascara came away with the paper. "I'm sorry. I'm just tired."

Gayle waited a beat, then asked, "Why didn't you go to the police when you found the necklace?"

"It's a long story."

"I don't have anywhere to be."

"Panicked, I guess." I shredded the napkin. "My friend was with me, and she thought we should leave."

Gayle's face was nonbelieving. "That's not a long story." She scratched her nose and leaned in. Her chin rested in her palm, and she blinked, waiting for the rest.

"Fine." I swigged the rest of my milk and set the carton aside before answering. "My parents aren't around because of a cop. Okay?" *Half-truths, all of it.*

"Okay, now"—Gayle's eyebrows lifted—"there's something with some meat to it. That's something I can understand."

"I don't trust 'em. They—"

"I hear you." Gayle gave a stern look I took to mean, *Stop talking.* So I did. She sipped her tea, then changed the subject. "You mentioned the school's database. What would that do?"

"I was only thinking out loud. But the diaries are supposed to be anonymous, right?"

"Mm-hmm." Gayle crumpled the tissue paper her donuts had been on.

"Except when you open an account, you have to use your name." I'd typed mine in last night. Excitement, like fizzy, bubbling pop, built inside me, tingling the tips of my fingers and making my heart speed up. I was on to something; I could feel it. "So, a list of real names connected to usernames exists somewhere. It's not really anonymous."

"Okay, okay. I see what you're saying." Gayle sat back in her chair, one eyebrow cocked. "Know any hackers?" She removed a lanyard from the pocket of her suede jacket. A plastic card—her press pass—dangled over the table. "Because I kept this."

"I do. I know someone." I bit my lip, trying not to smile too big. Because if I examined this moment any closer, I'd have to admit I was enjoying it.

"This can get you into the newsroom"—she slid the press pass across the table—"but it's only gonna get you so far. Plus, it's only bound to be good for so long. You'll have to move fast."

"I'll call my guy." *I'll call my guy! Who was even talking right now?* It sure as hell didn't sound like me.

"You know the police might have an easier time getting access to this, right?"

"I told you. I can't." Images long hidden and buried re-surfaced: a blurry, featureless mask of a face, an impressive navy-blue uniform, a gold shield, all supposed symbols of authority and trust. The bells above the donut shop door jangled and brought me out of the trance. I shook it off, pressed the phantom memories down, and continued where I'd left off. "If I can figure out the accounts are linked to real names, so can anyone, including whoever this dead_papers person is. If she wipes her account—deletes it before I can get her real name—all I'm left with are a handful of printouts and my bloody necklace."

"And apparently, motive."

"Right, that's all the cops will see."

"You're a pretty white girl. They'll see that too."

"You think they'll go easy on me?"

"I know that for a fact."

"They didn't go easy on my parents." My ears burned; my cheeks probably flushed with too many feelings. She didn't know the whole story, but I didn't know hers either.

Gayle shrugged. "Look, I'm not trying to upset you. I'm just saying, in your case, you probably have less to worry about than you think. The necklace is a coincidence, right? Looking at you and a good lawyer, cops could probably be made to see that."

Gayle applied a fresh layer of shimmery lip gloss, then continued, "If I were you, I'd be asking myself why that *friend* of yours was so keen to leave the crime scene too. You ever think of that?"

I hadn't, had I? Thoughts—accusations—ran circles in my head. *Maeve?*

"No." I shook my head. "She's helping me. The plan is to tie this case up in a neat bow, then hand it over. That way, nothing can get...misconstrued. Or mishandled."

I took out the slip of paper Gayle had given me earlier, with her lawyer cousin's phone number on it, and slid it across the table. "Can you put your number on here too?"

Gayle eyed me carefully. She licked her front teeth, either sizing me up or calculating how much involvement she'd be willing to risk. Finally, she took a pen out of her purse and clicked the top. She scribbled seven numbers on the paper. "I'll be at this number most of the day, but remember, once they deactivate this pass, the access is gone."

"Got it." I folded the paper and slipped it into my front pocket. "I'll be in touch. I'll need details—office layout, maybe some computer stuff."

"We'll talk later, then."

I collected our trash on my tray and tossed it in the bin. Right before opening the doors and setting off the jingle bells, I stopped. "Thanks. I know you don't have to help me."

"I'm a sucker for story, that's all." Gayle smiled, revealing a slight gap in her front teeth. She straightened her shoulders and sniffed. "Go on, Hazel. Clock's ticking."

"Right. See ya later." My heart fluttered and buzzed like a fly's wings. *Stick to the plan.* And I would, even though it was a new one.

Chapter Seventeen

Visitors

OCTOBER 23, 2000

Making my way back to campus, I realized I'd probably missed Maeve. We'd agreed to meet. Hopefully, she'd understand; a lead was a lead, and I had no choice but to follow through on this thing with Gayle. There were no other options. The journalism building was on my way back to the dorm, so I stopped to check for Maeve.

The lobby was more crowded, midmorning. Students lingered, lounging on the furniture or floor in groups of twos and threes. They held textbooks in their laps and talked over notepads. I wandered around them, looking for a body off by themselves—alone. There were a couple of those, too, with noses buried in novels and headphones signifying a desire not to be bothered.

Near the food cart, I nodded at the vender and asked, "Where are the phones?" Every building I'd been in had a row of pay phones and one campus phone somewhere on the premises.

"Back by the bathrooms. Toward the main doors, make a right." He looked tired. I wondered how many times a day he answered the same question or one similar, treated like the building's concierge.

"Thanks."

He opened a newspaper. An unflattering photograph of the police chief graced the front page. I expected one of Ryan's senior pictures would make tomorrow's, in all its soft-focus, all-American, in-no-way-a-predator glory.

In the hall leading to the bathrooms, the distant whirring of hand dryers grew louder and then softer as doors opened and closed. A few crumpled brown paper towels had been cast aside. No doubt some nasty-ass germs covered every surface of this hallway.

Two pay phones were attached to the wall, and farther down, a study carrel housed a standard-looking landline—free to use if calling someplace on campus. I picked up the beige receiver and dialed the number to check my messages. Sure enough, there were three, and they were all various versions of Maeve asking where the fuck I was. I deleted them and called our dorm phone. Nobody answered, but I pressed the number directed to Maeve's voice mail and left a message explaining I'd caught up with someone—I didn't want to put Gayle's name in a recorded message—and had had an *informational* breakfast. I hung up, hoping she'd check her messages soon, and left the journalism building.

Outdoors, the world went on as normal. Students bustled past me to get to class, or breakfast, or back to their dorms. Campus shuttles belched black smoke as they rolled away from their designated stops. Brown leaves whirled through a cold wind, dancing along the edges of the curb as winter geared up for a go-around.

I looked toward the Trap. Seemingly overnight, the trees had popped with their fall foliage: yellows, oranges, and red—all the warm shades of warning. Dead leaves littered the ground, and a stray piece of caution tape twirled and fluttered in the cold wind. In the center, the old oak stood tall and fierce, forever looking on. *God, what has it seen?*

I shoved my hands in my jacket pockets and walked the rest of the way home with my head down. And that was exactly how I didn't see Sara and her suitemate, Shirlee, until it was too late. When I finally looked up, Sara stood near the bicycle racks outside my dorm waving madly. I walked by without acknowledging either one of them.

"Hazel! Hazel, wait!" Sara shouted and ran after me, her friend lagging behind.

At the side entrance, I shoved my key into the lock. Sara had set the cops in my direction and might have left my necklace near the crime scene; I did not want to speak to her.

But Sara was quick. She grabbed hold of my fleece and said, "Please!"

There was no getting out of this.

"What do you want?" I practically barked.

Her mouth opened and closed. Her chest deflated with whatever nerve she'd gathered to get this far.

"Just go. You're the last person I want to talk to right now." I went inside, and the door slipped shut behind me.

"I wanna help!" Her voice, full and loud with dramatic training, made its way through the heavy metal door.

For whatever reason, probably sheer exhaustion, I homed in on the chipped paint of the push bar. I thought about my first day here when I'd fallen in this very stairwell, and only one person had stopped to make sure I was okay. Unlike out in the Trap, when I'd fallen harder, and everyone had avoided the crap out of me. *What could it hurt?* Sara was dramatic and flaky and self-absorbed, but she wasn't a murderer. I couldn't picture her physically hurting anyone, even if backed into an impossible situation. And I needed all the help I could get. Hearing whatever Sara had to say, especially when it came to what the police knew, wasn't going to kill me.

I opened the door to let her in. Anger flooded my heart when she came into view, framed by fall colors and campus life.

"Can Shirlee come too?"

I started up the stairs without saying anything; their stomping behind me told me they both followed. Our footsteps were the only sound until a group of girls on the floor above us entered, and their casual conversation took over the space, debating the talent of Britney versus Christina. How nice to be having that chat instead of this one...

I led them through the hall and to my room. Everything since Friday night had been a whirlwind, one adrenaline rush after another. I plopped onto the loveseat and didn't offer Sara a drink because, fuck her, she'd brought me further into this mess. She leaned against the minifridge with her hands clasped in front of her. Her friend stayed by the door, on lookout.

"This is cozy." Sara looked around our space, filled with the junk of four girls.

"Save it." I rubbed my eyes with the heel of my palms. The pressure created a pleasant sensation behind my eyes, a lingering sensation—something I could still feel when I looked back at Sara. "Why are you here?"

"I'm sorry for calling you out the other day. I know you were just trying to be helpful." She bit her lower lip.

"He was a dick," I said.

Shirlee's eyes flickered up and met mine. There was something there, something about her I couldn't put my finger on. I prided myself on studying people, catching glimpses of their characters, what they chose not to hide. But Shirlee's gaze wobbled between strength and weakness, like a candle flame flickering in the wind—unsteady one second, then bright and fierce the next.

I broke eye contact and asked Sara, "Have you seen the diaries?"

"Shirlee showed me after I got home last night."

At the mention of her name, Shirlee straightened her posture. I didn't meet her gaze again though. Her unsteadiness was off-putting and distracting.

"So you'd already told the police I had it out for him, then came home and saw someone had confessed."

"Yes. I mean, dead_papers isn't you, right?" She looked away, seeming nervous.

"Ohmygod, no!" I yelled indignantly. "I never saw him again."

"Look, I wanna help," she offered.

"Do you? I think you've done enough."

She teared up. *Great.*

"Have the police contacted you?" Shirlee finally spoke up. Her voice was firmer than her gaze and different from when I'd spoken to her last. Back then, she'd whispered, *I believe you.* Maybe she was guiding Sara through this. Maybe Ryan had tried something with her too.

"Not that I'm aware of. But I've been gone all morning."

"They'll probably want to interview you. It'll be similar to what Sara went through."

And until Shirlee mentioned it, I hadn't thought about what Sara had been through. *Gruesome* and *meticulous.* It was her boyfriend's dead body in the Trap. Someone was accusing him of horrible acts on the web, and the entire school was reading about it.

"How are you? Really," I asked, lightening my tone. I got up and grabbed some drinks out of the fridge. But when I offered, they both declined. "Whatever." I put the extras back and popped the tab on mine. It hissed as I cracked it open and tasted like a sugar rush.

"I'm okay, I guess," Sara said.

"It's pretty intense," I said.

Shirlee rolled her lips together as if she had something to say but couldn't decide if she should. Sara looked out the window.

"You were right about him," she whispered. When she looked back at me, tears pooled on the edge of her eyelids again. She was going to lose it for sure. "He didn't have to die though. Especially in that way." Sara crumpled. She brought her hands to her face and yelped like a wounded animal. Then she ran to the bathroom and threw up.

I sat there, cringing with each heave and then the awful stream of splashing. *Jesus Christ.* I refused to walk in there and hold her hair; I'd just end up tossing my donut. Shirlee could help, but she didn't move either.

"He *did* deserve it," Shirlee whispered. "Especially in that way." Her eyes met mine again. This time, there was nothing there but a barely contained, seething rage. Her fury reminded me of how my mother looked some days after she was attacked. When she was "all cried out" and wrath blanketed her whole essence.

"You believe the dead_papers account of what happened, then?"

Her eyes narrowed. "You don't?"

"I didn't say that."

"Can I borrow a towel or something?" Sara yelled. The flushing toilet swooshed in the background.

"There're clean washcloths on the plastic shelf in there," I said, still staring at Shirlee. I didn't know what to make of her. It wasn't like I disagreed. I knew the evil men were capable of inflicting. Mom had been ruined. So was dead_papers, by her own dad.

The faucet squeaked, and then came the sound of rushing water. When Sara emerged, pale and weak, she glistened with sweat.

"I'm sorry."

"No worries." I made a mental note to spray the bathroom with Lysol after she left. "They used the word gruesome on the news, so I can only imagine."

"He was ripped to shreds."

"What?" I leaned forward. "How do you know this?"

"Pictures. They showed me pictures of his body." She blinked rapidly and looked around the room as if she'd forgotten where she was. "It was...a lot." She breathed deeply, swallowing carefully. "His stomach..." She gagged, then shook her head.

"They'll show them to you too." Shirlee moved to Sara's side and rubbed her arm. "I think they wanna see your reaction."

"Tell me what else to expect." If I went in there knowing the routine, it might help.

"It wasn't like on TV. There was no good cop, bad cop. They were both just...direct. To the point."

"That's good."

"What happened between you two in the Trap just slipped out. I don't even know why I started talking about it."

The cops were experienced then. In Mom's case the police *somehow* got a neighbor to mention Mom struggling with addiction in an interview, which made its way to the papers. It had been pure gossip, a product of the sad, small-town rumor mill. But afterward, the cops stopped believing my mom and slipped in questions regarding how many pills she might've taken the day she "claimed to have been assaulted." It had been bad to begin with, but everything got so much worse once they started doubting her.

I pulled out a notebook and jotted down some notes. "Tell me everything."

AFTER SARA LEFT, I called Doug. During the few minutes it took for his roommate to jerk around with the phone, I nearly fell asleep.

"Hey! I wasn't sure if I'd hear from you," Doug said.

What was that supposed to mean?

"Uh, okay. Listen, I need..." This was way too big of a favor for a phone conversation. "...to ask you about something. Can we meet up?"

"Sure. My last class of the day is over on your side of campus. I'll stop by when it's over. Should be around five-ish?"

"Perfect, thanks."

"See you then." We both hung up. I had all day to figure out how to talk him into helping me.

The fan in my computer whirred, and I thought of Aunt Liddy. I hadn't even told her thanks for the computer yet. *One email, then sleep.* I wiggled the mouse, and the screen lit up. Clicking on the envelope icon brought up my inbox. An email from LeafLady7@aol.com appeared. I clicked on it.

Hazel,

I've seen the news. Let me know you're okay, okay?

Promise,

Aunt L

Of course news of Ryan's murder would have made its way throughout the state. A white dude slaughtered on campus would upset other white folks, and the media attention fanned what Ohio liked most about itself, that salt-of-the-earth vibe, the belief that such tragedy never occurred here.

I clicked Reply and stared at the subject line. How could I fill this in? "Send Help" seemed appropriate, but Aunt Liddy would have a heart attack if she knew how I'd been spending my time.

So I lied—by omission. My fingers tapped along the keyboard without putting too much thought into where they were going.

Hi! I came home the other night to find this rad new computer at the front desk. Thank you! Things are going fine here...busy. Saturday night was scary, but things have calmed down. Don't worry. I promise to call soon. -Hazel

I hit Send, and my note magically traveled to its location. Through wires and space and thin air, it would get to my aunt.

In the bedroom, I closed the curtains but opened the window. The cool air brought the smell of fallen leaves into our crowded space. I kicked off my shoes and didn't even bother changing clothes. I taco-ed myself into my comforter and closed my eyes.

Chapter Eighteen

Someone's Here for You

OCTOBER 23, 2000

I was shaking. *No.* Someone was shaking me.

"Hey, hey. It's time to wake up," Maeve's voice whispered softly. "Somebody's here for you."

I rolled onto my back. My shoulder and hip were stiff and sore; I'd slept hard. "What time is it?"

"Evening. You slept the whole day."

"Shit."

"The guy from the other night is downstairs. He says you made plans with him earlier today."

"Doug. Yeah, I did." I sat up, careful not to hit my head on the bed railing above me. "Sorry I missed you at the journalism building." I stretched as best I could, pointing my elbows above my head and elongating my spine. Maeve moved to the bunk opposite and sat.

"That's okay. Did you find out anything?"

"Yes. You should come with me and Doug. I can fill you both in at the same time. Did she post again?"

"Not since this morning. She's still on the site, last I checked."

"Okay, let's go then." I hopped out of bed and changed into a fresh pair of jeans and a clean T-shirt. Then I transferred my necklace from one pocket to the next, always keeping it with me.

"Where to?" Maeve asked.

"The cafeteria. I'm starving."

Maeve zipped up her hoodie while I brushed my hair into a quick ponytail. In the living quarters, Kim sat on the couch, braiding Trish's hair into an elaborate crown twisting around her head.

"Where are you guys off to?" Kim asked through a set of bobby pins held between her teeth.

"Get some food," I said.

"Bring me back some fries?" Trish asked, wincing as Kim tightened a strand.

Maeve and I nodded and left.

We picked up Doug in the lobby. He was slouched on one of the couches. His hands were tucked behind his head, and at first, I thought he'd fallen asleep. But then he looked up, and a moment of confusion crossed his brow as he took in not only me but Maeve as well.

"Hey! Maeve, right?" He stood and held out his hand. Maeve shook it. Then he looked to me. "What's up?"

I took in a deep breath; this was a lot to go over. "I need to talk to both of you about something."

Doug scratched his head. The crease between his thick eyebrows darkened.

"Is it okay if we go to the cafeteria for some food? I haven't eaten since breakfast, and this is a lot to ask."

Doug looked from my face to Maeve's, confusion blooming all over his features.

"Don't worry; it's not a sex thing," Maeve said.

"Uh—I—uh—didn't—" he stammered.

"Unless you're into that kind of thing." A mischievous glint appeared in Maeve's eyes, the same one I'd noticed when she made Sara cry. They danced with the drama, took delight in how uncomfortable she'd made Doug. And it *was* funny. I bit the inside of my cheek to stop myself from laughing.

Doug let out a nervous little *heh-heh* of a laugh and played with the straps of his backpack.

"Chill, dude. I'm joking."

"Can we go?" I swept my arm toward the front door.

"Okay," Doug finally managed.

"Lead the way," Maeve said.

With my eyes, I communicated a warning to Maeve. *Cool it.* She was goofing with Doug, but he didn't know how she played. And I needed his help; I couldn't have him running off into the night again because of a bruised ego or whatever.

A whoosh of cold blew over me as I pushed open the door. The temperature had dropped throughout the day. Autumn would be chased away by winter's icy fingers sooner than later. Gray clouds swirled overhead. My jacket didn't stand much of a chance against this weather. I huddled into myself, bracing my arms across my chest as we filed into the cafeteria.

The smell of french fries and fried fish saturated the dining hall. I grabbed a tray and plate at the start of the sneeze-guarded buffet line. The others joined me. In the kitchen area, sprays of water, clanging pans, and the occasional bit of Spanish could be heard. At the end of the line, a student worker scanned our IDs, and I led us to a corner table by the windows. This was the best spot for watching people without actually having to be among them. I'd learned more from this vantage than I ever did at an economics lecture.

I noticed people's patterns sitting here. A pack of hyper-masculine white guys always passed by during lunch; the one with a cleft chin had started casting longing looks at the oblivious blond one a week ago. At breakfast, a girl with an amazing red trench coat walked by with her nose in a new book every other day. A guy with black hair and brown skin sat at a nearby table, and he always left with an extra roll he'd tear up and scatter for the pigeons. Over the past few weeks, I'd grown to prefer this people-watching time to classes and my soap opera. These were real people with real-life dramas of their own. Sometimes I was sure I could see the whole story behind their behaviors.

I ate half my sandwich before addressing Maeve and Doug. I wasn't sure I wanted Doug to know every detail, but I couldn't expect him to help if he didn't understand what was at stake.

"So, you know about the—" I looked around. "—murder."

"Everyone does." Doug dipped a fry into the pile of ketchup on his plate and popped it into his mouth.

"There's a chance I might be brought in for questioning."

"That's ridiculous. You were with me."

"Right!" I slapped the table. Amid all the drama, I'd nearly forgotten I hadn't done anything wrong, and there *were* people who could verify that. "Here's the thing—I can't talk to the police."

"Why?" Maeve and Doug asked simultaneously.

For a second, I was back on my couch watching Channel 5 broadcast a sketch of the uniformed man who'd destroyed my family. "It involves my parents, okay? They're...gone. And I don't talk about it."

Nobody ever questioned what I was implying; they inferred it must be a dead parent thing. Doug and Maeve exchanged a quick pitying look, and then they both tried to cover it up.

"We'll call them and explain." Doug pulled a cellular phone out of his baggy pockets.

"Could you be any more male right now?" Maeve snatched the phone away from him. "She just said that's not an option for her."

"What's my gender got to do with it?" Doug looked back and forth between us.

"Are you sure you want to involve him?" Maeve asked me.

"Yes. We've all seen the dead_papers feed—"

"I organized them while you were sleeping." Maeve took a binder out of her backpack and plopped it on the table. "Anything having to do with the actual murder is behind the pink divider."

Doug and I leaned in.

I asked, "How did you group the rest?"

"Harassment, assault, random, and stuff about her dad."

"All you need is, like, a title sheet," said Doug.

"I'm waiting for the author's real name." Maeve smirked.

"That's where Doug comes in." I took out Gayle's press pass. It swung between us.

"Is that what I think it is?" Maeve asked.

"Yep, she gave it to me this morning."

Doug examined the plastic card with Gayle's picture on it. "I don't get it."

"This can get us to a campus database, right?" I asked.

"I don't know," Doug said, pocketing the press pass.

"What do you mean, you don't know?"

Doug's gaze homed in on something behind me, right over my shoulder. Peripherally, I heard their footsteps, out of tune with the squeaks of sneakers and rubbery boot soles. Theirs were the clomping of dress shoes. But still—the alto voice, the bomber jacket over pantsuit combo, the leather portfolio, the neatly combed hair—it came as a surprise.

"Do any of you know a Hazel Fischer?" The woman showed her badge. She kept it on a chain around her neck. The badge glinted gold, highlighted by a ray of sunset beaming through the window, traveling across the solar system merely to make the emblem glisten.

I couldn't speak. I couldn't function. I wasn't even there. My consciousness broke free and watched from above as Doug tried to explain. The detective held her hand up to silence him.

"We just need to ask a few questions." Her voice registered low and slow.

Time sped up when Maeve suggested the binder. "Take a look at these, ma'am."

"Hazel Fischer?" She ignored Maeve's offering. "Will you come with me, please?"

I followed but was only half present.

"Where are you taking her?" Maeve asked. "She hasn't done anything!"

The detective ignored my friends' protests and ushered me out of the building.

A man—her partner, for sure—sat on a nearby bench polishing off the remains of a candy bar. He set the silver wrapper down and pressed a stray strand of his overly gelled hair behind his ear. The little piece of trash took flight in the cold breeze, and he didn't try to stop it.

"This her?" He licked and sucked the chocolate remains out of his teeth, making awful smacking sounds. A stubborn spot among his molars required him to poke and scratch at his mouth until he spit some particle of cud at our feet. He was older—older than the detective who'd brought me out here, older than my parents would have been. That put him around Aunt Liddy's age in my mind, close to retirement and probably a know-it-all.

"According to her friends, yes."

"Did you check her ID, Patterson?" He seemed to be searching for something in the long pockets of his trench coat. "Ah, here it is." He brought out a miniature notepad and pencil stub.

"No, sir."

"Jesus, rookie." The detective asked for my identification as he stood.

An ID was in my back pocket, but so was the damned necklace. I'd kept it with me, feeling more comfortable with it nearby. Throughout the day, I would check on it, touch it, make sure no one else had it. I fumbled around, pulling my jacket pockets inside out.

"Where's it at if you don't have it on you?"

I pointed to Robin Hall behind them.

"We just came from there. Your roommates told us you were here."

I shrugged.

"Not one for talking, are ya?" he asked.

I stared at the tops of his ears. I looked at ears when I couldn't look at eyes. It was a trick Aunt Liddy showed me when this teacher had gotten all pissy about my refusal to make eye contact. I hadn't been trying to be rude. The teacher never understood. Her eye color matched my dad's, a near glacial-blue hemmed by a ring of navy, like a set of twin planets.

The pair of detectives clomped toward my building, and I followed. *I didn't* actually *lie*, I thought. My driver's license was in my closet, tucked into a wallet and kept in a purse I almost never carried. It was my student ID that rubbed between the necklace and my pocket. I could very nearly hear the metal charm scratch against the plastic with each step. I'd lied. They knew I'd lied. Or they would know when my pants actually caught on fire.

When we arrived at the room, Trish and Kim hurried out, exchanging curious looks and nervous giggles. I went to my closet to grab my license. The detectives were busy scrutinizing our décor, the way investigators scrutinize everything. I handed my license to the one called Patterson.

"Your birthday is..." She brought the card closer to her eyes. "In the summer. You're eighteen." She made note of something in her folio and handed my ID back to me. When no one spoke, Patterson broke the silence.

"So, Hazel, we're here today because a—" She checked her notes. "—Sara Gilchrist said you may have quarreled with the victim, Ryan Newsome, prior to his murder."

My nose twitched at the word *victim* being used to describe Ryan. But she hadn't asked a question, so I didn't provide an answer.

"Is that true?" Detective Patterson asked.

"Kind of." Somehow the quiet words scraped themselves out of my mouth. Maybe the brown coffee stain on her collar gave me enough confidence to speak. Either way, the words landed on the rug, twitching and gasping for air.

"Kind of?" She clicked the top of her pen and motioned for me to keep talking.

"We had an encounter."

The male detective—I hadn't caught his name yet—eyed my computer. He nudged the mouse, and the screen lit up. The diaries were still pulled up. He sniffed and acted as if the fact hadn't captured his attention.

"Could you describe this encounter, please?" Patterson asked.

"My friend and I were walking home the other night, and he—Ryan—approached us. He was really drunk." I bit my lower lip. The next part was embarrassing, and I didn't want to tell it again.

"Go on."

I closed my eyes for a beat and told the rest as quickly as possible. The male detective's gaze was on me now, not the computer. I could feel his eyes judging me, dissecting my story. Did he think I was making the whole thing up? Trying to make "the victim" look bad?

"And you told all of this to Ms. Gilchrist. Why?"

"I was trying to warn her."

"'Bout what exactly?" Patterson's partner spoke up now.

"How he'd hit me. And what he said to us." A prickling of indignation raised the hair on the back of my neck.

"Sounds like a little innocent fun to me. Boys blowing off some steam." Patterson's partner pulled a Tootsie Roll pop out of his pocket. He unwrapped it and stuck it in his mouth. "Know what I mean?"

Of course I knew what he meant. It was the excuse of the ages. Fuck his ears; I stared right into his eyes. They were dark, almost black—not like planets at all. "Boys will be boys, you mean. Yeah, I've heard of it."

"And where were you last night?" Detective Patterson turned the conversation.

"On a date."

"And what time did you get home?"

I swallowed. The date ended, and then I'd gone off with Maeve. "Uh, maybe nine?"

"You don't know when you got home?"

"Not exactly." I skirted around the truth, debating whether more details would pique their curiosity or squelch it. I gambled on silence.

A few quiet moments passed while Patterson scribbled in her notepad. "Okay, I think that's everything we need for now." Patterson clicked the pen and shut her folio. "Right, Detective Shaver?"

"Sure thing." He rubbed his palms along the breast of his jacket as if he were looking for something or wiping something gross off his hands. "I think so." He shook my hand and thanked me for my help and turned to leave. Or almost leave.

He turned back and asked, "That your computer?"

"Yes," I answered.

"You on the online diaries?"

"Yes, but I just joined the other day. I didn't know about them until Saturday."

Detective Shaver cocked his head and nodded, seemingly considering what to ask next. He'd tipped his hand, letting me know they were taking the diaries seriously. They must have been looking into them after Gayle's suggestion at the press conference. After a beat of awkward silence, he stepped into the hallway, whistling some random tune, with one hand in the pocket of his trench coat and the other holding his lollipop.

Patterson lingered. She handed me her business card. "If you think of anything else, call me." When she walked away, the leathery smell of her bomber jacket went with her.

The card's corners were crisp against my fingertips. Detective Lana Patterson's name was raised in smooth black ink. I'd call only when I could hand her the case on a damn platter and not a moment sooner.

Maeve and Doug entered the room soon after the police left. Doug handed me my drink, and Maeve carried the rest of my dinner in a to-go box.

"Thanks, you two." I was having trouble catching my breath, so I sat on the still-warm love seat.

"Do you want this now?" Maeve asked.

"Not really." I couldn't breathe, let alone eat.

Maeve opened the box and started munching on the leftover fries. Doug sat at my desk. They were watching me and waiting to hear what the police had said.

"It's fine." I cleared my throat. "They wanted to know what happened the other night in the Trap."

Maeve knew what I meant, but Doug looked confused.

"But you were with me..."

"No. Different night." Maeve offered up the explanation. "A while ago, we met the guy in the Trap—the one who was murdered. And it didn't go smoothly."

"Can someone please tell me what's going on?" Doug asked.

Maeve and I exchanged a look.

"We need his help," I said. "But can you tell him?" I didn't have the energy to go through it all again.

So Maeve did, and Doug listened without interrupting— not even to ask what we were wearing the night Ryan smacked me. I took over and explained the connections: Sara's boyfriend, how I'd warned her, and that being how the police had connected me to Ryan.

"Also, we found this near the crime scene." I pulled the necklace out of my pocket and unfolded the paper surrounding it. Most of the dried blood had cleaned off, but I was sure some still lingered in the nooks and crannies of the piece. I placed the whole thing, paper and all, on the rug as if it were some macabre offering.

"Is that...?" Doug kneeled next to it on the carpet.

"It's my necklace."

"Are you sure it's yours?" He leaned in, taking a closer look.

"Hers is missing," Maeve answered.

"And it wasn't just some charm necklace from Claire's. It's vintage; my mother bought it at an estate sale when she was my age."

Doug grabbed a pen and poked the leather cording and charm. "You wore this the day we met."

"I did?"

"Yeah, the afternoon in the theater. I complimented you on it."

"I don't remember ever taking it off or putting it away." Time had stretched itself out. It seemed impossible any of this had happened only two days ago. I scratched my head, underneath and around my ponytail, replaying the moment I'd met Doug.

"Is it broken?" Maeve grabbed a pencil and spread the necklace out, separating the clasping mechanism from the tangled heap.

I kneeled between them both—not afraid to touch because I already had—and examined the necklace. The cording—picked out at a Renaissance faire vendor a few years ago—was neither antique nor valuable. Sure enough, part of the clasp was stretched; it was no longer a complete circle, but an elongated *C*.

"It is broken," I said. "It could have just fallen off when I walked home that night."

"But..." The gleam in Maeve's eyes was gone, replaced with a thoughtful look of concern tinged with confusion.

"But what?" I asked. "None of this matters." My tone was deflated...*disappointed*. But how could I feel that way? The police didn't know about the necklace, and I'd told them I was with Doug. Those were good things. So why did I feel as though I'd lost something?

"You had the necklace when you met him." Maeve indicated Doug. "And then you went to Sara's dorm, right? To warn her?"

"Yes."

"Ryan ends up dead, and your necklace is at the crime scene." She laid out the facts in simple language—one step leading to the next. "Dead_papers mentioned it in her post. None of this seems like a coincidence to me."

"Then Sara tells the police of our...incident, or whatever you wanna call it, with Ryan," I continued. "Do you think she's *trying* to get me in trouble? Like, she's the one who killed him?"

"Maybe? It tracks." Maeve wrung her hands. "We considered it earlier, remember? It seems more probable now." Her eyebrows furrowed as she strung the bits of information together.

"But the stuff dead_papers said about her dad— I've met Sara's family." The image of her mild-mannered dad arose in my head. From the audience, his often-crooked wire-rimmed lenses glowed in the stage lights. "They don't—
"

"Maybe she's still covering for him. Lying about some of the details she puts in the diary. Who knows?"

"It's still my word against—" I folded up the necklace and put it away.

"And my word," Doug offered. "I don't mind talking to the police."

I didn't know how to explain it to him. How to tell him in my mind, in my experience, the police would simply write him off. He'd be a friend trying to help another friend. Luckily, I didn't have to.

He blew out a long breath. "But you need something else..."

"I do. You'll help us figure out who dead_papers is?" I asked.

"Hazel, I know for a fact you were with me, and that makes you innocent, even if someone's trying to set you up. So, yeah, I'll help."

I couldn't have stopped myself; I threw my arms around him and hugged him. He nearly toppled over, and we both laughed as he regained his balance.

"I don't think we'll need him," Maeve said. Her voice sounded strange, as if it were detached or disembodied. It floated above us like a ghost.

"He's some kind of computer whiz," I said, and Doug blushed. I turned back toward Maeve. "Of course, we—"

The color had drained out of Maeve's face. Her gaze hadn't left the screen.

"What is it?" I asked.

Her shoulders slumped, and she leaned back in my chair. Her hands fell away from the keyboard and drooped into her lap. She finally looked at me and said what I'd been racing against.

"Dead_papers is gone."

"What?" I let go of Doug and positioned myself behind Maeve as she retyped dead_papers's account name into the search bar.

"It's not coming up." She gestured at the screen. "Look."

The hourglass turned over and over again until, finally, a message stated no account by that name could be found.

"Damn." I clenched my fists. If Doug and Maeve hadn't been there, I might have thrown the monitor across the room. "It's too late."

"Not necessarily." Doug stood up and gathered his backpack off the floor. "Even if the user deleted it, there's still a record in the flat-file database. I'd just have to locate the reporting software. Maybe access the drives VTOC or run a restore. It's time-consuming. I'd have to guess at an admin password, but people aren't smart about those."

"I have no idea what any of that means," I said.

"Seriously?" he asked.

"Seriously."

"Well...basically, I'm saying I might be able to make this work."

"Okay. Okay, then. Let's go."

Without another word, we gathered our belongings. I wasn't sure why—or if—Sara was *trying* to point the police in my direction, but if we had tangible proof she'd written the dead_papers posts... Well, that would be more than our word against hers.

As Maeve locked our door she said, "Once this is over, I'm gonna have you teach me how to do all this. Got it, Doug?" She elbowed his midsection, and he agreed. His cheeks flushed with—my best guess—pride. Hell, I might take him up on lessons too. Computer shit seemed powerful.

I called Gayle when we reached the dorm lobby. She agreed to meet us at the journalism building and talk us through the newsroom layout and what to expect in terms of security.

It was dark out already, fall bringing such earlier nights. But out of the corner of my eye, I noticed someone reading a newspaper under a lamppost, which seemed odd and out of sorts for the time of day. They wore knee socks and a short skirt on the freezing metal bench slats. I couldn't make out facial features, except for a pair of gleaming wire-rimmed glasses. Something seemed familiar. Maybe they were in one of my classes? Or lived on another floor? I wasn't sure, but I didn't have time to ponder it through.

We continued toward the journalism building. Every now and then, I had to jog a few steps to keep pace with Maeve's long stride. She hadn't said anything since we left the dorm; none of us had. I was sure their thoughts were swirling around in their heads, like mine.

This whole thing was preposterous. I couldn't believe what Maeve and Doug were doing for me. I thought I understood why Doug wanted to help. He'd been with me the night of the murder and knew, without question, I was innocent. But what about Maeve? What *had* kept her from going to the cops when I found my necklace? Was it solely to protect me?

A stoplight's glare painted Maeve's strong profile red. I remembered back to the night on the banks of the river, right before the encounter with Ryan, back before any of this had happened, and we'd started becoming friends. She'd been funny and exciting and mysterious to me—still was all those things.

I trust her. I trust her. I repeated the mantra. *I want her.* Oh.

As we approached the journalism building, Gayle waited at the top of the steps. She blew out the smoke of a cigarette and then smooshed it with the same stylish boots she'd worn this morning. She signaled for us to stay on the sidewalk and descended the stairs. At the landing, Gayle led us around the side of the building. Her heels sank into the dirt ground, adding a hitch to her stride. She brought us to the building's side entrance, explaining the newspaper office layout as she went.

"The last classes should be finishing up"—Gayle checked her watch—"in about twenty minutes. The bad news is, with a murderer on the loose, posting blogs and what not, someone will surely be up there most of the night, working a story for tomorrow's paper."

"How can we get around them?"

"That's on you." Gayle huffed.

"Tell me about the chief editor," Doug spoke up.

"He's lazy as hell. In fact, he's probably already gone for the day."

Doug asked a few more questions regarding where his office was located and some admin computer program stuff.

"If his office is locked, y'all are out of luck. It's the only separate office up there, next to a conference room along the west-facing wall with all the windows. He's got two computers in there, and I'd guess one of them will have access to whatever it is you need."

"The reporting software," Doug said.

"Whatever." Gayle held up her forefinger. "One thing." She looked pointedly in my direction. "I want this story."

"What story?" I asked.

"This one. The inside scoop. I want to write it up."

"For the *Echo*?" It was the least I could do. "Fine." I shrugged.

"Wait," Maeve interrupted. "What do you plan on doing with it?"

"Scooping these guys, of course. I brought them dead_papers, but they didn't want to hear it. I knew it was important. That's why I showed up at that press conference. And they fired me for overstepping."

"We'll work out details later. I'm fine handing the story over to you, Gayle."

"After you take it to the police, though, right?" Doug asked.

God. So many opinions. "Yeah, sure. Of course." I didn't know what I'd actually do, but it hardly mattered now. We weren't even sure this was something we'd be able to pull off. I'd make promises now and decisions later. "Let's get this over with."

Gayle opened the side entrance door, and Doug and Maeve went inside. She caught me by the sleeve as I walked by. "You trust these two?"

I licked my lips, watching them walk on ahead of me. Their sneakers squeaked the whole way. "Yes."

"Well, good luck. Call me later."

"You wanna come with?" I asked.

"Nope." She shook her head. "I've got my future in mind."

"Me too."

"Go on, then."

I stepped inside and slowed the door until it closed with a quiet click. Maeve and Doug waited for me at the end of the hall, near the dim lobby. Maeve pointed to where the food cart was rolled up against the wall beyond the antique press. Nonchalantly, the three of us walked toward it. The cart's metal surfaces had been shined clean, and the cash register was locked under an acrylic case. Behind the cart was a wide set of open double doors, the lecture hall dark and empty beyond them. We stepped inside and waited.

"Is hiding necessary?" I whispered. Gayle had just told us the newspaper's work room was open all night.

"We don't want anyone to recognize us later, right?" Maeve said, and I didn't question her. If she wanted this to be more dramatic than necessary, well...that was what I liked about being with her anyway.

After a few minutes, Doug squirmed in the seat next to mine.

I leaned over and asked, "What are you doing?"

"Checking the time." The area lit up with the electric-gray light from his phone. "Class should be over in five," he whispered back.

As we sat there, my heart beat faster. A sense of urgency and pressure built in my stomach. My knee involuntarily bounced. I felt as if I could run a marathon or toss an over-turned car. If my future wasn't at stake, I might've called it exhilarating.

A distant eruption of chatter and footsteps grew increasingly louder, as a group made their way toward the lobby. We listened to the everyday, normal conversations of the students as they passed by. They talked of homework and weekend party plans—how boring. Maeve and I hadn't had a single conversation that wasn't murder-related since Friday.

Finally, a set of dress shoes clicked along the tiles. A couple of quick goodbyes were exchanged amid the backdrop of jangling keys. Then the only thing we heard was the ebbing, melodic whistle of someone walking through the lobby.

I was ready to give Maeve the "all clear" signal. She grabbed my arm and mouthed for me to wait. The room pulsed with silence. Something clattered to the floor in the distance; I assumed a janitor had dropped something, but a softball-sized lump of nerves formed in my throat anyway. I pushed it down and peeked beyond the auditorium door, then motioned for Maeve and Doug to join me. Together, we bypassed the lounge area by the antique press and followed signs leading to *The Campus Echo*.

A dim hallway opened next to the elevator. In it, we found the stairwell door and stepped inside. I covered my nose and mouth as we were met with the stink of old, wet shoes.

"Ugh, it reeks in here." Doug's voice echoed all around us.

Maeve held her finger over her mouth, and Doug mouthed an apology. Gayle had said the newsroom was on the top floor, so we had a climb ahead of us. I took my hand away from my nose, thinking I might as well get used to the smell since we'd be huffing and puffing our way through it.

Chapter Nineteen

The Hack

OCTOBER 23, 2000

When we reached the top floor, I bent over and rested my hands on my knees, gulping in deep, steadying breaths. Maeve and Doug were right behind me, plodding up the last few steps to the stairwell's end.

"Why didn't we take the elevator?" Maeve said breathlessly.

"Less chance—" I sucked in air. "—of anyone seeing us."

"Right," she said.

"Let's wait till we catch our breath," Doug suggested. "Before going on."

I agreed. Maeve locked her palms behind her head and paced around the landing, stretching her lean frame and forcing herself to take in slow, measured amounts of air.

Doug rotated his neck until I heard a cracking pop. "I should tell you guys—if the police or a superuser seized the dead_papers account, there might not be a way for me to get at it."

"You're telling us now?" I asked.

"So this could be a dead end," Maeve lamented.

"I just wanna make you aware."

"Okay, great." This wasn't going to work. With every step forward, dead_papers, or Sara, or whoever, outmaneuvered me. Unable to piece together a defense, I pictured myself in jail—like Dad. The similarities between my past and present were few, but every once in a while, they smacked together.

Enough. Even if this experiment failed, I had to go through with this. I had to at least try to *not* end up like my parents. I pushed away old memories, reached for the door handle, yet stopped short of opening it. Through the little square of glass, I could see a man in a gray uniform in front of the elevators. Next to him, a cart teemed with cleaning supplies. Maeve bumped into me.

"Sorry, I—"

"Shh." I pointed at the custodian. Together, we watched as he fiddled with a boom box. He adjusted the dial and tilted the antennae until classical piano music lilted through the space. More waiting.

All three of us took turns peeking at him through the small window as he emptied trashcans and mopped the landing.

"How much longer do you think?" Maeve asked.

"I have no idea," I said. "Hopefully, he'll be done soon."

"Do we have to wait?" Maeve asked.

"I mean, I guess not. Gayle said the newsroom was open all the time, so the guy's probably used to people coming and going."

"Uh, we're waiting." Doug lowered himself to the floor and crossed his legs. "I'm hacking into the university database, and I really don't want anyone to recognize me after the fact." He rested his head on the cinder block wall and closed his eyes. His heel bounced up and down.

"Fair enough." I hadn't even considered what would happen if we got caught. Why was I doing this to them?

Maeve chewed her bottom lip. She barely blinked as she watched the custodian work. "Something's happening." She motioned for me to look.

The custodian crouched in front of his cart, rifling through the supplies on the bottom shelf.

"He's already searched the other side. I think he's missing something," she whispered. And sure enough, the custodian stood, took off his hat, and swiped his hand through a mass of gray hair before pushing the elevator button.

"Doug, this is it," I hissed.

Doug's eyes blinked open, and in seconds, he was right next to me, straightening his too-long T-shirt.

The elevator door closed, taking the custodian to a lower level, and the three of us made our way out of the stairwell. The aroma of cleaning fluid hit my nose, smelling of black licorice and conjuring Mom's always-clean kitchen countertops. Maeve stepped toward the cart, in the opposite direction of the newsroom.

"What are you doing?" I asked. As I turned, my sneakers screeched over the damp tiles.

Maeve scanned the cart, picking her way around toilet paper rolls and generic spray bottles filled with a mint-green liquid. Looking for what, I had no idea.

"Maeve, come on!" I muttered.

Doug was already halfway down the hall. He stopped in front of the restrooms and motioned he would wait there, then disappeared under a sign marked Men.

"A-ha!" Maeve cheered. On her forefinger dangled a set of keys. "I thought I saw him stash them!"

"Great! Now let's go before he gets back." The lights over the doors lit up consecutively as the elevator started to rise. "We have to go!"

Maeve jogged toward me, the keys jingling until she wrapped her fist around them.

"Do we need those?"

"Gayle said the editor's office might be locked."

"Oh, wow." There were holes in the plan. Hopefully, I had gathered enough hands to plug them all up. "Good thinking."

We set off, catching up with Doug. Eventually, the hall splintered off in three different directions. A placard directed us to the newspaper offices. Doug's fingers grazed the sign's braille as we passed.

Classroom after classroom sat empty and dark until we came to a wall of glass with two large potted plants framing the door at the end of the hall. A stenciled sign read, "*The Campus Echo* est. 1840." As we got closer, the ID scanner Gayle had mentioned was right where she said it would be. I pulled Gayle's pass from around my neck, but Maeve set her hand on my shoulder. She pointed to an inconspicuous chrome bowl affixed to the ceiling ahead.

"Camera." She pulled her hood up; it flopped above her eyebrows. Doug and I did the same.

I scanned the newsroom beyond, an open area, aglow in the dim-blue fluorescence of the few bulbs left on, but noticed no other security monitors.

Swoosh. The lock's red dot blinked twice, then turned green with a beep and a click. We were in.

The temperature in the newsroom seemed cooler than the hallway. Desks formed clusters, some tidy, some not, each one topped with a laptop computer. A copy center took up one wall, complete with fax machines, a massive Xerox, five printers, and stacks of plain white paper. We walked quickly past an open break room with circular tables and a coffee maker brewing a fresh pot, the aroma competing with the overpowering smell of ink. The frosted glass of the conference room showed silhouettes moving within.

The chief editor's office looked empty, miniblinds pulled shut, door closed. When we tried the handle, it didn't budge—locked. This was where we were supposed to give up. There was no way of getting in. He had already left for the day, with all access to the computer stuff safely locked behind the door. There'd have been nothing we could have done unless one of us picked locks. Or there happened to be a beautiful assistant who had palmed the custodian's keys. I could've kissed Maeve. This whole endeavor would've been such a waste if not for her forethought.

The problem was the door's proximity to the conference room. The three of us were huddled right there, right next to it. If anyone thought to come out of the conference room—to refill a cup of coffee or sharpen a pencil or whatever—we would be doomed. Maeve moved with precision, trying each key without making a sound. Whoever was in the conference room was having a good time. The group's laughter provided an inconsistent soundtrack to our scheme.

"I've gone through all of them!" Maeve murmured, desperation tinging her tone.

"Let me." I took over, and on my fifth attempt, the lock unhitched. I turned the knob, and the three of us filed into the office.

Golf imagery and cheesy motivational quotes lined the walls. I immediately pictured a white guy with a pastel sweater draped over his shoulders. A large desk ran half the length of the back wall, paper and pens strewn all over the top, along with a selection of half-empty coffee mugs.

I stepped behind the desk and inched open one of the drawers. A long strip of condoms twisted around and through a plethora of sticky notes and packets of hot sauce.

Doug rolled the cushy chair to the corner section of the desk in front of the other computer—beige, chunky, and older-looking—then bent forward, basically hugging the machine.

"What are you doing?" Maeve asked. She'd been inspecting the view, and a metallic *ping* rang out when her finger slipped away from the blinds.

"Finding the power button." He felt along the back of the computer tower and must have clicked something because it started blinking and whirring.

"Why are there two computers?" I asked.

"Best guess..." Doug paused, standing in front of the monitor as it emitted a gray glow. Every now and again, a flash of bright-green gibberish filled the screen. "...they're in the middle of an upgrade. This baby will be obsolete soon."

"Will it get us what we need?" Maeve asked.

"As long as no one's wiped it, I should be able to get into either the catalog or database server and get the information. And bingo..." As the old computer booted up, Doug swiped something off the side of the monitor.

"What's that?"

"Passwords." He held up a sticky note with the paper's name written in Sharpie, followed by a string of consecutive numbers—echo123. "Although, I probably could have guessed that one." Handwritten underneath the first password, a second one said, "System Password: OUDatabase1111." Doug flicked the note. "Not sure when people are gonna smarten up about their password choices." He sat, and soon the office filled with Doug's tap-tapping on the keys.

I joined Maeve near the windows. Outside, the moonlight painted the tops of spindly, reaching branches in a wash of white shimmer. We sat on a low set of bookshelves placed under the window. I took a breath, my whole body registering with the deep pull of air. We were close to an end, and I inched toward a safer resolution. I would make copies of everything and take all the information to both Gayle and Detective Patterson without having to say a word. Then this would be over. Gathering clues, running down leads, hacking systems: all of it, done.

Maeve nibbled at her lower lip. I wondered what she was thinking, so I nudged her.

"What's up?"

She shrugged. "I don't know. Feels too easy, ya know?"

"It is possible for things to work out," I said. "Not always, but sometimes."

She nodded, the worry not leaving her eyes. The group next door belted out another raucous round of laughter, making me think they were drinking more than coffee over there.

"All right, I'm in." Doug stopped typing, a pregnant silence descending on the room.

"So, who is it?" I hopped up and stood behind him.

"Not anyone named Sara," he said with a questioning lilt.

"What?" Maeve stood behind me, her breath on my neck. "Then who?"

I recognized her name on the screen.

She'd whispered: *I believe you, he* did *deserve it, especially in that way.*

She'd typed: *I killed him.*

And a click once more, in the literal sense, as the door opened and closed, and Shirlee Hensen, Sara's suitemate, entered the room.

Chapter Twenty

All Wrong

OCTOBER 23, 2000

Shirlee's wire frames reflected the computer's light, creating glowing blue rings around her eyes. I thought of the figure on the bench. And then I remembered the night of the murder, a fleeting moment before Maeve had whisked us away from the scene when I thought I'd seen something—someone—in the bushes. From that night to this one, the orbs were the same.

"Surprise!" Her voice shook with a breathy excitement. "It's me."

"Who is this?" Maeve asked me.

"Eyes on me, Maeve."

"How do you know my name?"

"I've been following you both ever since Hazel picked up her necklace in the Trap."

"You were there?" I asked.

"You know her?" Maeve asked.

"She's Sara's suitemate," I said.

"I'd come back to watch." Shirlee twirled a strand of hair around her finger. "It was my handiwork after all." She stepped closer, a box cutter gripped in one hand. "I wanted to see if they could put Humpty Dumpty together again. All the king's horses..."

Shirlee's voice lilted over the words of the nursery rhyme, but there was something fake and manipulative to her manner. Something planned or forced. "You know the rest. But lo and behold, there you were. The girl I'd meant to run into in the first place."

"You were looking for me?" I asked.

"Sara found your necklace in her room but refused to return it. I saw the hallmark, and I'd heard your story about *Ryan*." She said his name as if it pained her. "Sara was being unfair. So I volunteered, but...well, we've all read the end. That's why you're here, isn't it?"

"But how did you get in here?"

"Oh, easy. I told the janitor I'd forgotten my pass, and he let me in. The question is what are you doing? What is it that led you here of all places?"

She didn't know. She was clueless regarding the database trail.

Doug twitched; the mouse under his hand made a traitorous *click*. Shirlee took a shaky step forward, pointing the box cutter at Doug.

"What's he doing?" She directed Maeve and me with a stern steadiness: "Move away from him."

"This is ridiculous," I said. "You can't threaten all three of us with just a box cutter."

Shirlee laughed at me, condescension dripping over each jeer. "Very logical."

She paused and reached into the messenger bag crossed over her shoulder. "I have this too." She pulled out a handgun. "Another little gift from my dad." She laughed. "I guess he *would* know how dangerous it is to be a woman."

The gun invaded negative space with its matte-black shape, a deadly shadow in and of itself.

"Step away from the little computer man. Okay?"

Maeve moved, and I followed her. What choice did we have?

Doug stared at the computer screen. Did his life flash before him in those emerald-green lines of code? Shirlee stepped toward him again; only the desk separated them.

"Now, tell me what you're doing." she said, her tone saccharine sweet.

"I-I," he stuttered, then cleared his throat and straightened his posture. "I was retrieving your name from the system." He sniffed. "For Hazel."

"How sweet. You got a real knight in shining armor over here, Hazel."

Where was the Shirlee I'd met at Sara's rehearsal? The one who'd believed me when I warned of Ryan. Somehow, she'd evolved into this? Had her experiences molded her into someone capable of destroying lives? Could she have ever escaped this fate? I didn't have time to ponder it. Not with a gun pointed at Doug's head. If something happened to him, it would be my fault. I was the only reason he was here.

"But why the need to out me? Hmm?" Shirlee kept the gun trained on Doug, her grip tightened. "Have the police visited you yet?"

"Yes!" I called out—overly loud and streaked with panic. "They spoke with me this afternoon. I'm pretty sure one of them thinks it's me. I-I can't go to jail. I won't sit in a police station. I. Can't."

She dropped the hand holding the gun to her side. "And why is that, Hazel?"

It was exactly what a needed—a break in the tension. I could breathe. But only for a moment because now I had to tell her and everyone else in the room what had happened.

"I've had some experience." I started with my usual style, skirting around my family's truth. I couldn't see Shirlee's eyes roll behind her glasses, but it was clear from the way her head jerked this wasn't going to cut it. I couldn't lie anymore. Not with my friends' lives at stake.

"My mom was attacked. Raped." I hated saying that word. It brought attention and judgment and preconceived ideas. "She was at home one day, and a stranger knocked on the door. He was dressed in a police uniform. Nobody knows if he was really a cop somewhere; they never found him.

"She reported everything. Did everything right. But after the shock wore off, someone leaked that she'd used drugs, as if she were an addict or something." The pace of my speech picked up, and words spilled out. I'd never told anyone this after the case closed, but now it seemed I couldn't stop. And if I was talking, Shirlee wasn't killing.

"She might've taken a Valium every now and then or smoked weed. But that's hardly an addiction." Truthfully, I had no idea how much or what Mom had been using—if anything. "They villainized her for it anyway. Started acting as if maybe she wasn't telling the truth, like maybe it didn't happen the way she said it did, if it even happened at all."

Shirlee had stepped closer to me as I spoke. I tried not to let her proximity unnerve me, but she was right there, her face only a foot away from mine. Her eyes darted back and forth, searching.

"She killed herself," I whispered. "Jumped off a bridge. In the end, I don't know what she thought was true. That's how bad it got."

"You said he dressed like a cop?" Shirlee quietly asked.

"Yeah." I wanted to step back, away from her, but was scared to make a move that might set her off. "Anyway, that's why I—"

"Did he have a tattoo?" Somehow, she seemed more agitated.

I was scared to answer, terrified of saying the wrong thing, and my mind could barely focus on what she was asking me to remember.

"Any identifying marks?" she asked.

"I-I—"

"Think!" she yelled.

"Yes," I blurted. Somehow, the memory clicked into place. "A Roman numeral, or something on his hand. She—"

"An *X*." Shirlee sank onto one of the chairs in front of the desk. Her guard was down. I didn't know what I'd said, but something had obviously overwhelmed her. And then—

"Oh." The air whooshed out of me as if I'd been kicked in the chest.

"What? What is it?"

I could hear Maeve's voice, but it was far away—off in the distance. Maybe in a different time.

"Hazel?"

I looked at her. Maeve, my first friend here. She shouldn't have had to learn about me in this weird and horrible moment. Her face was blurry because of my tears.

"Are you okay?"

I shook my head. *No.* I wasn't okay. Nothing was fine. Nothing was ever going to be all right. But I didn't say anything. It was Shirlee who finally spoke up.

"Where are you from?" Shirlee asked.

"Hillery...er, Danville, Illinois. Near Champaign," I said automatically. "Where are you from?"

"'Bout an hour from there. In Indiana."

"What is going on?" Maeve asked.

"It was my dad." Shirlee's voice was barely a whisper.

ANOTHER ROUND OF whoops and laugher bellowed in the room next door.

"You'll never get past them." Maeve changed the subject, diverting attention away from the truth connecting Shirlee and me.

Shirlee shook her head, coming out of her reverie. "What makes you think I care?"

"She's right," Doug said. "If shots are fired, they're coming in here. Your identity will be revealed no matter what."

The computer whirred, and Shirlee sat up straight, slicing the box cutter through the air in front of her. "Don't move," she growled at Doug, holding both weapons in front of her.

"I didn't," he said.

We all froze, except for the group in the next room. Their door banged open, and the footsteps of one, maybe two, of them passed by.

"They're working on the case, too, you know." I gathered whatever strength hadn't just been spooned out of me. Maybe if I pushed her, she'd make a mistake big enough for us to gain an advantage.

"Shut up." She pointed the cutter toward me.

This moment was bigger than what had happened in the Trap. There was something more between me and her; we were connected through time and space and a string of awful coincidences. A whole range of events had lined up so exactly, bringing us both here. A standoff. The air around her smelled of baby powder. I could make out a line of moisture on her upper lip. She was as rattled as I was.

"What tipped you off?" I ventured. "How did you know it was your dad who hurt my mom?" He was between every line of her diary, her weakness. So I pressed the advantage. Then I remembered the pictures she'd described and swallowed back bile. Unfortunately, he was my weakness too.

She rolled her lips. Her gaze flicked away from mine. "The uniform. He kept one in his closet." She looked at the floor. "When I was little, I assumed it was a costume. For dress-up or Halloween. But I never saw him wear it. It was just there. Later, I asked him, and he didn't have an answer. Said it was nothing. Told me to forget about it."

I'd always believed my mom, but this confirmed her account. The police had been wrong, had gaslit her until she couldn't take it anymore. I closed my eyes, unable to really function. All of this was too much.

"He had a hardware store. There's no reason he should've had that uniform," Shirlee said. A shudder, maybe of revulsion, moved over her.

Maeve was beside me. She curled her hand around mine. I assumed she was simply being kind, showing support and offering strength, and then I felt the little metal cannister between our palms. I pushed all my feelings away as a plan took shape.

"He almost got us too—Ryan." Maeve changed the subject. "The weekend before. If one of his friends hadn't pulled him away, I don't know what would've happened."

"Sara told me," Shirlee said. But her expression still seemed disoriented, far-off, in a remembering place—the same place I was reeling myself back from.

"You did every woman a favor," Maeve added, building her up. "And you were protecting someone else, right?"

"Well, I don't—" Shirlee seemed confused. "I *was* trying to help. With the first cut, yeah. But I couldn't stop. Everything went black." Her nostrils flared. "And then red."

"The police will understand," Doug said.

Anger flashed like lightning across Shirlee's features.

I held up my hand, hoping he'd catch the gesture and keep quiet. Maeve looked as if she might strangle him. There wasn't a man alive who could talk to Shirlee about this.

"What?" Doug said. "It isn't rocket science. Something illegal happens, you go to the police. You explain."

Shut the fuck up, Doug.

Shirlee's head tilted, and her cold knowing laugh descended upon the office, seemingly shrinking us and everything else inside. We'd been reduced to the size of dust motes, swirling in and around her ridicule. We were nothing.

"Of. Course." She basically spat her words. Yet, she kept both her weapons at her sides.

Good. She still wants to talk.

"I'm a skinny kid with a passion for computers. You think I don't know what it's like to be harassed?"

Both Maeve and Shirlee snorted.

"Poor little nerdy white man." Shirlee added, "Put yourself in someone else's shoes for once. Nobody will save us." Her shoulders shuddered as she took a deep breath. Shirlee looked to me and shook her head, then raised her gun once more, leveling it at Doug's head. "We're all drowning in it."

"Don't! If you shoot him, it's all over," I pleaded with her. She was making less and less sense the longer this went on. Doug was being dense as hell, but I could not let that cost him his life. I imagined his eyes pinched shut, but I didn't dare take my gaze off Shirlee.

"I don't plan on being caught, Hazel. Ever. Dad will help me. After all, he would know."

I had to think of something—anything. If Maeve maced her, Shirlee might pull the trigger.

"Shirlee, what do you need?" Maeve asked. She let go of my hand, leaving the pepper spray to me, and held up both of hers. She pointed to one of the chairs near Shirlee. When Shirlee didn't object, Maeve stepped closer. The leather seat cushion squelched as Maeve sat. At the sound, Shirlee tightened her grip on the gun, but her arm shook with its weight. She wouldn't be able to hold the pose for much longer.

And that was when I'd make a move.

"What I *need*?" Shirlee repositioned herself to address Maeve; the gun stayed focused on Doug, and the box cutter glinted at Maeve. "How 'bout a rewind button, hmm? That might help. Then I could go back and, what, not kill him? That would make things better. Or maybe I need to go back further and stop all those incidents I wrote about in my online diary because that shit was definitely cumulative. Or maybe I should've never been born. Obviously, this is all a part of who I am—my legacy."

"Okay." I gestured toward Doug. "Maybe he can—I don't know—wipe the system?"

"What do you mean?" she asked.

"Doug was able to find your name attached to the dead_papers account, so anyone who knows their way around a computer can too. But what do you think, Doug? Can you delete it forever?" I prayed for him to say yes, even if it wasn't true.

"Uh, sure."

Our eyes met, and I tried to telepathically tell him to sound more confident.

"Yes," Doug reiterated, nodding. "I can make that happen."

Shirlee stayed quiet, seemingly thinking it over. We waited, the silence in the office a contrast to the party next door. Could this work? And if it did, would that make us accomplices? It didn't really matter with our lives on the line.

It was Shirlee's move. She was in control here.

"Do it," she said.

A sprig of relief sprouted in my chest at the sound of Doug's typing. This would work.

"Done," he said.

"Good." A maniacal grin split Shirlee's face. "Unfortunately, there's no way for me to let the three of you go."

"That's not true," Maeve said. "We can all just leave. Go back to our dorms as if this never happened."

"Too risky." Shirlee wiped her brow with her forearm and then trained the gun back on Doug.

"We won't say anything," Doug pleaded.

"I doubt that very much." Shirlee's features screwed up, and then she shook it off. "You know my identity, which means you're an internet search away from my dad's identity. Who knows what you all have planned?"

Stick to the plan. But what was the plan? Mine had changed along the way. Or had it? Maybe there was a plan— one I hadn't been consciously aware of in the beginning. Some grand design where I was supposed to come to college, find my mother's rapist, and make him pay. A surge of adrenaline rushed through me at the thought of bringing that man to justice. My connection to Shirlee wouldn't be some sick twist of fate, but a key.

"I think it's pretty obvious that you all fancy yourselves as a bunch of do-gooders—"

I rushed at her and crashed my head and shoulders right into her torso. Both her arms swung to her sides, curling around my back. The gun rang out, and I barely registered a slice of pain in my arm as we toppled over the chairs. She punched at my head and face. I sprayed the Mace. She screamed. I screamed. The box cutter sliced the air, and as I grabbed her wrist, my hand was slick with blood. With all my weight on top of her, I wrestled her arms to the ground and set my knees on top of them. Maeve grabbed the gun nearby. Then the door shot open, and the lights came on. We all froze.

I could only imagine how this looked from their vantage: bodies sprawled on the floor, a young woman wielding a gun, all the blood.

"What's goin' on in here?" a slurred masculine voice asked.

I put my hands up by my ears. "Not what you think." I moved to get off Shirlee. Maeve placed the gun on the desk, clearly out of Shirlee's reach, and put her hands up as well.

As soon as she could, Shirlee curled into the fetal position and started whimpering.

"Is she okay?" a more sober-sounding voice chimed in.

"I know how this looks," Doug said. His chair squealed as he rolled away from the computer. "But you've got this all wrong. She was coming after us."

"All three of you?" A woman and another man shouldered their way into the room. They knelt before Shirlee, checking to make sure she was all right.

"Thank you for helping me," she whispered to the woman, who was now brushing Shirlee's hair back from her face. With a delicate touch, the woman removed Shirlee's glasses. They were broken, one lens totally askew.

"I'm calling the cops," some guy said. He flipped open a cell phone, then dialed. Stepping away from the doorway, he answered the dispatcher's questions.

A wave of nausea worked up my body. Soon, they'd all be here: heroic first responders, who touched everything and asked questions. So many questions.

The couple helped Shirlee sit up and asked her if she wanted some water. Shirlee nodded. They had a silent conversation with their eyes until the woman left to get what

Shirlee had requested. The man looked around nervously. His gaze rested on the three of us and then the gun on the desk.

"Joe! Can you come in here?" He called for a friend to help keep watch.

Shirlee looked only at me. Mischief glinted in her gaze, and she tilted her head in a way that indicated she had the upper hand and would do whatever it took to keep it.

The room got swimmy then. Something warm and liquid dripped down my side. My arm lit up with pain, and I instinctively clutched at it, which made everything a whole lot worse. I was aware my knees had buckled. I heard Maeve asking if I was okay. Black spots blotted out her face. And then everything faded into the dark.

"HAZEL..."

A dreamy, sparkling flash of Maeve's face—blurry, but there—filled my line of vision. I was shaking. My head felt like it rolled, decapitated and free, over the icy, blowing waves of one of the Great Lakes.

"Hazel!"

Bright and unrelenting lights flickered on, casting everyone in silhouette.

"Jesus, where are they?" Maeve was panicked, her voice screeching a little at the ends of her sentences. "Look at her color, Doug."

My head lolled to the side, and under the desk was the box cutter. The same one that had killed Ryan, only now, someone else's blood was smeared across the blade. And I knew it was mine. My body was slow and heavy and unresponsive to any of the actions that might have woven their way through my nerves.

"How bad is it?" someone asked.

"I'm not sure. I don't want to move her," Maeve said.

"My arm," I tried to say, but even to my own ears, the words sounded as if I were underwater.

"Shh." Maeve's hands were smeared and rusty-looking.

Was that all mine?

Then, everything got more technical as a stranger in purple latex gloves assessed the situation. They moved me around, bandaged, and strapped me to the gurney. Pain started coming then—great waves of it, rippling and licking my entire side. Every time they moved me, reality wavered with another searing reminder of severed nerve endings. The edges of existence blurred and mixed like watercolors. I could hear Maeve asking questions, but they faded as I was rolled out of the room.

In the larger office area, I caught sight of Shirlee as the paramedics examined her. As one of the EMTs unfolded a chrome-colored blanket over Shirlee's shoulders, she winked.

Bitch.

Outside, the night air enveloped me, crisp and clean. It filled my lungs, and I took in big great gulps before they locked me away in the ambulance. If I was dying, I wanted the cold, misty air inside me.

Life still swooned around me as unfamiliar things beeped, and official-looking people shouted orders and directions. Someone placed a smooth plastic mask over my nose and mouth, and two loud thumps sounded. In the distance the sirens blared.

"You're doing good, hun." The paramedic in purple gloves checked cords that were now attached to me and monitored the beeping machines.

By the time we stopped, reality and pain regained all its harshness. There was no more shifting back into a world of soft bucolic pastels. Instead, my whole body throbbed with hurt. The back doors popped open, and the paramedics wheeled me out of the ambulance, a carefully coordinated routine with lots of clicking and clacking. They weren't running, nor did they seem to be in a hurry, which I took to be a positive sign. A team of medical professionals met us near the doors, and I listened carefully as the medics listed my stats.

"Two wounds with a sharp object, one superficial, one with elongation...lower right quadrant...stable."

They wheeled me into a small room and went to work— on me.

"Do you know where you are?" a nurse with a sweet, dimpled smile asked.

"Hospital." I nodded as tears leaked out of the corners of my eyes.

"That's right. University Hospital. We've got you." He removed the oxygen mask and handed me a tissue, while a flurry of activity happened near my waist.

"What's your..." I struggled to bring my words together in the right way, tried to clear my throat, but pain seared up my side. "...name?"

"I'm Jamal. And you're gonna be just fine."

Jamal explained every procedural thing right before it happened. He told me when they'd roll me on my side. As information was tossed round the room, he noted it on the clipboard. He held my hand when they numbed me up for stitches.

And then, finally, everything quieted, and I was alone, which was not necessarily a great thing considering what I'd been through. The pain was numbed but tingly enough to keep me from moving too much. I stayed in triage and listened to all the emergencies around me. There were so many—high-pitched beeping sounds, crying, coughing, vomiting, all parts of the soundtrack.

Jamal came in to check on me. I was still on my side, and the pain meds were starting to wear off.

"How ya doing?"

"Getting sore."

"You'll have that." Jamal checked some of the machines around me and scribbled some information in my chart. "I don't think they're going to admit you."

"Really?"

"Really." Jamal indicated he was going to lift up the sheet. I was in a gown but had no memory of how or when that had happened. He checked the wound on my side. "It's a long gash but not too deep. At this point, the biggest risk would be infection. The one on your arm is a bit deeper." Jamal lowered the sheet and made more notes on my clipboard.

Inexplicably, I started crying again. The thought of leaving the hospital alone was too much. I needed someone, anyone, to help me through those doors. I'd been fucking stabbed.

Jamal came around to the side of the bed where I could see him. His face was blurry through my tears, but the kindness behind his dark eyes made me cry harder.

"Okay, okay, now," he said. "Shhh. You're okay."

"I-I don't think I am."

I had no idea if Jamal had any idea what had happened, how I'd stood with my friends at knife and gunpoint, while a maniac held court for what seemed like hours.

"You had your student ID on ya. And we called your next of kin. Your auntie, she'll be here soon."

Aunt Liddy was on her way. Some of the tightness in my chest unfurled. Aunt Liddy would take over, be in control.

"You won't be alone for too much longer."

"What about the police?" I asked.

Jamal's lips tightened. "They're here."

My heartbeat ticked up a notch. Jamal glanced at the monitor.

"Okay, don't panic on me now. We don't want ya passing out again. You're feeling pretty sleepy anyway, right? Those pain meds can knock a person out." Jamal checked his watch. "She said she was two hours away, so she should be here soon."

"Thank you."

"Just doing my job."

Jamal's presence was a river of calm and kindness. Thank god he'd chosen to be a nurse. Showing up for an endless sea of patients, keeping them relaxed when they were at their worst—what a gift. I wondered if it was inherent, whether he'd known all along what he was meant to be.

I snorted, thinking back to how and why I'd started at Oakley...to be a teacher. What a joke that had turned out to be.

"What are you laughing at?" Jamal asked as he checked the machines connected to me.

"Nothing." I was no teacher. I'd never had it in me. Sometimes you just had to face things head-on or, at the very least, pay attention to red flags as soon as you saw them. If I'd done that earlier, maybe I wouldn't be in this hospital bed. "Let the police in. I'm ready to talk."

Chapter Twenty-One

Lucky

OCTOBER 24, 2000

Moving brought on a shockwave of pain, but I did it anyway, reaching for a drink on the tray near the foot of my bed. The apple juice had been mixed with so much ice it looked like a Slushie. The foggy feeling lifted as the drink's crisp tartness simultaneously reminded me of my childhood and that I was still alive, in the present—still able to enjoy the flavor of an apple some machine had squeezed the life out of.

Two uniformed police officers strolled into my room, and a lump formed in my throat at the sight of them. Before I could change my mind about this, they were at the foot of my bed, asking questions regarding what had happened at the *Echo*.

What were we doing there?

Trying to find out the murderer's identity.

Why did you think the newspaper had that infor-mation?

It was just a hunch. (I might have found the nerve to talk, but I wasn't going to sell out Doug or Gayle.)

What happened when—notes checked—*Shirlee Hensen arrived?*

All hell broke loose.

Each question flowed to the next, another—always another. I answered them as best I could, but there was a haziness around the night, as if it were something I watched rather than experienced. I heard Aunt Liddy before I saw her. Her voice always carried farther than others.

"Hazel Fischer, please."

...

"I most certainly am her family."

...

"No, not her mother. I'm her legal guardian. You called me! Look, my niece has been hurt, and if you don't cut out this nonsense right this second, you'll have to get security down here. Because I'm 'bout to go off!"

A few seconds later, a nurse escorted my aunt into my room.

"What's all this?" she asked, eyeing the officers.

"We're taking her statement, ma'am."

"Can't this wait? She's wounded, for god's sake!"

The cops exchanged a look, and the one taking notes put his pad away. "We've got enough for now. If I were you, I'd expect to hear from one of the detectives soon."

I didn't know what that was supposed to mean. Was my description of the night not good enough? Aunt Liddy gave the men the evil eye until they were gone and well out of earshot. Then she turned to the nurse and asked about my injuries.

She explained, and Aunt Liddy held my hand while listening. But the nurse didn't have all the backstory. She only mentioned the number of stitches, pain management, and what to look out for. She wasn't even here when I was brought in.

"The doctor will go over everything with you before she's discharged," the nurse said and left the room.

Aunt Liddy looked down at me sharply and shook her head. The measure of relief was easy to spot in the way her eyes went soft when they met mine. She frowned and kept taking deep breaths, a streak of anger replacing her fear.

"I know there's more to this story." She pursed her lips, broke eye contact, and started pacing.

I closed my eyes. She was the person who knew the most about me, which meant she understood I'd tell her only when I was good and ready.

The doctor came and filled Aunt Liddy in again, saying the exact same things the nurse had said, adding a question regarding whether I'd had a history of fainting.

"Yes," Aunt Liddy said.

"No," I argued.

"Do you not remember last summer? When the drama department led a Shakespeare in the Park series? The doctor said it was probably the heat."

"A vasovagal response can be triggered by that—standing too long, the sight of blood, extreme fear...any of those things." The doctor handed her two prescriptions, and she gave one of them right back.

"Narcotics make her puke. Or at least they did when she had her wisdom teeth removed."

"Okay, good to know." The doctor addressed me by tapping my foot with the chart. "We'll find something else. I can write you a prescription for high-dose ibuprofen."

"Whatever," I mumbled.

"She'll still feel the pain, so it'll keep her resting." The doctor tucked his hands in his pockets. He explained we'd need to make an appointment with a primary physician soon.

"They can keep an eye on how she's healing." He lowered his voice and said, "I'm making a therapy referral too. Common practice when someone's been hurt in this way."

"Thank you, doctor. When can I take her home?"

"You're welcome." He shook my aunt's hand. "Discharge paperwork should be in the works now."

"We live a couple hours away. How would she manage in the car?"

"Getting in and sitting up—things will be tender. It's her call. I'd like to see her get up and walk around, with some help of course. Use the restroom. Maybe eat something. Those kinds of things, before releasing her."

Aunt Liddy checked her watch. I had no concept of time, except the windows were black and reflective. It was late, possibly the next day.

"By the time all of those things happen, it will be morning, and you'll be on your way home." The doctor made his way to my bedside. "Take it easy now, okay."

Aunt Liddy thanked the doctor and then left to speak to the officers herself. It took her a long time to come back, and when she did, they weren't following her.

"Are they coming back?" I asked.

"I have their card. They agreed to let you rest a while longer."

"I didn't do anything wrong," I said.

"I know that."

"They might think I did."

"If they thought that, you'd be handcuffed to the bed."

THE HOSPITAL DOORS swished open, and the smell of exhaust lingered on the walkway. Aunt Liddy crossed the street, bustling toward a parking garage, while Jamal, who was still on shift, wheeled and parked my chair near the curb.

"Thank you," I said.

"You keep saying that, but I'm just doing my job."

"Well, you're good at it."

An old pickup truck screeched to a stop nearby. A new emergency arose as the driver slammed the truck into park and tore out of the driver side.

"Baby's comin'!" the driver yelled as he raced to the passenger side and opened the door for a hugely pregnant, panting woman. The pair hobbled inside without shutting the door to their truck.

"That must be exciting."

"Yeah, those are usually the good kind of emergencies."

Jamal smiled as he stepped into the loading zone and closed the truck door. "At least he didn't leave the engine running."

"Will you get to help the baby being born?"

"Probably not. Typically, there's enough time to get up to labor and delivery."

From where I sat, I could see Aunt Liddy's car pull up to the parking garage pay window.

"So how did you know you wanted to be a nurse?" I was curious, and the mega-ibuprofen had me feeling decent.

Jamal unlocked the brake as Aunt Liddy parked in front of us.

"I wanted to help people," he said, wheeling me closer to the back seat. "And I don't mind a little gore."

I laughed, but that was a bad idea. Pain rippled around my midsection. "Don't make me laugh."

"You asked."

Aunt Liddy opened the car door, and they awkwardly helped me inside. I wanted to stretch out over the seat, but Aunt Liddy had me buckled in before I could. Then we pulled away from the hospital. Jamal's words banged around in my head as Aunt Liddy caught nearly every stoplight on the way downtown.

She clicked on the blinker, and we turned into an underground garage of a hotel she'd booked. She'd been up all night and hadn't liked the idea of driving home so soon. Plus, the officers had told her not to go too far. It was midmorning, but the garage was filled with orange, sporadically blinking overhead lights. She shut off the car, and we were cast in shadow.

Aunt Liddy rotated in her seat to face me and said, "I'll go check in and see if they have any wheelchairs to get you upstairs."

"I can walk." But I sucked in a wisp of breath when I moved to unbuckle my seat belt.

"Don't be ridiculous. I'll be right back." She dumped her keys into her satchel of a purse and hurried off toward the elevator across the way.

Every noise echoed in the garage: the screeching of brakes; a quick tap on a car horn; the slow, steady pace of a man's dress shoes on the pavement; someone whistling a familiar melody. I swallowed past the lump forming in my throat, but a swimming feeling reformed in my head. My breath came quick with a sharp pain as I slid down in the seat, not wanting to be seen by a living soul. Sweat broke out over my forehead and upper lip, but I couldn't tell if it was from fear or pain. What was this? Leftover shock? I thought of Shirlee, wondered where she was right now. And what about her dad? He would have been called too. He'd definitely be in the city. Maybe even this hotel. No. I was being hysterical. This was solely a creepy everyday parking garage with creepy everyday parking-garage sounds. I closed my eyes and wished the underwater feeling in my brain away.

Knock-knock-knock! I jumped and grimaced.

My aunt's knuckles tapped on the window. "You all right in there?" Her voice was muffled.

I nodded, but tears were perilously close to falling—*again*. I hated being injured and scared, and not just in that moment, but all the time. I carried around all this shit about my family, and it stopped me from doing—and feeling—so much.

Aunt Liddy unlocked the door and helped me into a wheelchair. Rolling toward the elevator, I caught glimpses of the gray world beyond. People hustled over the sidewalks, going about their dailies, while something mildly catastrophic had happened to me. The world went on as if it barely knew me, and... It didn't.

The elevator was cramped with my chair and the handful of other people in business attire who joined us.

"Where's your luggage?" I asked, my voice sounding loud and clumsy in my own ears.

Everyone stared at the numbers as they lit with our ascent.

"In the car," she whispered, not wanting to disturb those around her with minutiae. Randomly, I wondered if that was something that only happened here, in the middle of the country. Did Californians worry about being too loud in an elevator? It didn't matter. *Here* was where I was, and *here*, people whispered so that no one else would be bothered. It was smothering. We should all be shouting. Fuck the niceties. We lived in a world where mothers were raped. And dads were monsters. Daughters carried secrets. Sons were spoiled by toxicity. Teenagers slaughtered classmates. Wars never ended. And we were all just supposed to stay quiet?

I played with the zipper on my hoodie and seethed. This was all so wrong. Thank goodness Aunt Liddy had had the foresight to bring some of my old clothes from home. Because if people could be troubled by the volume of someone's voice, who knows what would have happened if I were still sitting in my bloodstained clothes.

The elevator let out a smooth *ding* of arrival, and we all poured into the lobby. Everyone let us through first, which was nice and polite and correct. The hotel was swank. Plush ivory couches cornered several planned seating areas. Crystal chandeliers sparkled near the ceiling and set off all the room's golden accents.

The wheels of my chair squelched along the marble floor tiles until we reached another elevator with shiny brass doors. Aunt Liddy pressed the button and away we went.

Our room—or suite—had a living room area, a kitchenette, and, behind a set of French doors, two queen-sized beds. The downstairs décor continued here, with lots of white-and-gold-trimmed things. But the carpet was a little worn and discolored in some areas.

"You went all out, huh?" I asked.

"Well, it's not every day your niece gets stabbed." Aunt Liddy set her big purse on the counter. "Do you want me to help you onto the bed?"

"No. Will you roll me over to the window?"

She did so without saying a word.

The gray and brown buildings pressed themselves into the blue sky. We were up high, overlooking the three muddy rivers that wound their way through and around the city. I couldn't help but think of Shirlee's posts: how she described watching the river, how it came to life for her, how she heard all the victims' stories. And now I knew; Mom was one of them.

Shirlee's posts seemed to be the ramblings of someone losing their grip on reality, yet more often than I'd like to admit, I understood what she'd meant completely. Everything that had ever happened to and around me still flowed somewhere, cutting through my thoughts, my actions, filtering my every perspective.

I fiddled with the knobs on the fan unit under the window. "It hurts to move."

"We've got a couple hours before your meds wear off, and I'll need to find a pharmacy to fill your prescription." Aunt Liddy looked around as though answers were hidden within the manufactured art and thick, yellow wallpaper.

"Maeve might be able to help." If she wasn't sitting in a holding cell.

"Maeve?"

"One of my suitemates. Do you want me to call her and ask?"

Aunt Liddy chewed on her lower lip, thinking it over. "It would save me a trip to your dorm. I brought some things from home, but you'd taken a lot when you moved. Contact case—you'll need your glasses. I can buy everything else."

"Hand me the phone."

Aunt Liddy dialed and stretched the receiver to me. "Do you need anything?"

"Could you grab me a pop and something from the vending machine to eat?"

"Yeah, okay. Then I'll figure out the pharmacy situation."

The phone rang in my ear, and each time, it was startling. I checked for a clock but didn't see one. My suitemates were probably all at class. Well, probably not Maeve. If she wasn't at our place, then I hoped she was cozied up with either her parents or a lawyer right now.

Right before I knew it would click to voice mail, someone picked up with a hurried hello.

"Uh, hi. Who is this?" I asked.

"Kim. And you are?"

"Kim, it's me Hazel."

"Hazel! Where the fuck are you? There was another incident on campus last night, and you guys didn't come home! We've been worried sick."

"I'm at a hotel with my aunt."

"What? Why?"

"It's a long story. Listen, is Maeve around?"

"I haven't seen her either."

Shit.

"Well, could you leave her a message for me?"

"Of course."

There was some scuffling. I pictured Kim in her cute pink sweats with print across her backside, reaching for the marker above the message board. I left the hotel name and room number and asked if Maeve could pack an overnight bag for me.

"You got it," Kim chirped. "How long do you think you'll be gone?"

"I—I don't know." I'd only been to the ocean a handful of times with my parents, but the truth of last night hit me like a breaking wave. It slammed into my chest, rolled me over, and stole my breath. Death always hovered over all of us, but last night, it had snuck around and faced me.

"Hazel? You still there?"

"Yeah, I'm here." And that was only because I'd been lucky.

I'D SLOWLY AND painfully been able to maneuver myself to one of the beds. I couldn't reach the remote, though, so I napped until the *swoosh-click* of the deadbolt lock woke me up. I startled, and the injury sent shockwaves through my body—again. A hissing sound came out of me.

Aunt Liddy set down her suitcase and tore open a little white bag filled with beautiful, wonderful medicine. She gave me one giant ibuprofen and handed me a bottle of Coke. I swallowed.

"How are you doing?" she asked, passing me a bag of Cheetos.

"Fine. I slept."

"That's good." Her shoulders bobbed with a weighty sigh. "Look, the police want to speak with you again. I gave them my cell phone number at the hospital, and they've already called." She sniffed. "Twice." Aunt Liddy twisted the cap off a Diet Coke and took a swig. "You need to tell me everything before I call them back."

And so I did. Midway through, she kicked her sneakers off and sat back against the cushiony headboard. She didn't say anything, merely closed her eyes and listened. She gave me a hard look when I told her about finding my necklace in the Trap and keeping it to myself. Everything could have turned out differently if I'd made another choice right then and there. But I hadn't. Partly because Maeve had been adamant, but also because I hadn't wanted to. It all connected—a thread of coincidences that didn't seem to be random. They led to something, piling up as I kept climbing over. I just wasn't quite sure what was at the top—yet. But if I was being super honest with myself, everything that had happened since Ryan's murder had made me feel alive again. The world was brand-new.

"What were you thinking?" Aunt Liddy asked after I finished.

"I wasn't, I guess."

"Hogwash." She stood and went to the dresser. She sifted through some of the bags we'd brought up to the room. "These are ruined." She tied up a clear plastic bag filled with my bloody clothes. "But I'm not trashing them here. No need to freak out housekeeping."

I couldn't tell if she was talking to herself or me. Either way, I didn't have a response.

"But this was mixed in with your things." She brought my necklace to me. "What would you like me to do with it?"

I wasn't sure I could even look at it, but I did. I took it from her and held it in my hands, touching the crevices and curvature of the charm. I didn't think I could ever wear it again; there was so much more attached to it now.

A soft tapping sounded, and Aunt Liddy gave me a questioning look. Someone was at the door. I shrugged, or at least attempted to, before she got up and checked the peephole.

"It's a young woman."

"Oh, right. Probably Maeve. I asked her to bring some of my stuff over."

Aunt Liddy opened the door and introduced herself. Maeve was quiet and kept her eyes on the swirling patterns of the carpet.

"Well, I'm sure you two would like a moment. Hazel, I'm going to call around for a lawyer, and then we're setting up your second interview. Got it?"

"Yes, ma'am."

"I'm going to the hotel bar..." Aunt Liddy mumbled as the door clicked shut behind her.

"How are you?" Maeve's gaze flicked to my face.

"Hey," I said. "I'm fine." I probably looked half-raised-from-the-dead.

Her breath hitched. She closed her eyes for a few beats before continuing. "We weren't sure."

"Just a flesh wound." I offered, and she laughed in a nervous-breakdown way.

Maeve set a plastic grocery bag at my feet. "Our book-bags were at the scene, so they've been collected into evidence. Listen to me, using those words like I have a clue."

She let out a heavy breath as though she might deflate and took a seat on the bed opposite me.

"I've had a couple of those moments myself." I asked her if she wanted some of my Coke. She nodded. I sucked in a breath as I reached for the pop. Maeve rushed over, but I waved her away. "Don't worry. I've got this." I handed her the bottle.

She poured some into a tumbler as I tucked my hands into the big, kangaroo pocket of my sweatshirt, letting the tingling jolts of pain run their course.

"They got you on the good stuff?"

"Nah, they make me puke."

"Bummer." Maeve sat on the edge of the other bed.

She handed me the rest of the Coke, and I set it on the nightstand.

"You haven't been arrested, so that seems like something good."

She nodded, staring at the umber liquid bubbling in her cup.

"Tell me."

"There's not much to tell," she said. "They questioned me. I gave them everything we had, and they let me go."

"Were your parents there?"

"I called them, but I'm over eighteen. They hired a lawyer for me, though, and told me not to answer anything else until she was present."

"They've been hounding my aunt."

"We probably should've talked to them sooner."

I shrugged. "It would've changed the course of things, for sure."

"What you told Shirlee last night..." She gave me a side-eyed look. "You never told *me* why you didn't want to go to the police."

"It's a fucked-up story."

She nodded. "Still..."

"Look. I've never said *any* of what I said last night out loud, okay? It's something I keep—" I placed my palm over my heart. "—here."

"I get it."

"Thanks," I said. But I barely believed she understood what it was like to carry such an enormous weight.

"Do you remember the day Trish and Kim got into a fight over that guy who spilled a drink on her? I'd come back to the dorm pretty messed up."

My hand was still over my heart. I felt its pace tick up. "Yeah."

"I'd been attacked. Shoved down on the trail that runs alongside the river. Groped."

I couldn't breathe.

"I don't know what stopped them from doing anything else, but the guy ran off. I tried to report it"—Maeve kept rubbing her thumb across her palm—"but I was pretty out of it."

I forced myself to breathe.

"I'd hit my head on a rock, I think. Campus police thought I was drunk, blamed me. So I figured everyone is all on their own anyway. Nobody ever helps. Once you touched the necklace, I guess that idea kinda went into hyperdrive or something. I was trying to protect you—us."

All this time, I'd been so focused on my aversion to the cops I hadn't paid much attention to Maeve's. But it was there, plain as day; she'd never been guilty. She'd been mistrustful. Our eyes locked, and I remembered how shaken she'd been that day.

"Holy shit, Maeve. Why didn't you tell me?" The words whooshed out of me as though a door had blown open.

"What was there to tell? It happens all the time."

"Jesus Christ." Fury billowed through me. How were we supposed to be okay with this going on every fucking day, in every fucking place? This casual violence, supported through dismissal or outright denial, chipped away at us. We either ignored it, or we broke. Like Shirlee.

"I'm sorry that happened to you." My feeble apology hung between us.

"Yeah, well..." Maeve didn't make eye contact. Her gaze fluttered around me, not settling on anything for more than a few seconds.

My breathing was off, shallow with pain and anger.

"Did they arrest Shirlee?" I asked, changing the subject. I thought we were alike in this way, unwilling to linger on anything painful for too long.

"I have no idea." Her tone switched back to its normal pitch and fluency. "Should we check the news?"

"Ugh. Probably." Although, finding out what had happened to Shirlee wasn't something I felt quite ready for. But what choice did I have? If she was walking around free, both Maeve and I could still be in danger. "Where are you staying?"

"At the dorm. My parents were out of town, but my mom will be here tomorrow."

"Maybe you should stay here."

"Your aunt would be okay with that?"

"*Pssh*, she won't care. Have you heard from Doug? Gayle?"

Maeve shook her head. "Only you."

"Let me have the phone."

She placed it on the bed next to me, then grabbed the remote.

I dialed; it rang and rang. The voice mail clicked on, and I warned Doug not to stay at his place.

When I hung up, Maeve asked, "You think she knows where Doug lives?"

"I don't know, but I'm not going to underestimate her." I called Gayle, but again, the call went to voice mail. I told her everything I knew, which wasn't much, and hoped for their safety.

Maeve flipped through the channels, landing on *Days*. She left it on, and we both zoned out to the soap opera's familiar themes. At the commercial break, she asked, "You'd met Shirlee before, huh?"

"For all of, like, five minutes."

"Did you suspect her at all?"

Everything inside me wanted to say yes, wanted to brag about how I'd seen something cold and calculated behind her eyes the moment we were introduced. But that idea was nothing but a big old lie. I hadn't noticed anything *off* regarding Shirlee. I'd shaken hands with someone capable of murder, the daughter of my mom's rapist, and it never registered.

"Not for a second." I hadn't even known of the dead_papers account when I first met Shirlee, but she'd been writing them. "Do you still have the binder?"

"The detectives have it."

"Shit. I told Gayle she could have the story."

"She can. I made two copies. I'll call her again tomorrow. Everybody's already seen the diaries. That's not the story, Hazel. The story is us."

How could that be? We were just two young people playing detectives. And we'd nearly gotten ourselves killed in the process. I wasn't sure that was newsworthy.

"I ordered to-go!" Aunt Liddy's lilt sounded like her two-glasses-of-chardonnay voice. She swooshed in with a Styrofoam boxed meal in each hand. With her purse swinging from her elbow, she handed one to each of us. "Here. I ate at the bar."

"Is it okay if Maeve stays tonight?"

"I don't care." Aunt Liddy flopped on the bed Maeve sat on, her forearm over her eyes. "You have an appointment with a Detective Patterson tomorrow at nine."

"Did you get a lawyer?" Maeve asked.

"Bet your ass I did."

Soon after, Aunt Liddy's mouth slackened, and she started snoring softly. Maeve moved over to my bed. We ate our grilled cheeses and watched TV. A breaking news alert interrupted the programming, and the screen flashed with a soft-filtered image of Ryan. The picture shifted to a polished blond reporter with twinkling blue eyes. I recognized the historic oak tree behind her, caution tape still wrapped and spinning around the trunk. She stood in the Trap.

"Police have verified an arrest has been made in response to what was earlier described as 'a grisly and meticulous' attack of Oakley University student, Ryan Newsome. The suspect is another student at the school, and while authorities are not releasing a name at this time, it's believed a confession was posted within the university's own online community."

"Well..." I sighed. "Now we know what happened to her." I couldn't bring myself to say Shirlee's name.

"Guess so. Oh, I almost forgot." The bed shook with her movement as Maeve got up and crossed the room. She stood in front of the dresser and rummaged through the grocery bag. "I got you this. A get-well gift." She held a book.

"Homework?" I said, but then realized it was too small to be one of my textbooks, and this one was leather-bound with golden-edged pages.

"A diary," she said, handing it to me.

"Oh...wow. Ha! Not an online one."

"I figured that's not really your style," she said.

"Thank you." It was thoughtful. And private. I could write the truth and hide it away—not a single soul needed to know everything about my life, except me. And I was fortunate enough to have someone who recognized and respected that in my life. A person who liked me even when I needed to hide.

Chapter Twenty-Two

Destinations

OCTOBER 25, 2000

The police station was busy in the way one would expect any major city police station to be. An officer in a dark-blue uniform sat behind a desk greeting people and directing them to different areas. She had us wait in an area lined with wooden benches.

Moving around still wasn't easy—wouldn't be for a little while more—so Aunt Liddy had slipped the hotel concierge an extra twenty to let us use the wheelchair for the morning.

Maeve came with us. Her eyes danced all over the station environment; mine were doing the same. I examined every person, every noise, sound, and smell. The place hustled and bustled as though it were a living, breathing entity. Walkie-talkies crackled with a static-edged language I had trouble understanding. Uniformed officers strode in an out of the entrance. Whatever their missions, they were still a mystery to us.

One policeman high-fived two kids and let them pick lollipops from a hidden stash while their mom thanked him. In another area, a group of officers scoffed and laughed at what I assumed was a drunk man, tripping over his own feet. Kindnesses and cruelty blended together, but that was true of any place where people were.

Detective Patterson strolled around the maze of desks. She wore the same thing she'd had on the other day: suit pants and a collared oxford shirt—pink this time. She kept her head and shoulders high as she passed through the room. Some of the other officers watched her as she passed their desks, a barely contained glint of contempt registering in their looks. I wondered how long it took her to figure out how to never show any weakness among this old boys' club of street cops—probably not long. Or maybe she'd been born knowing, an inherent survival trait.

She stopped at the front desk and spoke with the woman behind it, who motioned in our direction. Detective Patterson glanced at us, a tight, close-lipped smile curving around her otherwise sharp features.

"You must be the Fischers." The detective held out her hand, and my aunt shook it.

"Only one of us is a Fischer. I'm Lydia Greene, her aunt. And our lawyer isn't here yet. Hazel, introduce yourself."

"We've met," I said.

Aunt Liddy's head snapped around. "Excuse me?"

"She came to my dorm because I'd fought with Ry—"

"Shh!" Aunt Liddy cut me off, turning back to Detective Patterson. "You spoke to her without a lawyer or guardian present?"

"Ma'am, we had a conversation. We were simply tying up another line of questioning. She's an adult, ma'am."

"Barely." Aunt Liddy crossed her arms as an energetic-looking man rushed into the station. He wore a gray herring-bone jacket, and raindrops spotted his glasses. He hustled to the front desk and gave his name and who he was looking for, which was, of course, us.

"Sorry to be late!" he announced loudly. "Traffic." He held out his hand and introduced himself to both Aunt Liddy and the detective. "Manuel Sierra." His black hair was long on top and fell rather perfectly over his brow.

"Good to meet you," Aunt Liddy said. "Detective Patterson here was just explaining how she questioned my niece without my knowledge or a lawyer present."

The detective scratched her eyebrow. "Ms. Greene, as I've explained—"

"I didn't ask for a lawyer, Aunt Liddy." I tried rolling my wheels toward them, but a shock of pain shot up my side and back. Maeve took over, pushing me toward the center of their conversation. "It was informal. Now, can we get on with this?"

Detective Patterson took the lead, and Maeve pushed me through the station. People made sure to get out of the wheelchair's way, watching me pass as if I were a one-woman parade. The tiled floor changed to carpeting, and the wheelchair lurched forward as Maeve adjusted.

We approached a hall lined with doors and what I assumed were one-way glass windows. I figured we'd be setting up in one of those, but Detective Patterson led us past the interrogation rooms toward another office area. Here, a handful of uniformed officers loitered around some of the desks, their hands resting on their utility belts while they listened to instructions given by a gruff voice. I recognized the voice as the other detective who'd shown up at my dorm, but I couldn't remember his name. I only hoped he wouldn't be a part of today's proceedings.

He nodded at us as we passed and, luckily, did not follow. We stopped in front of a small office labeled as

Detective Patterson's, and she stopped with her hand on the doorknob.

"I'm afraid there isn't enough room for all of you. You're welcome to wait over there." She pointed out a seating area set up around a water cooler and coffee station. "The coffee isn't too awful," she added.

Aunt Liddy made as if she might protest but ended up keeping her thoughts to herself. Instead, she leaned down and told me to follow Mr. Sierra's lead. Then she gave him a look—a mom-look she had perfected in the few years we'd been forced together. He nodded. Maeve squeezed my shoulder; then it was just me and two representatives of the criminal justice system.

The two professionals stared at me, waiting for what I wasn't sure. I guessed they wanted me to roll myself into the office.

"Little help?" I asked.

"Oh! Yes, yes." Mr. Sierra shuffled his briefcase and jacket to the floor, resting them against the wall, and took the handlebars. He pushed me forward and deposited me in front of Detective Patterson's desk.

The room smelled of cinnamon-spice. A large white mug with a tea tag hanging over the edge sat on the desk. Frosted-pink lipstick curved along the mug's lip. The office was cramped, filled with bookshelves displaying everything from leather-bound spines with titles glittering in gold leaf to more modern textbooks. A heat register belched out warm air behind Patterson's desk, and an antique-looking ceramic pot sat atop a flickering candle ensconced by a grated metal covering.

"Would you like some? Those brutes out there don't do tea," Detective Patterson asked, noticing where my gaze had landed.

"Uh, no. Thanks. I'm a brute, I guess."

"All right, then." Detective Patterson took a file folder off the top of a fairly large stack and opened it. "Let's get down to business, shall we?" She indicated a recording device on the corner of her desk.

"Certainly," said Mr. Sierra, straightening his glasses.

"We need your formal statement regarding the night of October twenty-third. Okay if I record?"

The adults looked to me for an answer. I nodded my consent.

"They'll need a verbal, Ms. Fischer," said Mr. Sierra.

"Yeah, I'm fine with you recording me."

Detective Patterson pressed both the bright red Record button and Play. The cassette tape whirred to life.

"As I understand it, my client is prepared to offer you any and all knowledge gained through private investigations of the campus murder by one Maeve Drakos and Hazel Fischer."

"Private investigation?" I asked.

Mr. Sierra shot a glance at me and gave a terse nod.

"Yes, we've agreed upon that." Detective Patterson knocked a knuckle against a binder I recognized as Maeve's. She clasped her hands together. "Ms. Fischer, when we met the day of..." She paused and shuffled through some of the paperwork. "Ah, yes, here it is, October twenty-third. At our meeting, I asked about your disagreement with Ryan Newsome and his death, yet you mentioned nothing regarding Shirlee Hensen. Why is that?"

I checked with Mr. Sierra, who nodded once more, indicating I should answer. "We didn't know who was writing the online diary yet."

"And when did you know?"

"When she surprised us in the newsroom."

"And what was it you were doing there exactly?"

Mr. Sierra put his hand on my arm, leaned over, and whispered, "Stay vague."

"Gathering data?" I said.

Detective Patterson blinked slowly. "Through hacking into the university's server system?"

"Don't answer that," Mr. Sierra interjected.

"Fine." The detective sniffed. "What can you tell me about the attack?"

As I answered her question, a stage curtain of exhaustion fell over me. My shoulders gave under the weight of repetition. How many more times would I have to do this? But I already knew the answer. I'd been through this with Mom. I'd told and told and told. In the end, nothing good happened.

"So she showed up and attacked you?" Patterson asked.

"She said she'd been following Maeve and me. In fact, I had seen her right before we got to the journalism building. But I'd only met her once—no, twice," I corrected, remembering the visit she and Sara had paid me. "So she was just kinda vaguely familiar. I didn't think anything of it." There was some shame in those last words. How could I not have known? How could I make sure that no one ever surprised me with a darker side again?

"A necklace being left at the crime scene was mentioned in one of the online posts. Did you know anything about that?"

"No." I lied, and I hoped Maeve and Doug had too.

Patterson stopped the recording. "Well, looking through your file—" She *knock-knocked* on the binder again. "—and hearing your account is actually impressive."

She checked over a few slips of paper in a case file of her own, grabbed a pen, made some adjustments, and closed it. "Given the high profile and media coverage, I do expect the district attorney to be in contact with you soon."

"Am I in trouble?" I hated myself for asking. I sounded like a child.

The detective's eyes softened, and Mr. Sierra patted my arm. My stomach squirmed.

"No, Hazel. You're not in trouble," my lawyer answered.

"Quite the opposite," said Patterson, and she sipped her tea. "Ooh, that's gone cold." She twisted in her seat and grabbed the teapot behind her. Warming up her drink, she said, "In fact, you and your friends saved the day. This is off the record, and I'll deny it if anyone asks, but it would have taken us days to get to where you ended up. Warrants and all."

"Really?"

"Yes, the internet has proved a tricky thing for police work. There are gray areas where we're not sure how the law applies yet, so rules are being made up as we go. A reporter alerted us to the existence of the online journals, and the university was working with their information technology department. They were in the process of granting us permission to view them, but without a court order, we probably wouldn't have been able to gain access to the system database linking real names to usernames in a timely manner. We just hadn't gotten that far yet."

The information sank in, along with the fact that we wouldn't have been granted access either. It was one of those times when rules had to be bent.

"What happens to Shirlee?" I asked.

"She's been charged and arrested, right, Detective Patterson?" said Mr. Sierra. "So my client can feel safe in her home."

"That's a matter of public record, yes. She's been taken into custody. Our side of the job is done. Beyond that, I couldn't risk a prediction. The information concerning her father is...compelling."

I wanted to ask more, but I already knew she wouldn't be able to speak freely about Shirlee or her dad.

Mr. Sierra gathered his belongings. He fastened his suitcase, then shrugged on his trench coat. The two shook hands formally.

"One more thing." Detective Patterson came around the front of her desk and side-shuffled to a file cabinet. She opened the top drawer and flicked past the first few file folders. "Here we are. I gave one of these to your partner as well. Now, I don't know what you're currently majoring in, but I know aptitude when I see it. I run a few training courses for this program at Acorn Community College. Take a look, Hazel. If you need anything, be in touch."

It said *Application* on the header, but I folded the packet in half. Application for what? I was curious but not enough to be rude or risk showing any emotion in front of these two strangers.

"Thank you." I offered Detective Patterson my left hand to shake because it didn't hurt as much. Mr. Sierra awkwardly wheeled me out of the office. Without enough room to turn around, he slowly backed out.

Behind Patterson, and beyond the cheap metal blinds and grimy windows, a gray sky spat out the year's first snowflakes. In seconds, they grew heavy and fat, falling faster. They'd be collecting on the streets below, enough to stick. The view from her office included the muddy slick of the river, its rapids slowly churning around the city.

Outside the station, I waited on the sidewalk with Maeve while Aunt Liddy brought the car around.

"Do you want to wait inside?" Maeve asked.

"No. I want to feel the snow."

Tiny, frozen specks of white gathered all around us. They caught and melted in my hair, in my eyelashes, on my cheeks. After everything, it was hard to believe anything so pure could exist. But it did. Beauty endured like hope.

"Do me a favor?" I asked.

"Sure."

"Can you take me to the river?"

"What about your aunt? I don't think she'll be too long."

"It'll only take a second."

She agreed, and we backtracked toward the crosswalk. The river flowed just beyond this block, and I wanted to see it before I left town. We passed a tall building with a courtyard that edged along the river. Maeve took a shortcut over the cement pad and stopped near the railing.

The water churned. I knew the river hadn't caused Shirlee to break; she'd been broken before she got here. And there was no such thing as the witch she'd described in her diaries. But still, there was something magical about the ever-presence of this river. How it had been here for eons and contained the power to tear down, change, and heal.

I'd been holding Mom's necklace all morning. The charm created impressions in my palm. I brought it to my lips and closed my eyes. I couldn't carry all of this anymore. So I held it over the water and dropped it.

The two of us watched until it disappeared with the current. Her necklace could be carried downstream or sink to the bottom. That wasn't up to me. The only thing I had control over was letting it go.

"Ready?" Maeve asked.

"I am."

Maeve pushed me back toward the police station. "What now?" she asked, coming to my side to press the crosswalk button.

"I'm going home for a while. You?"

"I'm not sure yet. Probably finish out the quarter. After that?" She stood next to me while we waited and shrugged. "Detective Patterson. She brought up the police academy program at the community college."

"She gave me an application."

"What do you think about that being something we do together?"

"Too soon to tell," I said.

Across the street, people hurried toward a bus stop, brushing icy weather off their shoulders. Someone slipped and fell a few yards before reaching the shelter. A few people rushed to check on them. They helped the person stand and get to the bus station. As a group, they held on to one another and took each step carefully through the freezing wet snowfall. The bus slushed through the already-gray sludge collecting on the side of the road, and they got there. They made it. Each of them fumbled through pockets and purses and boarded the massive hunk of metal. The bus, its windshield wipers blinking the snow away, headed toward a bunch of different final destinations. Its passengers probably all had preconceived notions about how their days, weeks, lives were supposed to go. But plans didn't matter all that much.

Epilogue

DECEMBER 9, 2000
Eight Weeks Later

Everyone has told me I have to put all this stuff—*feelings*—somewhere. So this was her—Dr. Lin's—idea, along with Maeve's, I suppose, since she gave me this journal. The therapist's office was, and is, an extremely uncomfortable place. While I'm there, I can't stop thinking what might happen if I said *all* the words out loud. My mind gets stuck on a never-ending loop. What consequences might erupt were I to speak what was true next to what I wanted?

Dr. Lin says if I can write it, maybe I can read it. Okay, fine. *Fine.*

I tend to skip right over what happened to my dad. Sometimes, I let people infer he's dead. He's not, but it's so much easier than explaining. Mom was sent over the edge. And my dad... He definitely followed her, just in a different way.

I was the one who found her when I came home from school. The front door was open. I walked in and could hear her crying in the bathroom. When I knocked on the door, it unlatched and opened. Through the crack, I saw her blood-ied face. The scratches on her ribs.

I asked what happened, and she jumped at my voice. She was scared of me, or for me; I won't ever know which. She started screaming then and wouldn't stop. I called Dad at work. He told me to call 911 and said he'd be there soon.

We all tried to do the right thing, employed all the right channels. But it turned out to be useless. Mom never stopped crying. Dad started drinking. Our family was done for. They both endlessly spiraled, and everything was so out of anyone's control. That man, Shirlee's dad—dressed up as someone we were trained to trust—knocked on our door and turned a picket-fence life into a series of grave markers.

Mom threw herself off a bridge; Dad basically did the same thing. He was drunk all the time. His school made him take a leave. Then one night in a bar parking lot, he beat a man with a rock for talking shit about my mom. They charged him with assault and battery. A felony. So he's in jail. Not the man who ruined everything, the person who set all this in motion; he's still free as far as I know. Nope, my dad's the one in a tan jumpsuit, talking to us from behind plexiglass, begging us to stop visiting. Which we did.

And now, Detective Patterson and Maeve think I might want to play a part in this system. What a fucking turn of events. How could I ever put that uniform on my body? And what does it mean if I want to? Guess I'm about to find out.

Acknowledgements

If you've gotten this far, thank you. I'm forever grateful for readers. You invest money and time and brain space, trusting in an adventure of someone else's making. I hope this one was worthy.

To Elizabetta and everyone at NineStar Press, thank you for your work and dedication to story.

Special thanks to those who let me pick their brains about publishing every once in a while: Sarah Armstrong-Garner, C. Vonzale Lewis, Daphne McClean, and Autumn Lindsey. A critique partnership was an integral part of this process, and I don't know if I'd ever finish anything without Sarah Armstrong-Garner and Pam Dunn, who are always willing to see past my snail's pacing and into the heart of the stories I write. I'm also grateful to Pam Dunn's insight regarding early internet and databases, and any mistakes at this stage are my own.

Thank you to C. Vonzale Lewis, who provided much-needed vision, and Lauren Emily Whalen, who, just when I thought I was done, made me go deeper. I'm so glad to know and work with all of you.

To my husband and final-final-final draft reader, Josh, thanks for always supporting my endeavors and all the kind ways you say I'm going on and on and being confusing. While I lose the courage to write on the regular, I'm lucky enough to know people who still believe in me, especially my two sons. Thank you, for always knowing your mom can do anything.

About Jessica Cranberry

Jessica Cranberry lives in the Sierra Nevada foothills and spends most days striking a balance between parenthood, teaching, and writing suspense novels or eclectic short stories.

Email
booksbyjessicacranberry@gmail.com

Website
www.jessicacranberry.com

Coming Soon from Jessica Cranberry

Amid the Haze

Hazel & Maeve: The Campus Mysteries, Book Two

Cool blasts of April air blew her hair around the car, swirling around her head, whipping against my cheek every now and then. It had grown longer, the weight of it suppressing some of her natural wave. We were headed to Indy—just the two of us. Behind us had been hours and hours of nothing but long, straight road, pumping music, Funyuns, and countless cigarette butts streaming out the windows as I drove full throttle across I-70. Acres of farmland surrounded us, mounded rows extending beyond the horizon, prepped for corn or soybean seed, but now a new city emerged with tall buildings cutting through a span of sky and a falling orange sun. As we navigated through downtown, through the maze of asphalt and concrete, the open fields fell away as if they ceased to exist.

Hazel flicked the radio off and lit another cigarette. She'd started smoking again, and I wasn't going to complain about it. That probably made me a shitty friend, but I was glad to have a smoking buddy.

"I brought you something." I reached into the backseat blindly, keeping my eyes on the road, and felt around in my bag until my fingers grazed the thin pages of the city newspaper. "Here. Check out page three."

Hazel unfolded the *Ledger Dispatch* and found our story, the one Gayle Jackson had interviewed us for, detailing last autumn's campus murder of Ryan Newsome (asshole and sexual predator, although most media outlets left those bits out) and how we'd pieced it all together...not totally unscathed.

"Good for her. She said she wasn't going back to the *Echo* after they canned her last year." Hazel carefully refolded the paper along the creases as if it contained nothing more than the crossword.

"You're not gonna read it?"

"I know how it ends."

Hazel hadn't gone back to school after Newsome's murderer attacked us. She needed time to heal—physically and emotionally. We all did. But I couldn't escape the feeling something else was keeping her away, distant. Before today, I hadn't seen Hazel since October, the morning I'd followed her into the police station to give a statement. We'd been emailing back and forth, but neither of us ever mentioned what had happened all those nights ago—what it had been like seeing her blood soak through her clothes, fear as thick as fog, a death so close you could taste it on the air like the salt and sand of a new shore. No, we'd skirted around all of that.

It didn't stop me from wondering how she felt or what she thought about it. Hazel could be a bit of a mystery to me. Most folks, I could see right through, not her. She kept everything wrapped up so tight inside herself, I didn't think I'd ever breakthrough. And maybe that was okay. Maybe even better than okay.

"I haven't been in a real city for months. I forgot how pretty it can be," she said. "All the bustling around. Life, I mean, you can see it happening." Her cigarette bounced with the motion of her lips. She tucked it between her fingers and blew out a long, lingering exhale as though she'd been born knowing how to do that.

"Have you been here before?" I asked.

"As a kid, I think we hit up the children's museum."

"Really?"

"Yeah, when my parents... We used to live right on the border of Illinois and Indiana."

I still couldn't believe it took her so long to tell me what she'd lived through. But knowing the ways people have been hurt changed relationships—sometimes for the better, sometimes not. So I get it; she didn't want pity anywhere near us.

"You're a regular child of the corn, then, huh?" And this seemed to be how we handled the big traumatic things, poking fun around what caused the most pain. Joking. Deflecting. Sidestepping anything that hurt.

"I told you my middle name is Malachi, didn't I?"

I laughed and pressed the cigarette lighter. Hazel instinctively reached for the pack in the cup holders and got one out for me. I rolled down my window just as the lighter popped back up, its coils burning orange and hot.

"Do you know where we're headed?" she asked.

"Not really. I printed out a MapQuest for it though. It's in the glovebox."

She took out the directions and spread the folded papers over her lap. "What street are we on?"

"Ohio."

"We're close. If you can find a place to park, do it."

Brake lights glowed red in front of us. I slowed down and watched the last of the sunset, streaking pink and purple behind the high-rise buildings of the Midwestern city. The air smelled of exhaust. I followed the inching traffic into a parking garage.

"You think all these people are going to the same place we are?" Hazel asked.

"Maybe? She has a following."

By the time I parked, night had fallen. Streetlights clicked on and cast the sidewalks in a tangerine glow. Hazel folded the directions and tucked them in her hoodie pocket.

We ended up not needing the map. A decent-sized crowd of mostly women seemed to all be going in the same direction. We just fit in and followed. As we got closer, a line had already formed, and we waited, stuck behind a rowdy group of college-aged kids with dark lipstick and short flowery dresses. They were probably the same age as Hazel and me. They seemed so much younger, though, with all the laughing and the screeching.

Hazel surveyed them; her right eyebrow cocked the way it always did when she tried to puzzle out someone's behavior I handed her the silver flask I'd slipped in my jacket pocket. Elbowing her, I told her to relax.

"I'm relaxed," she said and took a swig of the peppermint schnapps.

Spring flowers and just...joy scented the air. Yeah, that was it. Joy. After such a dark year, I barely recognized the feeling. The line shuffled forward. Ani DiFranco's name, in black block lettering, stood against the marquee's glow.

"I can't believe you scored tickets," Hazel said.

"I told you we should go."

Hazel's expression lightened whenever I pressed Play on *Living in Clip*, and in the middle of all the shit that had gone down at school last fall, there'd been a notice in the paper about this tour. I figured right then and there I'd pay whatever price to get Hazel to this show if we made it out of that mess.

"I didn't really think it would happen. Especially, in the middle of...everything."

"So, how've you been dealing with all of that?" Asking was a risk, but I wanted to take it. While I gave her a pass on talking about her family, I needed to know about this because the nightmares hadn't stopped for me. I still woke up in a sweaty panic, Shirlee's glowing glasses disappearing and reappearing like pieces of the Cheshire cat.

Hazel shoved her hands into the pockets of her hoodie and stared at her feet. "Honestly, I don't know that I am." Her eyes met mine. "I just ignore it mostly."

"Me too." Time heals all wounds. Unless it doesn't.

She fiddled with her hair, braiding the ends absentmindedly. We moved forward a few more steps. At the double doors, security guards shined flashlights in purses and patted down coat pockets.

Hazel pushed her hair back from her face. "I feel kinda frozen in place, ya know?"

"I do."

"Aunt Liddy says not to rush anything. That everything will settle back to normal in time. But what if it doesn't?"

"Maybe this is the new normal."

"Exactly."

"They haven't filled your space in our dorm yet. You could always come back."

"No. I withdrew."

"You did?"

She laughed in that self-mocking way she had sometimes. "You know I'm not meant to be anybody's teacher."

The thought of her surrounded by little kids made me laugh too. "There are other programs."

She shook her head. "I don't belong there. I knew it on day one. The only good thing that happened was meeting you and Doug."

"You guys still talk?"

"Yeah, through email mostly. Like with you."

"That's cool." But my heart said, *Oh.*

At the front of the line, an elderly security guard asked me to turn out my pockets. After she felt sure I wasn't carrying a weapon, I stepped into the theater lobby.

Gilded: that was the best way to describe the old lobby. Thick and lush maroon carpeting added an honest-to-god spring to my steps. Its floral pattern led to three partitioned sets of stairs. I stood under the chandelier, waiting for Hazel. She came through security smiling her real smile, the one I hadn't seen since we'd sat on the banks of the Skullkey and gotten high.

"This is amazing," she said.

"I know, right?"

Ticket masters stood at the top of each stairwell. We climbed up the center, and I handed our tickets over. The lady tore off an edge and gave me back the stubs, tossing out a set of quick directions I could barely hear.

We followed the crowd past the main theater toward another room. Here, there were no seats, standing room only—the more to dance in. I grabbed Hazel's hand and led her closer to the stage. *This is going to be an experience, damn it.* I looked back to catch her expression as she tucked hair behind her ears and examined our surroundings. She was probably busy making snap judgements about the people around us and locating the exits.

"Are we going all the way to the front?" she yelled over the din of the crowd.

"You know it," I answered.

I got us as close as possible. I found a spot nearly center stage, next to the girls who'd been in front of us in line. They were still very bouncy and squealy, but when the lights dimmed, an excited hush ran through everyone. For a second, I'd forgotten I was still holding Hazel's hand, but she squeezed it when the stage lights came on. Faces glowed in the light that remained, but hers most of all.

She let go of my hand to clap as some of the band members came onstage and lifted their instruments into their arms. A stray beat from the bass drum filled the room. The musicians jammed for a few minutes, playing a rhythmic string of notes that weren't quite a song yet, until Ani jogged onto the stage.

Her voice evoked something in me. Something feral and wild. Something that came before the constraints of *this* world. Before I knew it, one of my favorite songs floated through the speakers. The whole crowd cheered, then danced. My body, her body, their bodies: we all moved together and apart, like a living, breathing organism. And it went on and on, song after heart-thumping song. Until the band slowed things down, playing a quieter song.

The audience swayed and sang along. The words of "Untouchable Face" haunted the room.

Hazel's eyes glistened, her cheeks flushed, strands of her hair stuck to the sweaty sheen covering her skin, but she smiled. I touched her arm. And she looked at me, wiping her cheeks.

"Thanks for this," she said, coming in close so I could hear.

"You're welcome." I wanted to suggest something, but I didn't know how she might react. *Who am I?* I never worried about that kind of thing. Most of the time, I relished any reaction. But with her, I hesitated. Worried. I motioned toward the back, where only a few fans loitered along the walls. A crease formed between her eyebrows, but she followed me.

Standing there, with the music still filling up every inch of the room, I brought her closer. The heat radiating off her met the heat radiating off me. I could've kissed her, but I had something else in mind—stupidly.

The song ended, and the band rested for a few beats, riffing with each other through Ani's introductions of each member.

"I think we should fill out those applications Detective Patterson gave us," I said.

"That's what you wanted to tell me?" She scoffed, then trained her eyes back on the stage. "You want to switch schools?"

"The program looks promising, and they have a police academy built in," I explained as if she hadn't read the brochure.

"Do it. There's nothing stopping you from switching programs, Maeve."

She didn't get it. What I knew for sure, after everything we'd been through together, was that the feeling of us working together, fitting the puzzle pieces of a campus murder together, was something I wanted to hold on to.

"I want us to go together, Hazel. I don't know how to... *process* what happened last fall, but I loved working with you. I felt alive for, like, the first time."

She bit her upper lip, exposing the top edges of her bottom teeth. She wasn't making eye contact, which was purposeful. Everything was purposeful when it came to Hazel. "You know how I feel about all of this."

"Actually, I don't because we never talk about it." I felt a little trapped, panicky. I'd gotten myself into this conversation, and now I had to go right through the middle of it, whatever the outcome. Hazel saw through the moments when I manipulated people; she must've seen that's *not* what I was doing now. I wanted this, and I needed her. "We might be able to do good, help people, set things right. Didn't you enjoy working through the mystery of it? I fucking did."

"I did too." She glanced back at me. "It's funny you're bringing this up."

"I don't think it's funny. This is what I want, and I want to do it with you."

"Good." Hazel reached for her back pocket and brought an envelope folded over many times. "Because I got my acceptance letter last week."

"Shut up!" I shoved her playfully.

She stepped back with the momentum, laughing. "I have to pass a physical, then start next fall. If you're going to join me, you better get that application in quick."

"Why didn't you tell me? You said you didn't know what you were gonna do."

"I *still* go back and forth about whether I'm actually going to go. Not totally convinced police work is for me. Plus, I want you to do your own thing, follow your own path—whatever that is. But if you're into this, I think...so am I."

The band picked up the set's pace, starting up another fast song. With the music blaring, we had to keep coming in close to talk, practically screaming in each other's ears.

"I don't want to talk you into anything you don't want to do!" Hazel yelled.

I moved in, near her ear again. Her brown waves, glowing pink in the changing stage lights, brushed my cheek. "So, we're doing this?" I asked. "Together?"

"Yep, together." Her eyes met mine.

What did I see there? Her seriousness, her willingness to just be who she was without really caring what others thought, her sense of humor that no one else knew about. A future.

Connect with NineStar Press

www.ninestarpress.com

www.facebook.com/ninestarpress

www.facebook.com/groups/NineStarNiche

www.twitter.com/ninestarpress

www.instagram.com/ninestarpress